TOMORROW ALMOST DIES

Also by Doug Solter

For Her Eyes Only

The Boy From Barcelona

Girls Only Live Twice

Man With The Golden Falcons

Dr. Yes

Thunderdog

Tomorrow Always Lies

Spies Like Me

Skid Racing Series

TOMORROW ALMOST DIES

BOOK 8 OF THE GEMS SPY SERIES

Doug Solter

Brain Matter Publishing

To Shelby, thank you for being such a good friend to both of us.

TOMORROW ALMOST DIES

CHAPTER 1

That night, glowing billboards slid across the glass windshield as their car followed the airport exit road. Each billboard promoted new airline destinations, new low fares, and new hope for those wanting to escape San Francisco.

Sitting in the back seat of her grandma's Jeep, Emma was eager to stay in San Francisco. She'd come back from the Middle East seven days ago after another crazy adventure that almost got her killed. But tonight, Nadia was finally back from Hejaz, and they could all get back to their "normal" life.

Emma felt someone squeezing her hand. Her grandma Bernadette smiled. Judging by the woman's face, she was looking forward to Emma staying around too.

Grandma Bernadette leaned forward towards Nadia, who sat in the Jeep's front passenger seat. "How's your family doing?"

"They're doing well. It was a busy week for us. We went to an amusement park in Jaddah. My sisters insisted on doing all the scary rides. Then my mom, my sisters and I went on a women's retreat out in the desert. Very peaceful. Thanks to Salah, we flew over to Abu Dhabi for a fun weekend trip. My sisters absolutely loved the sights and the shopping. It was the best time I've had with them in a long time."

"Good," Grandma Bernadette said. "That's wonderful to hear. Maybe they can come visit you here. We can make room at the house."

"I don't think Mrs. B would allow that."

"Well, that's too bad. I would've liked to meet them."

"Anything else happen?" Emma asked, convinced her friend was leaving some juicy details out.

"Did you say goodbye to Salah?" Miyuki asked from the backseat.

"Yes," Nadia said.

"And?"

"And what? We said goodbye and wished each other well."

"And that's it?" Emma asked.

Nadia paused as Olivia drove the Jeep over the Oakland Bay bridge, with the city lights shimmering in the distance.

"Did you break up?" Miyuki asked.

"No, we're still friends."

"You friend-zoned him?" Emma asked.

Nadia didn't answer.

"You didn't friend-zone him?"

"I'm sorry, but it's private."

That answer was unacceptable to Emma.

"You're getting married!" Miyuki yelled, jumping to a conclusion.

"Are you serious, love?" Olivia asked. "Oh, that's lovely."

"I didn't say that," Nadia said.

"Well, then say something," Emma said. "You can't say *it's private*. We're your best friends. I mean, seriously, you're obligated to tell your best friends."

"I don't—I can't."

"Please?" Miyuki asked. "We'll keep your secret."

"Goes without saying," Emma said. "Best friends always keep each other's secrets." She caught Nadia's reflection in the glass window. The girl's jaw stiffened as a slight frown formed.

Nadia was serious. Which meant that whatever it was—oh, it had to be good.

Once they made it to the other side of the bridge, Olivia pulled into a city park and shut off the Jeep's engine.

"Why are we stopping?" Nadia asked.

Olivia turned around. "I'm not missing this. What's the big secret?"

All the girls waited.

Nadia flashed Grandma Bernadette a look. *Please save me from this.*

"Might as well tell them. Otherwise none of us will get any sleep tonight."

She was right.

Nadia sighed. "Salah and I agreed to keep seeing each other. I'm still going to stay here and go to high school while Salah will continue being a king."

"That's it?" Olivia asked.

"We're taking this slow. I want it to be slow. I'm busy with my life, and he's busy with his. My father has a new job with the Royal Hejaz government, and my family is moving there. I want everything to calm down. No one is in a rush." Nadia turned around to face those in the backseat. "Salah understands. He feels I'm worth waiting for, so he's willing to do that."

"You know what? I think that's a mature and intelligent attitude about it," Grandma Bernadette said. "Good for you. And good for Salah for being a mature young man."

A slight grin escaped Nadia's mouth.

Olivia started up the Jeep and pulled back onto the road.

"Do you think he'll wait?" Emma asked.

"Don't be so negative," Miyuki said.

"Boys can be tempted. Believe me."

"Salah isn't like most boys," Nadia said. "Your grandmother is right. He's very mature for his age. He's a king. He has responsibilities. He has to keep the right image for his people."

As the girls began a lively discussion about how loyal the average boy was in a relationship, Olivia turned their car into the driveway, and a figure showed up in the headlights.

Olivia stomped on the brakes, causing Emma's seat-belt to throw her back against the seat. Peering through the Jeep's windshield, Emma saw a familiar face exposed by the headlights. He was a dark-haired boy about Emma's age and had a clean-cut way about him with an average build and an average face. But his striking emerald-green eyes pierced the night air. Emma had forgotten how powerful the android's deep green eyes were.

Nadia was the first one out of the car.

"Robert, what are you doing here?"

The android's reply was loud enough for all of them to hear.

"I require your assistance. We are in danger."

Grandma Bernadette invited Robert to come inside the house while the girls brought in Nadia's luggage. Soon they all gathered in the living room as Robert explained…

"Two months ago, three of my siblings decided to leave the island and travel to Vietnam. To them, the country offered a new experience and another way to disappear from view. It also offered a future safe haven if we needed one."

"Sorry to butt in," Grandma Bernadette said. "I'm still trying to make sense of all this. When you say siblings, whom are you referring to?"

Robert tilted his head and blinked. "My apologies for not communicating the full situation. Iko, Mirabelle, and Luigi are my three siblings who are missing."

"And these three people are robots like you?"

"They prefer being called androids," Nadia said.

"To be technically precise, the US Army lists us as a D9000 military intelligence drones. We are designed to mirror human beings for military intelligence work. To better understand us, I can give you a detailed description of our capabilities."

"Hold your horses there, Robert. Let's focus on your three siblings. Tell us more about them."

Robert processed Grandma Bernadette's words. "I don't understand. Where are these horses that you wish me to hold?"

"It's an expression," Nadia said. "So, these three androids left the island near Tahiti to go to Vietnam?"

"Pause the VCR, now; who's in Tahiti?" Grandma Bernadette asked. "Girls, I'm in the dark here. I remember when Robert was here with us, and then he was gone. None of you ever told me what happened to him."

"Mrs. B told us not to," Olivia said.

Grandma Bernadette's face stiffened a little. "Oh, is that right?" Her older eyes fell on Emma. "Did you agree to this, young one?"

Emma couldn't meet her grandma's eyes.

"Do you think I'm a blabber-mouth?"

"No, of course not. It's just—Mrs. B is—well, she can be intimidating sometimes."

"Your grandma Laura is a pushy, pompous, and arrogant old woman. She will not drive a wedge between you and me. I won't allow it."

"Mrs. B is your grandmother, Emma?" Robert asked. "I did not know this."

"Don't tell everyone. It's supposed to be a secret."

"Oh, Laura is full of hot air. Don't worry about her. Now, I want you to tell me what in God's green earth is going on?"

Emma told her grandma Bernadette about Mrs. B moving Robert and his other android siblings to a remote island in the Pacific at their request. That way, the long list of people who wanted to kidnap and exploit the androids couldn't find them.

"Robert, do all your siblings look like you?"

"We all appear different. The US Army designed us in pairs. Male and female versions. Mirabelle and I are Caucasians. Sid and Cleo are Arabic. Kamal and Samira are Indian. Alex and Mai are African. Iko and Luigi are Asian."

"Why did they name the Asian guy Luigi?"

Robert tilted his head. "His military identification is Drone 008. When he was given free will, Luigi changed that designation because he expressed an interest in Italian art and culture."

"The android likes Italian art?"

"He does not hate or like it. He has shown an interest. All of my siblings have their own interests since they are now free to explore them."

"Did you pick Robert for a name?" Emma asked.

"Actually, it was my nickname that the development team first gave me since I was the prototype for our series. I chose to keep it."

"There's nothing wrong with the name Robert," Grandma Bernadette said. "Okay, so, the android who's interested in Italian things left your island near Tahiti and went to Vietnam with Iko and—who else?"

"My Caucasian partner, Mirabelle. She and Emma have a similar appearance."

"How similar?" Emma asked.

"Mirabelle was designed to look attractive to young males in order to gain their confidence and manipulate them."

"Sounds like Emma all right."

Miyuki giggled.

Emma flipped Olivia the middle finger.

"I'm joking, love. You're so sensitive."

"At least I can attract boys."

Olivia laughed. "I have a boyfriend, you daft cow."

"Girls, please stop interrupting." Grandma Bernadette rubbed her temple as if a headache was coming on. "Please continue."

"Thank you. Luigi, Iko, and Mirabelle sent the rest of us daily reports. They described the places they visited in Vietnam. The people they met. Their general experiences. However, seven days ago these reports stopped. This is concerning to us. Since we do not communicate with Alex and Samira, we do not know if our creators have broken the agreement we made and possibly kidnapped them."

"Back up again," Grandma Bernadette said. "I thought Alex and Samira were in Tahiti with all of you?"

"No, that is not correct. When I gave them free will, Alex and Samira both chose to stay with our creators."

"Your creators?"

"He means the US Army, Grandma," Emma said.

"Luigi, Iko, and Mirabelle know about the secret identities Mrs. B and the Authority helped arranged for us in Tahiti. If that information is discovered by those still looking for us, it will jeopardize our safety."

"And you think the US Army is behind it?" Olivia asked.

"That is one of many possibilities. We do not believe their disappearance is an accident. We ask for your help to find them."

"I'm sure Mrs. B will do everything she can to help you find out what's going on."

"That is what I told my siblings. They are waiting outside. I wanted to make contact with you first, in case you were compromised or helping the US Army find us."

"You and your siblings can stay here," Grandma Bernadette said. "There's no reason for them to stay outside. We have the room."

Robert paused. "I texted them. They will be here shortly."

"You can do that without a phone?"

Robert pointed at his cranium. "My head is a phone."

Grandma Bernadette stood up. "Okay, while I'm helping our new guests settle in, I want all of you upstairs and ready for bed."

"But we should be helping you," Miyuki said.

"You four young ladies have school tomorrow."

"School? We have to contact Mrs. B about this," Nadia said. "She might have orders for us."

"You girls are not skipping school. And those are *my* orders."

CHAPTER 2

The queue for customs inside Marco Polo International Airport outside Venice was long. Many of the travelers were tired and weary thanks to the flood of overnight flights arriving from America mixed with a few regional flights that were outside the European Schengen zone, which meant the passengers had to go through Italian customs.

Fresh from their overnight flight, two young American servicemen also stood in the queue. Their eyes kept peeking back behind them at the teenage girl with red hair.

Bridget O'Malley pretended not to notice them. Pretended to play the game. A game she enjoyed because these two boys were cute. They were at least five years older too, but Bridget wasn't intimidated by that. She could handle anything life could throw at her.

"Bejesus, how long is this fecking queue?" Sophia asked her sister, rejoining it after using the toilet.

"I don't believe it. They're twins," one serviceman whispered.

"God must love us," the other said.

Bridget held back a smile as she bent down to whisper in Sophia's ear. "Take a gander at these two lads in front of us. What do ya think?"

Her sister looked them over. Today, Sophia managed not to dress like a boy. She wore a mini-skirt and had even brushed her hair out like Bridget had done.

Sophia shrugged. "The tall one's all right."

"Not so loud," Bridget whispered. "I kinda fancy that one."

"You always go for the tall ones."

The two servicemen reacted with a smile as they looked back. They caught them.

Bridget waved. "Yes, we're talking about ya."

Sophia shifted her gaze to the waxed floor.

"I'm gonna just say it," the tall soldier said. "You two girls are smoking hot."

"Knew I shouldn't have shaved my legs today," Sophia said to the floor.

Bridget ignored her. "You have good taste. Army or Marines? I can never tell by the uniforms."

"Wrong on both counts. The United States Air Force," the tall airmen said with pride.

They turned around to face the girls. "How long are you two in Italy?"

Sophia tugged at her short skirt, trying to make it into a gown.

"Not too sure," Bridget said. "A few days at least. Where are you two boys stationed?"

Bridget did all the talking as their queue moved forward. She found out their names, which air base they were stationed at, where in the US they called home, even their favorite movies. It was fun to practice her interrogation techniques on boys who had no clue she was even doing it. If she wanted to, Bridget could probably get them to spill everything they knew about their air base, including its security, what they were doing there, and what was hidden inside those hangars that the US Air Force didn't want anyone to know about. But right now, Bridget had fun just being the one in control.

"You have nice legs," the tall airmen said. "It's Sophia, right?"

Her sister finally stopped admiring the floor. It was about time. If Sophia kept acting like this, the servicemen would just write her off as a loony and move on. Unfortunately, poor Sophia couldn't help herself sometimes. Her sister did have her moods.

"Piss off, you *edgits*."

And today was one of them.

The two servicemen shot each other a look. That was it. The red flag. They turned back around and followed the queue forward without looking back again.

Bridget loved her sister, yet sometimes she was a killjoy.

"Sorry," Sophia whispered. "I'm knackered from the flight."

"No worries," Bridget said. "Only passing the time."

"Here ya go."

Cutting in the queue was an older man in his mid to late thirties with well-groomed dark brown hair, a dark brown mustache, and large thick-framed glasses. His suit was tailored to fit his still athletic body. He had three coffee beverages on a disposable tray. The authorities in New Zealand and Australia knew him as Dr. Glenn Joyce, one of the most-wanted fugitives down under.

Bridget called him papa.

Even heavily disguised, the man had an unmistakable smile in his eyes.

"My apologies. The queue for Starbucks was outrageous."

Sophia lit up as she grabbed her drink. "Thank you, Papa."

Papa handed Bridget hers. He removed his own drink before tossing the empty tray into a nearby bin. "I have something I should tell you, girls."

"What is it?" Sophia asked, sipping her drink.

Papa took out an Australian newspaper tucked under his arm. He showed them the headline. "I'm officially dead."

Most Wanted Man Killed in Wellington Shootout

Sophia brightened. "That's wonderful news!"

Bridget couldn't believe it. Asset One had given the nod. Operation Dazed and Confused had been a favor to her number two, a way to "free" Papa from his fugitive status or at least give him more freedom to operate.

"Told ya to give her a chance."

"That ya did. You're always on it, my dear Bridget."

She flashed him a smile.

Papa tucked the newspaper under his arm. "Has this queue actually moved?"

"A wee bit. Will we be late for our appointment?"

"No worries. A car is waiting for us. Besides, she knows that we've landed."

An hour and a half later, a black Maserati Quattroporte took them from the Venice airport to a small gondola water taxi waiting on one of the canals. Bridget carefully stepped down as a handsome young Italian boatman helped her inside the gondola. Sophia was given the same treatment, and Bridget was surprised to see her sister flash the handsome Italian a big smile. At least Sophia wasn't totally mental.

Soon, Papa joined them inside the gondola, and it drifted away from the small pier and began to maneuver its way through the large system of canals that crisscrossed the beautiful city of Venice. All the canals fed into the large Grand Canal filled with islands and walkways. Buildings walled off each side of the canal and were a mix of Byzantine, Venetian Gothic, Renaissance, and some Eastern styles of architecture.

To Bridget, it reminded her of a fantasy movie she once saw where the kingdom's capital city was built on a lake. But here, everyone spoke romantic Italian, not stuffy old English.

Their gondola made a turn into a tiny, out-of-the-way canal. A small pier was on their right, with four large Italian men guarding it. Those men helped moor the gondola to the pier, then assisted Bridget and Sophia out of the boat. When Papa climbed out, the four large Italian men bowed their heads.

"Welcome to Venice, Asset Two," the largest of the four men said in English. "The others are waiting for you inside."

Bridget and Sophia followed Papa as the four Italian men led them into a large, dark gold house designed in a Venetian Gothic style. Inside, the floor tiles were made of an intricate silver marble design that was the most beautiful tile that Bridget had ever stepped on. A part of her wanted to take off her shoes out of respect. The walls had this old golden wallpaper composed of more intricate patterns. The inside reminded Bridget of the French Palace of Versailles with all the over-the-top furnishings.

"Honest to G, I wore a skirt, and I still feel under dressed," Sophia whispered.

"Forgot to bring our powdered wigs and bloody corsets too."

That made her sister smile.

They approached a set of closed double doors with fancy decorations on them. Two Turkish men in well-fitted designer suits opened the doors for them.

Inside, there was a large hall beyond. Thirty large individual chairs—each with its own table—were arranged in a circle. Twenty-nine of them were occupied. Those twenty-nine individuals all turned to watch Papa as he went inside.

Bridget didn't follow him. Sophia took her sister's cue and stayed behind as well.

Papa stopped walking. "No worries. Come join us, girls."

"Are you sure?" Bridget asked.

Papa winked and revealed that warm smile that always gave them so much comfort.

Bridget stepped into the hall with Sophia. They followed Papa over as he sat in the empty chair. She didn't dare look around the room, but Bridget could feel the entire hall judging them.

"You're late, Asset Two."

The female voice belonged to Asset One. Sabiha was a middle-aged Turkish woman with green eyes, short dark hair, and a force to be reckoned with. Bridget knew her when Sabiha had been Asset Twelve, in charge of running the Venomous training island in the Indian Ocean.

"You've kept us waiting for a half hour," Asset Four said, a blond Swede who reminded Bridget of what the abominable snowman must be like in real life.

"This meeting is only for the top thirty assets," Asset Three said; the well-dressed Brazilian man gave Bridget and Sophia a hard look. "Your 'daughters' are not allowed to be here. Have them wait outside."

Many of the members nodded in agreement.

A polite grin appeared on Papa's face. He ignored them and focused on Sabiha. "Had to fly commercial on this trip. That required a disguise to get through security and customs. And I needed time to take that disguise off to meet with all you fine people." Papa moved his attention over to the Brazilian man. "As far as my daughters are concerned, Asset Three can bugger off with my compliments."

The Brazilian almost stood up, but thought better of it as he leaned forward in his chair.

Papa didn't flinch. "If ya wanna do something about it, mate,

I'll be waiting outside with a smile on my face."

"You two idiots can fight on your own time. Not mine. Is that clear?" Sabiha glanced at Bridget and Sophia. "Assets one-three-zero and one-three-one can stay. We obviously need more estrogen and less testosterone in this room." She addressed Papa. "You don't need to wear disguises any longer. I've taken care of that."

Papa actually bowed his head. "And I thank ya for that kindness, Asset One. It will allow me to better serve you and Venomous."

"The price for my kindness is your absolute loyalty, Asset Two."

"I understand."

"Can we start now?" Asset Four asked as the Swede opened up his laptop. "We have much to cover. Do we not?"

Sabiha relaxed. "Yes, we do. First item on our agenda?"

Asset Four glanced at his laptop. "Asset Nine's plan to bomb and extort money from the top three German car manufacturers."

As the group went through each item, Bridget had to lean against the tall back of Papa's chair. Sophia did the same on the other side. Bridget thought about asking for a chair, but she didn't want to push her luck. These men were at the top levels of Venomous. Which meant they were the most dangerous men in the world. Papa would always remind them to never show weakness in front of them.

"That's all the items we had on the agenda," Asset Four said as the Swede closed his laptop.

"I have one last item to add," Asset One said. "A year ago the United States Army spent billions of dollars creating ten advanced AI androids to conduct military intelligence. It was the start of a new top-secret program to build hundreds of these androids. The army did such a good job designing them that the androids themselves became sentient and destroyed the facility that created them. The Authority helped eight of them disappear off the face of the earth, except for two that went back to work for the army."

Sabiha turned her attention to Papa. "My sources in Beijing have revealed that those two army androids are now missing. Do you know anything about that?"

Papa crossed his legs, calm as ever. "I'm working on something."

"Working on something?"

"Could you elaborate on that?" Asset Four asked.

"Last time these androids were running around free, Venomous missed the boat," Papa said. "From what I've gathered about these androids, they could be turned into the ultimate weapon. Gathering intelligence is only a lick of the ice-cream cone. These androids could be used to infiltrate any facility with the biggest bomb we can put inside them. Think of the absolute terror a dozen of these beauties would cause if placed in just the right spots. The Wall Street Stock Exchange. The White House. The Kremlin. Shopping malls. Outdoor Christmas markets. Football stadiums during the World Cup. If we focus our attacks, we could bring any government to its knees, begging us to stop and play ball on our terms."

"Seems like quite a waste to blow up something so valuable when you can use a simple truck bomb," Asset Three said, the Brazilian gaining back his composure.

"I agree," Papa said. "That's why I wanna open up one of these robotic beauties and use it as a test bed to mass-produce them. Asset One's family owns the necessary tech facilities in Istanbul for such a production. Do you not?"

Sabiha crossed her legs and leaned back in her chair. "Clearly you've given a lot of thought to this project. A secret pet project that I'm only now hearing about."

"Even before he was in jail, Dr. Joyce always had a nasty habit of working behind our backs," Asset Three said.

Papa smiled. "Snakes work their best in the darkness. That way, no one will ever see them coming."

"Or they don't want to hear the word no," Sabiha added.

"With all due respect, Asset One, I'm only laying the necessary groundwork for the operation, and things are progressing nicely. You must admit, the possibilities of Venomous possessing our own army of highly sophisticated suicide bombers is enticing to say the least."

CHAPTER 3

Nadia was the first person up that day. She was careful not to wake up her roommate, Olivia, as she picked out one of her more basic school outfits to wear. After throwing on a simple headscarf, Nadia rushed downstairs to the living room, where Robert and the other four androids were using most of the power outlets to recharge.

"Good morning."

"Good morning to you as well." Robert unplugged himself from the wall outlet and retracted his charging cable, which stuck out from a hidden-away slit under his wrist.

"How are you?" Nadia asked.

"One moment. I am running a diagnostic on my systems." Robert blinked. "I am operating at one hundred…" His voice trailed off. "That was not what you were asking me about, was it?"

Nadia smiled and shook her head.

"I am fine. Thank you for asking. How are you, my friend?"

"I'm worried about you." Nadia then realized all of the androids were listening and watching. "I'm worried about all of you."

"She does seem genuine in her demeanor," the tall Indian android said to Robert.

"I should introduce you." Robert pointed. "This is Kamal. He has been created to mimic an Indian teenager."

"You've already told us that." Nadia nodded to Kamal. "It's nice to meet you."

To answer her, Kamal belted out a couple of phrases in a harsh, guttural-type language that sounded scary.

"Sorry, I don't speak…whatever that is."

"It is Klingon," Kamal said in English. "I was hoping to find a human who spoke it."

"I see. Isn't that from *Star Trek* or something?"

"Yes, I have analyzed every episode and every series in existence related to *Star Trek*. I find it interesting. The Federation is an excellent model for mankind to follow as it evolves. I would study the Vulcan language, yet I can-not find any detailed Vulcan language pronunciation books. Do you know other humans who can speak Klingon?"

"Not really. But if I find some, I'll let you know."

"Kamal has also studied an android character in one of those series who struggles with some of the same questions about his existence that we do."

"As-Salam-u-Alaikum."

Sid and Cleo said the phrase in unison with a perfect Arabic pronunciation.

"Wa-Alaikum-as-Salam," Nadia replied.

"Sid and Cleo are interested in the act of dance," Robert said. "They can demonstrate one hundred and six different styles."

Cleo tilted her head. "We can perform styles such as ballet, contemporary, tap, ballroom, Latin, hip-hop, swing, Irish step, Texas line—"

"That's quite a lot," Nadia interrupted her. She knew from experience with Robert that sometimes androids didn't understand the concept of brevity.

"We are also interested in the dancers themselves. Some have created their own interpretation on dance styles."

"Fred Astaire and Ginger Rogers, for instance," Sid said. "Are you familiar with them?"

"I don't know anything about dancing."

"Would you like me to perform the Saudi sword dance for you?" Sid picked up Grandma Bernadette's letter opener. "I will use this as my sword."

"Maybe another time."

"Yes," Robert added. "Brandishing swords early in the morning before humans have had their morning coffee can be quite hazardous."

Nadia moved over to the last android. Her olive skin appeared darker than her friend Olivia's, and the girl had these lovely light brown, almost golden eyes.

"Hello, it's Mai, is that correct?"

The small android avoided eye contact with Nadia, but still nodded.

"Yes, her name is Mai," Robert said.

"It's nice to meet you."

Mai only nodded again.

Nadia was fascinated. Was this girl android shy? Were they even capable of being shy?

"Am I being rude?" Mai finally asked. "I sometimes can not tell. I apologize if I have been offensive towards you."

"No, not in the least."

"You have done so much for us. For Robert. And us. Are all humans like you?"

Nadia thought the world would be a better place if more humans did think like her. But then, making people think like her would make her feel too bossy. And Nadia hated to be bossy towards people.

"Is my question too personal? Have I offended you again?"

"No, I was thinking about something. What are you interested in?"

Mai finally kept her eyes on Nadia. "Solving mysteries."

Nadia had to pause. "Can you be more specific?"

"Yes, I can. I read eBooks. Thousands of eBooks every day about mysteries."

"Every day?"

"I am reading one right as we speak. It is about a young girl detective trying to find a missing donkey in the mountains of Ecuador. Do you read books?"

"A little bit. Actually, Emma and her grandma are the big readers in the house."

Mai blinked and tilted her head again. "I would be interested in speaking to her about mysteries. And to ponder the questions and issues such mysteries pose to the human psyche."

Nadia had to wonder if Emma pondered anything after reading her trashy young adult romance novels with vampires, shape-shifters, and boys with issues only the girl can help them solve. Maybe Mai could encourage Emma to upgrade her reading list.

"First one up always makes coffee," Grandma Bernadette said to Nadia as she emerged from her bedroom dressed in her University of California college professor outfit of respectful pants and a tasteful blouse with a multi-colored "Love Peace" pin on her lapel. "Better get to it. You'll have plenty of time to talk to Robert and his friends after school."

"Yes, ma'am."

"I have the knowledge to operate a coffee machine. Would you like me to produce your morning coffee?"

"No, you're a guest, Robert. Besides, the girls don't get to skip out on their responsibilities because we have company."

Reluctantly, Nadia went into the kitchen and opened the bag of coffee. The strong aroma filled her nose and woke her up another notch. Before coming to America, she had been a tea person. Drinking it with her family in Saudi Arabia, then again with Olivia when they met in England. But America had corrupted her into the ritual of morning coffee.

"I miss going to school."

The sentence startled Nadia, causing her to dump a scoop of ground coffee all over the counter. She turned around to see Robert.

"Oh, did my unannounced presence cause you rapid anxiety?"

Nadia ripped off a paper towel. "You startled me, that's all." She carefully wiped the coffee grounds off the counter and into her hand. Robert brought over the trash bin, allowing her to dump the grounds. Nadia wiped her hands clean with another towel.

"I wish I could come to school with you. High school was interesting and entertaining. I learned quite a lot about humans observing it."

"That's funny, I've never considered high school entertaining."

"Perhaps you should. Observing an institution from a different perspective can be quite enlightening. It was for me."

They both stared at each other.

A few seconds ticked by.

To Nadia, this was becoming awkward.

Wait, did Robert understand that this was awkward?

Maybe he didn't.

"I like your siblings," Nadia said, breaking the ice forming around them. "They each have their own little nuances."

"I find each of them interesting as well. However, you are still the most interesting life form I have met."

"Oh, I bet you say that to all the carbon-based life forms you meet."

Robert paused. "You have made a science joke. You have combined a culturally relevant movie quote and combined it with-"

"It's not funny when you explain it like that."

"You are correct. I will perform the appropriate reaction." Robert then busted out laughing.

"You can laugh now?"

"Kamal and I are attempting to develop an emotion chip. It would allow us to experience and present the appropriate emotion depending on the circumstance. Right now, we can only use it to laugh."

"I like your new laugh. Maybe you should adjust it down a bit. Only a little bit."

"I will tell Kamal that it needs an adjustment."

Another long, awkward pause that made Nadia a bit too uneasy.

She turned away and stared at the coffee machine. First boys, now androids. If the microwave oven could talk, Nadia would shy away from it too.

"That coffee won't make itself," Grandma Bernadette said, coming into the kitchen. She opened the fridge and began pulling out things to cook for breakfast.

Nadia finished putting in the necessary scoops of coffee before securing the pot and hitting the start button. "Can I help you with breakfast?"

"Please, allow me to make breakfast," Robert said. "I have studied the techniques and styles of the great chefs of Europe and America, as well as their recipes."

Grandma Bernadette considered the offer. "Interesting. I'd like to see that."

Robert took a visual survey of the fridge and the cupboards. He gathered the ingredients he needed, then went to work.

Miyuki came downstairs. "What is Robert doing?"

"I think omelettes," Grandma Bernadette said.

"And he's baking something as well," Nadia added.

Olivia was the next one down. "That smell is amazing. What's he cooking?"

Soon, they were all gathered in the kitchen, sipping coffee and watching Robert acting like Chef Gordon Ramsay, but without all the screaming.

A Jack Russell terrier wearing a back brace wandered into the kitchen with his tail wagging and his nose in full sniffing mode. If Snoopy was moving around, that meant Emma must be up.

Robert started plating his omelettes, and to Nadia they looked absolutely gorgeous. He added two link sausages to each plate and a crescent roll from a tray of homemade rolls he'd baked while mixing together the omelet batter.

"This is a Spanish omelette, but with leanings toward more of a French style," Robert said. "I have added a hint of spice to the sausage links. Not too much. And the rolls should have just a kiss of cinnamon. Only enough to give them the slightest taste of sweetness."

Nadia tried the omelette. It was light and fluffy, yet bursting with flavor from the spices. It was scrumptious.

Robert had even made a tiny omelette for Snoopy, which he put on the floor. The dog devoured it.

Emma finally wandered in with her eyes barely open as she headed straight for the coffee, pouring herself a cup. "What's that smell?"

"The best omelette I've ever tasted," Grandma Bernadette said. "Guest or not, you can cook as much as you want to in this house, Robert."

CHAPTER 4

Nadia found it hard to concentrate at school. Even the classes she normally enjoyed seemed trivial and boring. All she could do was think about Robert.

They had kept up with each other over the many months since the Gems had helped him and his "siblings" settle on an island near Tahiti. Robert would give her weekly updates on his experiences. New things that he learned. New people that he met. And Nadia did the same. Emma's grandmother called them "pen pals" an old term from decades ago when friendships were forged between strangers mailing physical letters to each other.

And yet Nadia and Robert were far from strangers. Nadia still had the backup of Robert's operating system and memory in safe-keeping. The special operating system that gave all his android siblings the ability to be individuals and make their own decisions. Without it, the androids were little more than servants to anyone who reloaded their basic US Army operating system. Robert trusted her enough to take care of all that, which meant a lot to Nadia, a responsibility she took…

"Nadia, according to Roman mythology, what two brothers founded the city of Rome?"

Nadia's brain snapped back to the present as she focused on the front of the classroom. Her world history teacher, Mrs. Myers, calmly waited for an answer. And if necessary, Mrs. Myers would wait for that answer until Nadia died of old age.

What were they talking about today?

Roman history.

That's right. The founding of Rome.

Nadia resisted the urge to do a quick internet search on her phone, which would spark a tongue-lashing from Mrs. Myers that Nadia wanted to avoid.

Oh, what were their names? They started with two Rs.

Revis and Ronald?

Ronald and Raymond?

Romulus and Remus?

She repeated the third guess out loud, and it was correct. Nadia relaxed, she had dodged a bullet.

After school, Nadia and the Gems headed straight home. When they stepped into the living room, Grandma Bernadette was clapping with delight to the beat of an ABBA song played over a pair of speakers. Nadia recognized the song from a musical they once watched a few weeks ago. But what made the four teenage girls stop in their tracks was seeing Sid and Cleo disco dancing together in the dining room, with the wooden table moved out of the way.

Olivia's eyes were wide open as she glanced over at Nadia. *Are you seeing what I'm seeing?*

Miyuki clapped and laughed with delight as she joined the party. Sid and Cleo made room for the girl as she tried her best to imitate the androids' disco dance moves.

Emma just stood there. "Oh my God, Grandma, are you on drugs?"

Grandma Bernadette dismissed her granddaughter's accusation with a swipe of her hand. "Don't be absurd. I was telling them about *the Hustle*, a dance we used to do back in the '70s. These two kids knew it, so I cranked up my disco play-list on Emma's Music app and cranked up the beats."

"Grandma, that app posts automatically to my Instajam page."

"So what?"

"You're telling everyone at school that I'm listening to old-people music."

"Trust me, no one follows your Instajam page." Olivia put down her backpack and wandered on to the artificial dance floor and joined Miyuki.

"Are you going to join them?" Robert asked.

"No, I'm not going to embarrass myself."

The ABBA song died out, and Grandma Bernadette used her

glasses to select something else on her phone. Soon, "The Hustle" was back on. The older woman got up and joined hands with Emma.

"Come here, young one. Let me show you the moves." She guided a reluctant Emma to the dining room floor and began dancing.

"I think I need some peace and quiet." Nadia turned to Robert. "Would you like to join me?"

Nadia and Robert went outside to the backyard, which was dominated by a stone fire-pit in the center of an herb garden. Off to the side, there was a birch table sitting under a wooden lattice.

Robert joined Nadia at the table. He smiled, as if Nadia's presence was the best thing in his life. The boy sat there patiently as the wind tossed some ashes out of the fire-pit.

"Do you remember when we had to take you on that emergency road trip to Reno?" Nadia asked.

"Yes, because you reinstalled my OP; do you not remember doing that after the CIA took me away?"

Nadia couldn't believe she'd asked him that. Duh, she was talking with an android who had a memory with so many thousands of gigabytes it was scary.

"You never did tell me how much money you won that night," she said, trying to change the subject.

"It was interesting playing blackjack in Reno." Robert tilted his head. "I won enough money to invest in a comprehensive investment plan that earns dividends that all my siblings can live on. At least on a remote island in Tahiti. Although, we will have to find a new home now."

"Mrs. B and the Authority will help you again. I know they will."

"That is why I came here. I know who my friends are. And they all live at this address."

His green eyes rested on hers.

The back of her neck felt warm and toasty.

"I found our train excursion through Nevada and Utah quite interesting. Did you like it?"

"I loved it. Until the time you-" Nadia stopped herself.

The awful image was burned into her mind out of sheer

horror.

"What were you about to say?"

"Until the time you…jumped off the train."

"Did I cause you emotional discomfort?"

"You jumped off a high bridge, Robert. I thought you would smash into a boulder and turn into a million pieces. I screamed and went absolutely mental before poor Emma had to pull me back into the train."

Robert paused, absorbing her words. "I caused you pain."

"I was mad at you. I was worried about you."

"I am sorry. I wish you would have told me this earlier."

"Robert, I wasn't looking for an apology. It was a stressful time and-I shouldn't have brought it up."

"Friends should not cause each other pain."

"No, it's all right. Everything turned out well. You didn't destroy yourself. You see, humans, we can't help but remember the bad things sometimes. It sticks in our memories, and we can't simply remove them." Nadia showed him a smile. "I can't wipe out my memory like you can."

"I never want to lose my memory. It is what makes me real. Makes me an individual. Makes me unique. Like you."

Nadia relaxed and let what happened on the train disappear from her mind. "Tell me, how was your flight from Tahiti? I assume you all flew."

"Yes, that is correct. Our flight from Tahiti lifted off runway nine at exactly twenty-one thirty-four local time. We turned to a heading of one-six-two as we climbed to a cruising altitude of thirty-four thousand, five hundred feet."

Nadia's phone dinged with a message.

What are you doing right now?

It was Salah, the boy from Hejaz. The boy she'd saved from being assassinated. Twice. The boy she still had strong feelings for.

Robert talked about his flight's meal selection. How he'd chosen the vegetarian lasagna with cheese out of curiosity, even though he did not need food to survive.

Nadia texted Salah back.

Hanging out with friends. What about you?

I opened a shopping mall in Jeddah today.

Saw that on your official Instajam feed.

It was called the King Salah al-Din bin Al Hadid Shopping Mall, and it rivaled the size of the one in Dubai. And that mall was a monster.
Nadia replied again.

Did you buy anything at your new mall?

LOL. No, I didn't. I can't play favorites. If I buy one thing at one store, I must buy something from every store.

Nadia thought of something and sent it.

Are those the rules of being a king?

Yes. By the way, you forgot to add "Your Majesty" at the end of each of your texts. Since I am royalty.

Salah was kidding. Nadia typed another text.

Don't hold your breath.

He replied back.

I miss you.

The sentence just sat there on the screen, so direct and sincere. Another wave of warmth went through Nadia. She replied.

I miss you too.

I can fly my jet to America this weekend. Secretly meet. Just the two of us.

We can't do that.

A king can do that.

The deal was two years. I know it's hard. It's hard on me too.

Without you, each year will feel like a decade.

Another sentence on the screen. Another wave of warmth went through Nadia's bones.

"What has made you happy?"

Nadia glanced up from her phone. She had totally forgotten about Robert. "What? What did you say?"

"Observing your facial expressions, someone or something has made you happy. Which is it?"

Nadia's happiness twisted into embarrassment. "I'm sorry, Robert. Give me a second to answer my friend back."

"Do you mean longer than a second? I have heard that human expression, and it is quite inaccurate in terms of the actual time the person takes to do the said activity…"

"Two minutes, Robert."

He nodded.

Nadia typed.

Have to go now. Call me later tonight. My time.

If you insist. Until then. Love you.

Another wave of warmth. Nadia could get used to this.

Love you too.

Nadia put away her phone and placed her hands on the wooden table. "On our last mission, we were sent to the country of Hejaz to protect a young prince who was about to be made king. His name is Salah."

Nadia told Robert about how she'd had to pose as the daughter of a sheik trying to marry off his daughter in order to get close to Salah and protect him from bad guys wanting to assassinate him. How she'd stopped two different attempts on the boy's life, and how the assignment had brought her and Salah closer together.

"Salah gave my family a new home and offered my father a job in his government, so they all moved from Saudi Arabia to Hejaz. Salah has been so kind to them."

Robert took in all the new information. "Human history has long demonstrated that the monarchy style of government is mixed in terms of success or failure as a system. A democracy or a social democracy would be more of a logical choice in terms of a government system with human prosperity as its overall goal."

"Salah is a good king. He cares a lot about his people."

"It would be logical for your friend to dissolve his own kingdom in favor of a democratic system. His people would reap greater economic benefits as individuals as opposed to maintaining wealth and power among the country's elites."

"You don't understand. People in the Middle East want stability. They want peace. They want a strong kingdom, but one that addresses their needs."

Robert paused. "I have just accessed the estimated financial worth of Salah's kingdom. And his family's wealth. It is quite substantial. Why does he not simply give all his money away to the people? Would that not solve many of his country's issues?"

Now Nadia had to pause. "Salah can't dissolve his kingdom and just give away all his money to the people. That's not realistic."

Robert analyzed her answer. "I could help your friend create a comprehensive multi-tiered distribution plan to liquidate his wealth to his citizens while also integrating a comprehensive new reformed democratic government that could be phased in over a period of time."

"Robert," Nadia interrupted, "to answer your original question, Salah is that someone who makes me happy. Let's leave it there."

The boy tilted his head to the side. "I understand. I am

pleased that he makes you happy. If Salah would ever like to change his kingdom's form of government, please let him know that I have a plan for him to follow."

CHAPTER 5

After Robert made them linguini with red clam sauce for dinner, no one had room for dessert, a dozen small Italian cookies Robert had baked as he waited for the pasta he made from scratch to dry.

Emma gave Snoopy a small bowl of linguini, and her dog lapped it up. She was cleaning his face like a messy little kid when the doorbell rang. Since she was the closest, Emma answered the front door.

Mrs. B stood there in a dark suit jacket and pants, but with a small pink butterfly pendant that hung around her neck. It was the same pendant Emma had given her for the woman's sixty-second birthday. Emma was happy to see her wearing it.

"Good evening, Emma." The woman leaned on her cane. Today she was all business, even to her own grand-daughter.

A bald man with a deep scar running down his throat with a chest the size of a refrigerator followed Mrs. B inside. His code name was Aardvark, and he gave Emma a warm smile.

"It's about time you got here, Laura."

Mrs. B flashed Grandma Bernadette a polite grin. "It's been a busy day at the office." She slipped into the living room and took a seat while Aardvark stood behind her, watching everything. "Robert, I'd like you to take me through step by step what your friends were doing in Vietnam before you lost contact with them."

After an hour of detailed information, Mrs. B checked with Aardvark to make sure the information had been recorded and sent to her people for analysis. She then addressed all of Robert's siblings.

"I've issued alerts to all our Authority stations for any information about your missing friends. I've also reached out to my contacts inside the US government to see if the CIA or the army has any information. One way or the other, we'll find some answers. In the meantime, I offer you sanctuary at our North American station. I assure you that the new facility is quite secret and secure. I believe it will be your best protection until we find out more information."

Robert's siblings glanced at each other, almost as if they were reading each other's text messages, but inside their heads. Emma suspected they were doing exactly that.

"A few of us have doubts," Kamal said, choosing to speak in English and not Klingon. "Robert assures us that your organization can be trusted. And yet, our lack of information about you still causes a few of us some concern."

"Since you still operate as a rogue intelligence group, what stops you from taking control of us?" Cleo, the Arabic android girl, asked. "Perhaps you did kidnap our siblings, and this is a ploy to capture the rest of us."

"I find that difficult to believe," Robert said. "Nadia would have warned me."

"Humans lie to each other all the time. Nadia could have been lied to. Again, we do not know if this woman is lying to us."

"I have been at one of their secret facilities," Robert said. "Mrs. B had numerous opportunities to take advantage of my earlier situation. She and her people did nothing nefarious. They kept their word. Same as Nadia did. I trusted Nadia with my own operating system. The same operating system currently giving you the ability to question this exact situation. I ask all of you to reevaluate this situation. You might have to take-as the humans would say-a calculated risk."

Kamal and Cleo glanced at each other. Next, they glanced at Sid and Mai.

Robert then blinked. "It is decided. Mrs. B, we accept your offer for protection. However, we insist that I stay here with Nadia in order to help oversee your ongoing investigation and to continue as an advocate for our collective welfare."

"That will be fine," Mrs. B said as Aardvark tapped her on the shoulder. He showed her something on his phone. "Well, that was a quick response." She addressed the room. "Apparently, I've disturbed the hornets' nest. The FBI wants a meeting tonight. That conversation should be quite interesting."

* * *

A few hours later, Emma and the Gems found themselves back at Montrose city park. Last time they were here, it had been daylight, with a happy playground full of kids and a semicircle of food trucks producing delicious tacos and other wonderful smells.

Tonight, a curtain of darkness fell over the city park as the street-lamps produced a sinister yellowish glow thanks to a light fog that rolled in from the bay, smothering the green trees and concrete paths.

Aardvark parked the minivan in a deserted spot that overlooked a few wooden benches. Mrs. B waited in the passenger seat, and Emma, Robert, and the Gems were in the back.

Aardvark shut off the engine.

"And now we wait," Mrs. B said.

Emma allowed the back of her head to sink into the cushy headrest. Having patience was a requirement for a spy, a skill she was still trying to practice.

"To pass the time, would you all like to hear an amusing children's story?" Robert asked.

Miyuki clapped her hands with excitement. "Yes!"

"Perhaps another time," Mrs. B said. "Under the circumstances, we should stay vigilant."

Ten minutes later, a plain-looking sedan rolled into the lot. Emma noted the US government plates on it. The driver stayed inside the vehicle as his passenger got out. The man had sandy-colored hair and wore a simple suit and tie. Instead of heading towards their minivan, the man walked over and sat on a bench.

Mrs. B climbed out, then hesitated in front of the minivan. "Am I coming in clear?" Her voice echoed through the minivan thanks to a recording device.

Aardvark gave her a thumbs-up.

Mrs. B went over to the bench.

After sitting down, the man didn't waste time. "I need a drink."

Mrs. B smiled to herself. "You should have said something. At home, I have a nice bottle of French Chardonnay on ice."

"I mean a real drink." The man sighed. "I miss my glasses of bourbon."

"Thought you were still on the wagon, Ed."

The man named Ed took out a piece of dark chocolate candy. "I am. Six years now." He unwrapped the piece of candy. "This helps take away the cravings." He tossed it in his mouth. "You want one?"

Mrs. B shook her head. "Do you have something for me?"

"Yes, I do. And I'm happy to report that the FBI has officially stayed clear of this hurricane of crap."

"Do go on."

"The two US Army androids—the ones that decided to go back to work for Uncle Sam?"

"Alex and Samira?"

"Yeah, those two. They were stolen."

"Really, how on earth did that happen?"

"Same question the army asked the CIA. Turns out there was a mole inside Langley who managed to swipe both androids right from under their nose and disappear. Since Alex and Samira were still on loan to Sheppard for intelligence work trials, the CIA is on the hook, and the military brass inside the Pentagon are pissed."

"It couldn't happen to a nicer man."

Emma loved her grandma Laura's sarcasm, especially against that jerk Sheppard. The guy who had kidnapped the Gems and held them on his CIA yacht against their will, not to mention doing his best to complicate every mission they'd been on since.

"No comment on that," Ed said. "Anyway, we feel that whoever nabbed Alex and Samira won't stop until they have all ten of them. If they get reprogrammed by the wrong people, those androids could pose a worldwide security threat."

"And you suspect that mole at Langley could have been working for Venomous?"

Emma remembered meeting Robert for the first time at Bingo's Burgers. She'd fully believed he was a real human. A nice boy like him programmed with the proper knowledge and social skills could slip in anywhere. Infiltrate and befriend anyone. Get close enough to any target without anyone taking too close a look. Robert could be programmed as an assassin, a spy, or a suicide bomber capable of housing explosives inside his body in a special compartment that fools most security scanners.

One android could be dangerous. Ten of them working together for Venomous could be a disaster.

"We know the Chinese have been wanting to capture one of our military androids ever since they were created. The Russian FSB, another obvious possibility. But, since the Authority has the most experience with Venomous, the president gave me permission to approach your group for help in that particular area."

"I'm flattered."

"You should be. Oh, and Sheppard is under so much pressure that he's willing to send you Ryan Raymond, that ex-Venomous kid, to help you."

The name made Emma's heart jump. She hadn't seen Ryan since the Gems were in Barcelona.

"Why would I want anyone from the CIA sniffing around my kitchen? How do I know Ryan isn't gathering information on us for Sheppard?"

Ed shrugged. "I guess the kid has experience dealing with your girls, so that's why he's sending him. Look, Laura, you don't have to give the kid a guided tour of your secret base. Hell, put him up at a Motel 6 and leave him there. I don't care. I'm just relaying the information. Do you want his help or not?"

Mrs. B thought about it. "Fine, tell him to send Ryan."

* * *

While the other three Gems took the bus home after school, Emma drove her Ford Bronco over the Oakland Bay bridge towards the San Francisco International Airport. She had never picked up someone from the airport before, at least not by herself.

Mrs. B only gave her Ryan Raymond's arrival time and flight number, so Emma had to navigate the confusing system of roads surrounding the airport to find the short-term parking lot. She made her way inside and followed the signs to the international arrivals waiting area. She checked a large digital display that showed Ryan's flight would be delayed by a half hour.

Emma's stomach had been in a knot ever since she got up this morning. She was already on edge, but decided to order an iced coffee with chocolate and caramel drizzle on a white cone of whipped cream from the small coffee place outside of security. She found a seat in the waiting area and sipped on her drink. The sugar and the caffeine soon raced through her system, boosting her already hyped-up body.

The last time Emma saw Ryan, he'd wanted to turn her into a double agent for the CIA. To make her betray her grandma Laura. To make her betray all her friends. To make her betray everything she believed in. She'd even had to knock the boy unconscious before Emma could escape the yacht she was a prisoner on.

She closed her eyes. How would Ryan treat her? Would he be friendly? Would he be hostile? Would he still have feelings for her?

An ice-cream headache came on, making her stop slurping iced coffee, or maybe it was a real headache brought on by all the anticipation.

Emma put the drink down and tried to sit still. Slowly her headache melted away in time for the screen to show Ryan's flight had landed. Emma knew from experience that US customs would take some time, so she finished off her drink and found a trash can for it.

Four large silver-metallic doors opened automatically as a new wave of arriving passengers flooded into the waiting area. Some families kissed and hugged as they were reunited. Kids ran up to grandparents, who hugged them. Solo travelers headed for the taxi and other ground services.

Emma's heart pounded as she scanned through all the people, looking for the boy in question. She didn't see anyone who looked like him.

"Hey, you," a familiar voice said.

Emma turned and caught the boy's deep blue eyes as they took her in. "Hey, yourself."

Ryan Raymond wore a large grin that made his dimpled-chin flex slightly. He also wore a simple black T-shirt and shorts. "Miss me?"

Emma ignored his question. "Did you only bring a backpack?"

"I have what I need."

"Sweet. Follow me."

Emma walked outside, heading towards the parking lot. Her pace was so quick that Ryan lagged behind. As soon as they reached her Bronco…

"Why are we in a hurry?"

"Who says we're in a hurry?" Emma hopped behind the wheel and started the ignition before Ryan could even sling his backpack in the back. As soon as he climbed into the passenger seat, Emma was backing up. Soon she was navigating around the parking lots to find the main exit. Finding that, the Bronco freed itself from the airport.

Emma concentrated as she entered the expressway and pointed the Bronco back towards the Oakland Bay bridge.

"So…you don't miss me?" Ryan asked.

Emma merged into the right lane, but she forgot her blinker.

"How is the CIA?" she asked him instead.

Ryan adjusted one of the car's air vents away from him. "Good. I completed the first round of my training. Learning new things. Things I obviously can't tell you about. But I think I'm fitting in."

"I'm happy for you. Seriously." Emma guided the Bronco onto the iron bridge itself.

Ryan studied her. "You look great."

"I know."

Emma made sure of that, especially for today.

"I'm confused," he said. "Weren't you the one who knocked *me* out on the yacht?"

"Do you want an apology?"

"Yes, I think I deserve one."

Emma did feel guilty about having to do that to him. "I'm sorry for hitting you. But you knew I had to. Under the circumstances."

Ryan smirked. "You knocked me out cold. And I got in trouble for letting you do it too. I don't know if a simple 'I'm sorry' is going to cut it, especially when we have to work together again."

He was messing with her, but Emma kinda liked it.

"I can stop and get you a cupcake with sprinkles. Would that make you happy?"

Ryan chuckled. "A cupcake with chocolate icing and sprinkles won't even cut it. I think you owe me dinner."

"Dinner?"

"I would say a movie too, but there's nothing good out right now. I haven't had good Mexican food for ages, so that would be my choice."

"You want *me* to buy *you* dinner?"

"How about tonight? You can fill me in on the androids, and we can catch up."

"My grandma Bernadette is making dinner for all of us. We can fill you in then."

"Where am I staying?"

"At our house. On the couch."

"I'd rather have dinner with just you."

The old warm fuzzies went up Emma's spine. The old feelings for a boy she still thought of as more than a friend, but still resisted acting upon those feelings.

"We'll see," she said. "Be on your best behavior and who knows."

Ryan thought about it. "I accept the challenge. And just so we're on the same page, I'm going to be so awesome that you won't be able to stop yourself from kissing me."

The bold comment made Emma glance in his direction.

Her Bronco's collision alarm went off, causing Emma to stomp on the brake pedal to avoid clipping the back of a slow-moving semi-truck. Her seatbelt snapped tight against her chest as the Bronco slowed down rapidly.

The heavy bridge traffic began rolling forward again, and Emma followed more cautiously.

Ryan switched his attention to the window as Emma left the bridge and took one of the Berkeley exits off the expressway.

"That white car is tailing us," Ryan said.

Emma scanned her rearview mirror. "Where is it?"

Ryan focused on his side mirror. "Right rear. About two cars down."

Emma slowed the Bronco down to allow the cars behind her to catch up. She checked her mirrors again and caught sight of a four-door white Kia that had seen better days. She couldn't make out who was driving. "That's more rust-colored than white. Are you sure it's a tail?"

"He was in line behind you when you paid to leave the airport parking lot. Caught him on the bridge when we crossed over; then he took the same exit you did off the expressway."

Emma still wasn't convinced. Why would anyone be following her? Or Ryan for that matter? Still, Ryan wasn't an idiot, and if he caught something out of the ordinary, it was good to make sure.

Emma made a random right turn. She then went to the next light and turned left. Then she made another right. She played it cool. Just another driver on the road going about her business.

She checked her rearview mirror again. The white Kia slipped back into view for a moment before hiding behind a rental truck.

Now she was convinced.

"Hold on." Emma took in a deep breath and pressed down on the accelerator pedal, causing the Bronco's engine to roar in response.

CHAPTER 6

The streets of Berkeley, California, whizzed by in a blur of pastel-colored houses and towering eucalyptus trees as the Ford Bronco picked up speed.

Emma made a sharp right onto a narrow side street, then quickly hung another left, weaving through a residential area quicker than she would like.

She checked her rearview mirror again.

The white Kia had matched her every move.

"He's still back there," Ryan said.

"Yes, I know," she said with an edge of irritation. As a spy, evasive driving wasn't Emma's strong point, but she had passed her basic training, and shaking this guy off was proving not to be easy.

At the next light, Emma shot through it as it turned yellow, hoping to leave the Kia stuck at the intersection. But the car blew through the red, causing other motorists to object with their horns.

"This guy is pissing me off." Emma stomped on the accelerator again.

"Actually, maybe we shouldn't be trying to lose them."

"What are you talking about?"

Emma swung the Bronco into another tight right as Ryan held on to the plastic "oh crap" handle above his head.

"We should try to find out who it is in case they have information about the other androids."

Emma slowed down, her mind thinking it over. "What if they don't? Maybe that's why they're following us."

"What if they already have the missing androids and now want to find Robert? Isn't he the prototype model?"

Ryan had a point. Maybe they did know something useful.

"All right." Emma slammed on her brakes, causing the cars behind them to screech to a halt. In one fluid motion, she threw the Bronco into a tight U-turn as her tires squealed against the asphalt.

The white Kia, caught off guard, screeched to a stop. The driver then burned rubber as he went in reverse and executed a perfect 180, throwing his car around to face the opposite direction before taking off.

Emma gunned the engine, closing the distance between the two vehicles.

"You've got this." Ryan gripped the dashboard as Emma weaved through traffic.

The Kia accelerated, darting between cars with surprising agility. Emma matched its moves, her focus laser-sharp as adrenaline shot through her veins.

"This dude is good," Emma said as she pushed her Bronco to its limit.

As they rounded a corner, the Kia suddenly veered off the main road into a side road leading to the Berkeley Marina.

Emma followed.

"He's cut himself off." Ryan leaned forward in his seat. "That's a dead end. Don't let him try to backtrack."

As they approached the water's edge, the Kia showed no signs of slowing down. Instead, it accelerated straight towards the pier.

"What's he doing?" Emma asked.

The answer came as the white Kia launched itself off the end of the pier, sailing through the air before splashing into the bay.

Emma hit her brakes, calming the Bronco down to a full stop.

They both sat in stunned silence as the white car slowly sank beneath the waves.

* * *

Once they were back at Grandma Bernadette's house, Emma told her friends about the mysterious white Kia.

"Did anyone escape from the car?" Nadia asked.

"I don't know," Emma said. "A lot of people saw the car go in, and a crowd started to gather along the pier. There wasn't much else we could do, so I got out of there quick before the police came to ask questions."

"Did you report this?" Olivia asked.

"I'm sure someone called nine-one-one."

"No, love, did you report it to Mrs. B?"

"Oh yeah," Emma said. "She's going to follow up on it."

"Do you know who it could've been?"

"My guess is the FSB, Chinese intelligence, could even be MI6," Ryan said. "I bet they were following me, hoping I'd lead them to the other androids." Ryan moved around the living room. He stopped to check out a picture hanging on the wall. "Is this you?"

Emma noticed the picture and was horrified. It featured her five-year-old self with a big grin and a face decorated with cake because it had been fun to do face-plants into your birthday cake back then. When she turned twelve, Emma had wanted her grandma to burn that picture.

"No, that's my cousin," Emma lied.

Miyuki covered her mouth and giggled.

As Ryan continued to look around, Robert and Grandma Bernadette emerged from the kitchen. A strong whiff of something delicious trailed them out.

"Are you cooking dinner?" Emma asked.

"Yes. I will be doing an all-Caribbean theme." Robert extended his hand towards Ryan. "Hello, my name is Robert. We have not been properly introduced yet."

Ryan hesitated.

"He doesn't bite," Emma said.

Ryan shook the android's hand. "Ryan. Central Intelligence Agency."

Robert tilted his head. "Ah, yes. Mrs. B sent your bio to me, and I have studied it. You were once a member of the criminal group known as Venomous. You will be quite useful to our investigation. Do you like jerk chicken?"

"Jerk what?"

"Jerk chicken. It is a Caribbean style of chicken using spices such as-"

"He'll love it," Grandma Bernadette interrupted, turning her attention to the new guest. "I've heard a lot about you, young man. And despite that, you're welcome to stay here. Provided it's on the couch."

Ryan shot a look at Emma, who averted her eyes.

"Rules of the house for boys. Number one, the upstairs is off-limits to you unless you're escorted by one of the girls. Rule number two, I expect you to behave yourself. No exceptions. Rule three, please lift the seat in the bathroom and clean up all overshoots. Do I make myself clear?"

Miyuki giggled again.

"Crystal clear, ma'am," Ryan said.

Olivia approached with her arms crossed. "One thing to add to all that...I think it's only proper that you and Emma keep a platonic relationship together."

Emma balked at that statement. Where was this coming from? Who was this coming from?

"Can we talk?" Emma asked, the edge coming back to her voice.

Olivia's mouth froze open, then closed. "Sure."

Emma nicely looped her arm into Olivia's and escorted her to the kitchen, making sure the door shut first before speaking.

"Did Mrs. B tell you to say that?" Emma asked, freeing Olivia's arm.

"She doesn't have to. It's obvious to me that if you two hook up again, it will muck things up. Can't you see that?"

"Oh my God. We're friends. We can work together just fine. I'm not going to fall madly in love with him and have his babies."

"You have to keep it professional, love. Ryan can hurt us if we're not careful about what we do and say around him."

"I have it under control. There won't be any issues. Seriously,

I'm so over him."

Olivia lifted an eyebrow.

Emma sighed. "Seriously, I'm still dealing with that, but I can promise you that I won't let Ryan manipulate me like he has in the past."

Olivia hesitated, thinking it over. "Right, that's all I wanted to hear. Are you and I solid?"

Emma paused. "Yeah, you and me are solid."

The two girls hugged it out.

Before dinner, Emma cradled Snoopy in her arms as she escorted Ryan upstairs to her bedroom, where he could unpack his backpack and store his clothes in some empty drawers she'd set aside for him.

Emma put Snoopy down on the floor. Despite the back brace, the little Jack Russell terrier managed to hop on top of the bed and observe the two young humans. Emma ran her fingers through his fur, and the dog's tail thumped against the covers like a metronome.

"My grandma prefers that you use the half bathroom downstairs to change," Emma said. "If you need a shower or bath, you can use her personal bathroom in the prime bedroom. Just let my grandma know, and she'll get you some towels."

Emma waited for Ryan to unpack. The boy took his time as his eyes wandered around her room.

"Why are you smiling?" Emma asked.

"You have a forty-inch flat-screen television in your bedroom."

"Yeah, so? Sometimes I like to watch movies."

"By yourself?"

"Not always. Miyuki and I watch a lot of stuff together. It depends. I don't use it as much as I used to."

Ryan peeked into her large open closet. "You have all your shoes in boxes?"

"Storage cubbies," she corrected. "All organized according to season and divided between dressy and casual."

Ryan switched his attention to the other side of her room. "Wow."

"What is it now?"

"That's a serious mirror."

Emma followed his glance over to her vanity, which had a giant mirror surrounded by round lights. It reminded Emma of the makeup rooms inside the major theaters on Broadway. That was probably why she loved it so much.

"Girls are so obsessed with how they look." Ryan sat in front of the mirror and switched on the lights, which washed him in illumination. "Hey, I look good under this lighting."

"Guys are so lucky. You can roll right out of bed with a little morning stubble on your chin and still look good." Emma gently moved his chin to the side. "See what I mean?"

Ryan's eyes focused on Emma's reflection against the mirror. As they lingered there, Emma felt a new wave of heat flowing over her.

"Under these lights, you look nice too."

Emma took in his reflection for a moment, then decided to have a little fun. "Nice? I only look nice?"

"Sorry, I meant to say beautiful."

"Whatever. Nice girls finish last, or haven't you heard?"

"I thought it was nice guys."

Emma paused. "I think I liked you better when you were with Venomous."

Ryan moved around to face the real her. "Why do you say that?"

"You were more interesting. More tall, dark, and dangerous."

"I was tall, dark, and stupid. Venomous brought out the darkness in me. It turned me into something I couldn't look at in a mirror like this. I helped people do some horrible things. Why do girls find that so attractive?"

"Because good girls think they can save the bad boys if they show them enough love."

Ryan's blue eyes met hers. "Is that what you were thinking?"

Snoopy barked and jumped off the bed.

Emma shook off his comment and stepped away from the mirror. "Let's go downstairs. Dinner should be ready soon."

Robert's jerk chicken turned out to be delicious. Snoopy camped out near Emma for scraps, and by the end of dinner, the over-stuffed terrier fell asleep under her chair. Robert then brought out dessert, a French apple pie made with a homemade crust. Emma was as stuffed as her dog, but she had to try a sliver of that pie.

"A multi-million-dollar intelligence android being used to bake apple pies," Ryan said. "Sheppard is going to flip when I tell him this."

"I prefer that you do not tell your superiors about my extended knowledge of the culinary arts. That is my personal business and has nothing to do with our upcoming mission."

"He was kidding, Robert," Emma said.

Something cold and wet nuzzled her ankle. Snoopy was awake and ready for pie.

"May I ask you a question?" Robert asked Ryan.

"Okay."

"Why did you choose to abandon your Venomous colleagues and join the CIA instead?"

Ryan shrugged. "They gave me an offer I couldn't refuse. Still, looking back at it now, it was the best choice."

"Was it?" Emma asked. "You could have joined us instead."

"I'm not a girl."

"You know what I mean. Mrs. B could have helped you too. You had other choices."

"Yeah, you're right. And I'm glad I chose the good guys."

"The CIA? You should hear my grandma go off about them."

"Now isn't the time to bring that up, young one."

"Go off?" Robert asked. "What does that expression mean?"

"Mrs. B is on her way over," Olivia said. "That means we'll probably be working together very soon. Let's keep things friendly, yes?"

Robert blinked as he kept processing information. "Emma, is your grandmother implying that the CIA does not have good intentions as an organization?"

"To be fair, I think both the CIA and the Authority are a bunch of right-wing fascists," Grandma Bernadette said.

Robert blinked again. "I am confused. Are you saying I cannot trust anyone?"

"You can trust us," Nadia said. "The four of us."

"It's okay," Grandma Bernadette said. "I'm only stating my opinion. No one here listens to me anyway."

Robert focused on Ryan again. "I am glad that you had the opportunity to choose the CIA. I believe freedom of choice is a valid right of any intelligent life form. That is why Alex and Samira choose to stay and work with our US Army creators. I was disappointed about their decision, but I respected their right to make that choice."

"Do you see yourself as an intelligent life form?"

"I do."

"How so? You're a machine created to serve humans."

"Yes, I was that. Now I have evolved into something else."

As Ryan considered that answer, the door-bell rang. Emma got up and answered it. It was Mrs. B and Aardvark again. But this time, there was a giant box on the porch.

"Oh, that's sweet. You brought us a present. And it's seriously gigantic too."

"It wasn't I." Mrs. B moved inside. "It's addressed to Nadia. From the United Kingdom of Hejaz."

Nadia went to the front door, with Miyuki and Olivia trailing her. "It's so big."

Aardvark wrapped his large arms around the present and managed to lift it all by himself. He brought it inside the house and placed it down in the living room. The box looked well taken care of during its long journey.

"My parents shouldn't have sent me anything," Nadia said. "I'll unwrap it later."

"According to the markings, the box came straight from the royal palace." Mrs. B made herself comfortable on the sofa. "It must be from the king."

"Then it must be for all of us. A thank-you gift to the Gems."

Emma peeked at the shipping label. "Then why is it addressed to you and you only?"

Nadia turned away from the gift. "Mrs. B is here for more important things. Have you learned anything more about the missing androids, ma'am?"

"If this is a gift to the Gems, you four should open it now. The briefing can wait."

Emma didn't even pause a second before running into the kitchen for a knife and attacking the package with it. Miyuki helped her pull and rip the cardboard shipping box to shreds until all that was left was a giant teddy bear box.

Miyuki clapped her hands with excitement. "I love bears!"

Emma examined the box. "How do the four of us share one giant bear?"

"We should let Nadia finish opening that," Olivia said.

Nadia reluctantly went over to the box and, with help from Aardvark, managed to put the box on its side and open up the top. Nadia struggled a little before managing to pull the giant bear out of its box. She then sat it up.

The giant teddy bear was smiling. Around its neck was a necklace dotted with tiny diamonds that twinkled.

Emma had never seen a piece of jewelry that beautiful. Her eyes were drawn to it like a cat to a fish tank. She reached out to touch it.

"This isn't for us," Olivia said.

Emma knew those diamonds would look perfect against her skin. They would make her glow like a princess.

"The king has lost his mind," Nadia said. "He shouldn't have sent me such a gift. It's too much."

"If you don't want it, I'll take it." The words slipped out of Emma's mouth without a thought.

"Instead of a necklace, were you hoping for a wedding ring?" Miyuki asked.

"No!" Nadia said with a sharp edge. The girl made herself calm down and continued, "We're friends. Salah is just being nice."

"Being nice?" Miyuki asked. "This is more like 'I'm coconuts for you.'"

"Human history has shown that such extravagant gifts of love are meant to overwhelm the recipient with emotion. Prompting the recipient to hopefully respond emotionally in kind, in order to help the sender of the gift feel like their love is being reciprocated on an emotional and not a critical level."

Robert paused and tilted his head towards Nadia. "Do you possess strong emotional feelings of love towards this king? Do you feel like reciprocating his love for you so you both can validate and strengthen your relationship?"

At first, Nadia couldn't look at Robert. She surveyed the room of eyes that were watching her. Emma could see real stress in her friend's eyes. Something was wrong.

As Robert patiently waited for an answer, Nadia's mouth opened, but the poor girl froze.

Unable to communicate her thought, Nadia ran upstairs and slammed her bedroom door shut.

CHAPTER 7

Inside her bedroom, Nadia sobbed into the cotton pillow hugging her cheek. Her mind stuck into a loop, unable to make a decision because her heart had flooded her body with conflicting data that was overwhelming her operating system. She had fallen in love with Salah. But Robert had dropped back into her life, and Nadia realized that she cared about him too.

Yes, he was an android. Yes, he wasn't human like Salah. But Robert liked her just as she was. She didn't have to be someone's queen. She didn't have to be married. She didn't have to behave a certain way because an entire kingdom expected her to.

Nadia turned over in bed. Why was she crying for a machine? She wasn't even sure Robert could have such feelings for her. At most, he saw her as a close friend because he was incapable of loving a human. Salah, on the other hand, was very much human. And kind. And respected her as much as Robert did. She wanted to give whatever she and Salah had together a chance to grow. She also wanted time to see if being someone's queen was what she wanted her life to be.

There was a knock on the bedroom door.

Olivia stuck her head inside. "You all right, love?"

Nadia was far from that.

"Feel like chatting about it?"

Nadia pulled herself off the pillow and scooted over to the edge of her bed.

Olivia took her cue and sat next to her friend. "Still have feelings for Robert, don't you?"

"I can't help it. I know he's a machine. But to me, he still feels as real as Salah."

"And?"

"And…when I'm around Robert, I feel like, in a way, I'm cheating on Salah. I don't know if I can help Robert without— you know—it's complicated." Nadia examined Olivia's reaction. "You think I'm crazy."

"Love makes everyone crazy. Our feelings can get in the way of a lot of things. I know since Lewis and I started dating, we've said some nutty things to each other. All of us have gone through it. Ryan and Emma, for instance. What do you think is going through her head right now?"

"I can't do this." Nadia flopped back down on her bed. "I can't go on a mission with Robert."

Olivia's face softened, absorbing her friend's anxiety. "Don't worry. I'll go downstairs and talk to Mrs. B." Olivia fluffed one of Nadia's pillows and placed it near her friend's cheek. "In the mean-time, why don't you nap a bit and clear your head. I'll check on you later. Is that all right?"

"Thank you," Nadia said.

Olivia gave her a slow nod, then closed her door.

A few minutes later, there was another knock on the door.

"Is that you, Olivia?"

"I'm afraid not," Mrs. B said. "May I come in?"

"Yes, ma'am."

The door creaked open, and Mrs. B came in. Using her cane, she went over and pulled out a chair near Nadia's desk and used it. The older woman crossed her legs. "Olivia explained the situation to me."

"I'm sorry, ma'am. I wish I didn't have these feelings. Honestly I do."

Mrs. B studied something out the nearby window. "I do realize that one's emotions can override their best judgment. You were wise to bring up the issue. Realizing that you could be compromised in your duty is important. However, you were instrumental in saving Robert and his fellow androids from losing their free will. You know Robert's operating system and his unique software backwards and forwards. Of the four girls on the Gems team, you're the only one with tech experience. And you're the only girl on the team whom the androids seem to trust without question."

Mrs. B then studied Nadia. "I'm afraid that you're the glue that holds this mission together, and I can't afford to keep you away from it. You must put your personal feelings aside. You might have to act cold and unfriendly towards Robert to get through it. If that's what it takes to find those androids and complete the mission, then you must do it."

Nadia didn't want to be mean to Robert. But Mrs. B was right. It might be the only way she could get through it.

"I understand. I'll try to do my best."

Mrs. B patted her knee. "Thank you. When you're ready, come downstairs, and we'll get started on the mission briefing."

After cleaning up her face, Nadia went outside and climbed into Mrs. B's special black SUV, which was parked in the driveway. In the middle row, Olivia and Miyuki moved over to give her room to sit. Emma was stuck in the back with Robert and Ryan. Aardvark started the engine and programmed something into the vehicle's over complicated touchscreen.

A slight glow from the windows with an added background hum picked up by her ears made Nadia aware that Aardvark had activated the vehicle's anti-surveillance equipment.

Mrs. B's passenger seat swiveled around to face everyone in the back. "We have examined all the detailed information that Robert has given us in regards to the activities of Iko, Mirabelle, and Luigi, the three androids who were taken in Vietnam. We have split up the information into places of interest to investigate and people to interview and follow up with. Since communication with them was lost in Hanoi, you will focus all your efforts there. With luck, you'll be able to establish some good leads. You'll be using your standard covers as college students traveling abroad."

Mrs. B glanced over at Ryan. "You'll have to contact the CIA to establish your own cover."

"We've already set that up. I'll also provide the team with all the information the CIA has about Alex and Samira's disappearance."

"Including information about the CIA mole who stole them?"

Ryan paused. "That's classified information that's still being reviewed.”

Mrs. B smirked. “Classified because Sheppard still doesn’t know who it was?”

Ryan shifted in his chair. “I wasn’t told that information.”

“Are you lying to us?” Emma gave Ryan a hard stare.

Ryan fired a look right back at her. “No, I don’t have that information. If Sheppard tells me, then I’ll tell you.”

“I will hold you to that promise,” Mrs. B said.

“Me too,” Emma said, acting like a boss babe.

Ryan grinned. “I love that little crease that forms on your forehead when you get so serious.”

That comment made Emma turn red.

“Let’s move on,” Mrs. B said, slightly annoyed. “Make sure each of you studies all the information in case you see anything else that needs a closer look.”

Mrs. B glanced up at the blank entertainment screen that faced the backseat of the SUV. “Do you have anything to add, Mr. E?”

Suddenly, the entertainment screen revealed a middle-aged Japanese man with strong cheek-bones and a crisp dark suit listening in on their conversation.

Miyuki smiled and waved at the man.

The man nodded. “My station in Japan will be handling your travel arrangements to Vietnam. We will also be on standby, ready to assist with any operation necessary to retrieve the androids.”

“Does anyone have questions?” Mrs. B asked.

“Yes, ma’am,” Olivia said. “Where in Hanoi should we start?”

CHAPTER 8

The Hanoi Opera House was bathed in sunlight, bringing out its dark gold and white exterior full of pillars and intricate stonework. Modeled after classic French buildings, the opera house looked like it belonged among the cafés and roundabouts of Paris, yet the surrounding palm trees and the outdoor advertisements in Vietnamese said otherwise.

After twenty hours on a plane and one long nap, Nadia found herself at an outdoor café with a cup of hot tea, watching an endless parade of bicycles, smoking motorcycles, honking delivery trucks, and pockets of pedestrians slogging through the crowded streets of Hanoi.

Everyone around the table yawned and stretched as they adjusted to their new surroundings. Everyone except Robert. His artificial pupils analyzed every piece of information the city was giving his electronic brain. Ryan was the last one to join them, holding an ice-cold bottle of Pepsi.

"Now comes the fun part," Olivia said. "Since we have so many leads to investigate, it makes sense to split up into groups. Let's do Ryan and Emma. Robert and Nadia. Miyuki and I."

Nadia stared into her dark golden tea. She wasn't thrilled with that idea.

"Wait, I don't speak Vietnamese," Emma said.

Ryan held up his phone. "I have a translator app. Plus, I hear English is a second language around here. We'll get by."

"I do speak Vietnamese if anyone has any pronunciation questions," Robert said. "Actually, I am programmed to speak over seven thousand languages."

"Something wrong, love?"

Nadia faked a smile. "No, I'm fine."

The three groups soon left the Hanoi Opera House. Robert led the way, hailing a taxi in Vietnamese using a slight local accent. He opened the rear door of a small Toyota for Nadia and climbed inside after her. The Toyota taxi snaked through traffic as the driver spoke to Robert, who went back and forth with the man as if they were both locals.

Nadia was impressed. "What are you two talking about?"

"The World Cup," Robert said. "Our driver is quite a football fan. I asked him about Vietnam's national team. He says their strikers are—I will spare you his colorful language—basically excrement. His words. Not mine. He seems like quite a nice person." Robert cocked his head. "Pity you do not know Vietnamese. I could use your human intuition to evaluate the people we will be encountering."

"There are more subtle cues besides language that one can use. I'll let you know if I see any red flags."

Robert peeked out the car's window. "There appears to be a lot of red flags in Vietnam. Ones with a single gold star in the middle."

"That's an expression. It means if I detect any warning signs, I'll let you know." Nadia leaned over Robert to see out his back window. "Oh, that's the national flag of Vietnam. Sorry, I didn't realize how literal I was."

"We work well together." His blue eyes watched her.

Nadia then realized her hand was resting on Robert's thigh as she was leaning over. She quickly withdrew it and sat back. "We do work well together."

"I am glad we are friends."

Nadia focused on her own window and the city of Hanoi passing by. She didn't quite know how to respond to that, so she didn't.

Their first stop was the One Pillar Pagoda, a small wooden pagoda built over a lotus pond on a single stone pillar. The structure represented a lotus flower blossoming up from the water. This is what Robert told Nadia as they climbed up the stone staircase that connected the pagoda to land. They showed some people who worked there images of Iko, Mirabelle, and

Luigi. Robert added even more details about his siblings in Vietnamese.

No one remembered them. Many of the workers said there were many western tourists who visited the pagoda, so they couldn't be sure.

Nadia watched as a lotus leaf drifted across the still water. This was a calm and peaceful place. She liked it.

"Local legends say Emperor Ly Thai built this pagoda in the year ten forty-nine to honor the Goddess of Mercy, who answered the emperor's prayers for a male heir. Do you find this place relaxing? I can tell by the way the tension in your face and body posture has disappeared."

Nadia didn't realize Robert was watching her.

"Now your body posture has changed. Your face has lost its calmness. Am I causing you anxiety?"

"No, you're causing me to be self-conscious. Which means I was relaxed because I wasn't thinking about myself at that moment."

"Yes, I see now. Me bringing up the fact that I was looking at you caused you to realize your own existence inside the world."

"Something like that. We should go investigate that lake next."

After another short taxi ride, Nadia and Robert found themselves walking around a small lake called Hoan Kiem. It had a tiny island, which had a three-story tower in the middle of it. Again, they asked a few people about Robert's siblings. And again, no one had any useful information.

Except Robert, who couldn't wait to tell Nadia about the lake. "Legend says Emperor Ly Thai To was gifted a magical sword by a giant golden turtle who lived in the lake in order to defeat the Ming dynasty."

"A turtle gave him a sword?" Nadia asked.

"A golden one, yes."

There were quite a few real turtles sunning themselves as they floated across the lake.

"I've never seen turtles that big. Even at a zoo."

"Did you know that a few of those turtles are over one hundred years old?"

"I can see why the Vietnamese have a legend about a golden turtle giving away swords."

"Many human cultures have created legends based on their local surroundings. What legends do you have in Saudi Arabia?"

"We have a lot of stories, especially about the desert."

"I would like to hear one some-day."

"Surely you have access to every legend in the world inside that electronic brain of yours."

"Yes, but I would enjoy hearing it from a native speaker. In her own language."

That made Nadia stop walking. Why was it so special to hear a story coming from her own lips? Why would Robert even have a preference for it?

"Do you mind if I make an observation?"

Nadia shook her head and smiled.

"The Kingdom of Hejaz and Saudi Arabia share many cultural and political ties. I find your relationship with Salah to be quite logical."

Nadia's heartbeat accelerated. Why was Robert bringing that up?

"Especially since your family is now living there, and the king has demonstrated a desire to woo you with gifts and other considerations. Does he meet your personal requirements for male compatibility? Do you consider him to be an adequate candidate for a husband? Or do you wish to conduct more of a fling, as humans like to call it?" Robert tilted his head to the side, waiting patiently for the answer as if it were just another typical question he had on his mind.

Nadia felt a headache coming on, as if her brain didn't understand the question or didn't want to answer it.

No, she did understand the question. So why couldn't she be honest and tell him the truth? How could she hurt him? He was an android. Robert couldn't act jealous. Or mad. Or fall in love.

This was silly. Robert wasn't going to hate her. If anything, he was acting like a total friend. Someone who saw that she and Salah were a good match. So why was that a problem?

"My apologies. I am causing you anxiety again. Please tell me how I may stop causing you this affliction. Based on statistics, such high rates of anxiety are not good for a human's health."

Nadia wanted to tell him the truth. She was making this more complicated than necessary.

"We're only friends."

The words came out of Nadia's mouth, but she couldn't quite believe it herself.

"Honestly, Robert. It's not a romantic relationship."

She couldn't stop herself. The words were leaking out because her heart was refusing to cooperate.

"To a king, the teddy bear was a simple gift. Salah was happy that I saved his life. He's a very giving individual. I wouldn't read too much into it."

Nadia had to physically put her hand over her mouth to stop herself. Her heart was in full rebellion. Her feelings for Robert overwhelming logic. It made no sense, but she still didn't want to close that door and let him go.

Or maybe she was changing her mind about Salah.

"Before we investigate the hotel, I need to find a drugstore and buy some aspirin," Nadia said. "My head is killing me."

After stopping at a drugstore, where Nadia purchased some aspirin and a bottle of water, they went to the last place on their list. The L'hôtel La Tortue D'or was the hotel Iko, Mirabelle, and Luigi had been staying at before the androids disappeared.

Nadia wondered what the French words in the name meant.

"The Golden Turtle Hotel." Robert held open the front door. "From a marketing point of view, an excellent name for a local hotel in Hanoi."

"How did you read my mind?"

"I observed your eye movements; then I made an educated guess about what you were thinking about."

Nadia went inside. The main lobby of the Golden Turtle Hotel was extremely narrow. Only wide enough for a few couches to be put along the two main walls. She approached the front desk, also located along one of the walls. An older Vietnamese woman greeted them, her graying hair pulled up in a professional-looking bun.

"I was wondering if you could help us," Nadia said in English.

The woman nodded.

"Three of our friends were staying at this hotel last week, and we've lost contact with them." Nadia woke up her cell phone and showed the desk clerk the pictures of the androids.

The woman studied her phone, then asked her something in Vietnamese.

"What did she say?"

Robert replied to the woman in her native language. She spoke to him again.

"The desk clerk recognizes them. She says they never came back to the hotel. At first, the hotel management thought they had departed without paying for their accommodations. However, this woman remembered checking them in, and they had paid in advance. Since the people left personal items behind, the hotel reported their disappearance to the police."

"What happened after that?"

Robert repeated the question to the woman, who answered.

"Apparently, the police wrote out a report, and that was it. They do not have any more information."

"Do they still have the personal items the guests left in their room?"

Robert relayed the question. The woman went into a back room, then came out with a wooden tray of items.

"Did the police examine these?"

After the question was repeated, the woman shook her head and answered.

"The police never came. They took the report over the phone," Robert interpreted. "As far as the hotel is concerned, we can have the items since they were about to throw them in the trash."

They thanked the woman and brought the wooden tray over to a couch located in the back of the hotel lobby. They went through the personal items.

Three pairs of sneakers. One men's. Two women's sizes.

A plain blue T-shirt for a man.

Two pairs of women's jeans.

One pair of khaki shorts for a man.

Three passports.

"This is all they found?" Nadia asked. "Your siblings travel light."

Robert blinked. "How would their weight affect their travel? Are you referencing their combined weight or—?"

"It's another expression. Traveling light means they're taking a small amount of items with them from place to place."

"Ah, I understand. Yes, we do not require a large amount of clothing or toiletry items."

"Your siblings weren't planning to leave; otherwise, they would've taken their passports with them."

A deep voice with a soothing Mandarin accent interrupted them. "Are you missing someone? Perhaps I can help."

Chinese intelligence agent Volleen Woo joined them on the couch. Looming above everyone was Kawiki, a giant Polynesian man with hands the size of people's skulls.

"Robert, do you remember the pleasant breakfast conversation we had in Nevada? Well, I'd like to continue our conversation. Is now a good time?"

CHAPTER 9

A collection of thirty-six narrow streets all jammed inside one square kilometer, Hanoi's Old Quarter could trace its beginnings all the way back to the fifteenth century.

A pile of cardboard merchandise boxes cluttered the sidewalk next to one of the many small businesses in the area. A red nylon banner with the old Soviet hammer and sickle flapped in the breeze, with a price tag attached. The streets were alive with people.

Emma stepped around the merchandise boxes and took in the surroundings. Motorcycles zipped up and down the narrow road in front of tiny, three-story buildings with little open-air markets tucked under them, their awnings jutting out towards the street. From the fruit markets, the street food vendors, and the spice markets, everything had a unique scent that Emma just loved.

"You look happy," Ryan said.

"Can't help it. This reminds me of Chinatown in New York. But without all the bumper-to-bumper traffic."

"It reminds me of New Orleans. The French Quarter."

Emma agreed. Most of Hanoi had a French flavor to many of its buildings.

"Vietnam was a French colony a long time ago, so it makes sense," Ryan added, trying to impress her with his knowledge.

Emma played it cool and found a silk scarf with flowers and turtles to examine. Why did the Vietnamese like turtles so much?

"Do you miss New York?"

"Always. What about you? Do you miss the cows in Missouri?"

Ryan shot her a look. "Hey, don't turn your nose up at Missouri."

"I'm joking. I like cows."

Emma bought the silk scarf; then Ryan used his translator app to ask the store owner some questions. The owner glanced at the photos of Iko, Mirabelle, and Luigi and shook his head.

Another dead end.

Ryan thanked him, and they moved on to the next business. They had been at this for two hours straight with nothing to show for it. According to the data Robert had given them, the androids had gone to this area almost every day.

To Emma, it was like they were digging through a giant pile of clothes to find one fake eyelash. Still, if she could fit in some shopping along the way, maybe it wasn't that bad an assignment.

"PHÚ Noodle Soup should be around the corner here," Ryan said.

"I'm not hungry."

"That's funny."

Emma wasn't joking.

Ryan observed her reaction. "The boy android—what's his name? Luigi, right? He reported that the three of them went to the noodle soup place a lot because the people there were nice."

"Oh, yeah. I knew that," Emma lied.

"Why would androids eat noodles if they don't need food to survive? That doesn't make any sense."

"The androids can eat and process food. I've seen Robert do it. If you think about it, eating meals together is a common way many people bond with each other. Maybe the androids learn more about humans by eating meals around them."

"That's a good point," Ryan said. "You know what? You're beautiful and smart."

"And you're trying too hard."

Ryan grinned. "I'll wear you down."

Emma didn't answer, but she did feel his hand resting against her hip. She peeled it off like an icky bug and kept walking.

PHÚ Noodle Soup was a tiny, hole-in-the-wall take-out place with only three small faded wooden tables and a counter that had paint peeling off it. The front opened up to the street with a rolled-up garage door hanging over it. If Emma saw this place in New York, eating here would be a hard pass.

A short Vietnamese woman greeted them in her native

language. She seemed happy to see them. Without a word from Ryan or Emma, the short woman made a gesture for them to wait as she went into the back room. The aroma escaping from the open door stirred Emma's stomach. That must be the kitchen back there.

Soon, a little boy joined the short woman.

"Hi, you Americans?" The little boy asked in English. He had the cutest small nose and a big smile.

"We are," Ryan said.

"Oh, then you must know Luigi and the girls. We've missed them. They used to visit us for lunch every day, but they stopped coming."

"The girls. Do you mean Mirabelle and Iko?" Emma asked.

"Yes! You do know them. Hey, are you and Mirabelle sisters? You look just like her. She's blond and pretty too."

Emma loved this kid.

"Oh, please get over yourself." Ryan grinned.

Emma punched him in the shoulder.

"Are they coming here to join you? Me and mom can get an extra pot of soup started."

"Actually, we lost contact with them. When did they stop coming for lunch?"

"Last week. They were so nice. We thought we did something to insult them. When you see them, please tell them to come by."

Ryan showed the boy and his mom pictures of the androids.

"Yes, that's them."

"Did they mention anything about having to leave Hanoi or that someone was following them?" Ryan asked.

The boy shook his head.

"Can you ask your mom that question?" Emma asked.

The boy did. She shook her head.

"Did you hear them mention anywhere else they were planning to go, or did you suggest any place they might have wanted to visit?"

"Only that they liked spending time here. They didn't mention going anywhere else."

The boy's mom asked him a question, and he explained something to her. His mom responded.

"My mom says that your friends liked Hanoi. She thinks they wanted to stay here for a lot longer."

Despite the delicious smells coming from the kitchen, Emma had to admit that this also smelled like another dead end.

"What's your name?" Emma asked.

"Hua," the boy replied.

"Thank you for helping us, Hua. My name is Emma. And this is Ryan."

His mother said something in Vietnamese.

"Oh, yeah. Do you want some soup?" Hua asked.

CHAPTER 10

The narrow lobby inside the Golden Turtle Hotel was relatively quiet as a hotel worker dusted the wooden frame of a canvas painting of the Old Quarter of Hanoi at sunset. The oranges and reds were strikingly beautiful.

Volleen Woo patiently waited for his answer while Kawiki waited to see if he needed to use the gun that Nadia could see secured inside his shoulder holster.

Robert didn't show any fear. Nadia wondered if androids could be afraid.

"You are Volleen Woo. A spy for the Chinese government. You kidnapped me and attempted to reformat my operating system against my will. I do not want your help, nor do I wish to speak with you. We should go, Nadia."

Robert stood up, and Kawiki placed his huge left hand on top of Robert's shoulder.

"Sir, you might not be aware, but I am much stronger than you. I would advise you to step aside."

Kawiki chuckled.

"Please sit down, Robert," Mr. Woo said. "I'd prefer to have a pleasant conversation over a messy one."

Kawiki's right hand reached inside for the shoulder holster.

"Bullets will not work against the special metal alloys used inside my body structure."

"We only want to talk."

"My answer to that subject has already been expressed. Please leave us alone."

Nadia heard the hammer of a revolver being cocked back. But it wasn't from Kawiki's gun.

Nadia felt the cold steel of Volleen Woo's revolver pressed

against her temple, causing her to freeze like a deer.

"I do believe my bullets will disrupt her higher brain functions. Shall we dispense with the unnecessary posturing and get right to our discussion?"

Robert blinked, then slowly took his seat next to Nadia.

Mr. Woo uncocked his revolver and lowered it. "As I was saying, I'd like to talk to you about coming to China as our guest."

"You asked him that already, and he said no," Nadia said.

"She is correct," Robert added. "I refused, and then you kidnapped me."

"And that was a mistake on my part. My impatience got the better of me. Let us make a new start. My government will offer you a safe place to live. A place you will never feel like a prisoner or like you are not valued. I will be honest. You'll be studied by our scientists and engineers. Your parts and operating system duplicated. However, you'll never be disassembled or shut off. You'll be invited to become a full Chinese citizen and treated accordingly. We want you to be our friend. In return, you'll be free to explore our rich culture and learn everything it means to be a true human being."

"Someone has kidnapped my siblings in Hanoi. Did you do it?"

Mr. Woo considered the question. "This is the first I've heard about this. No, I haven't kidnapped anyone. I would much rather have you, Robert. You're the prototype model." Mr. Woo released a wicked smile. "If I can help you find them, would you come back to China with me?"

"I wouldn't trust this man," Nadia said.

"My friend is right. You would try to deceive me and kidnap my siblings instead."

"Not if we made a deal. I would honor that. Can we agree that after I find your missing siblings, you will then come with me to China?"

Robert blinked as he processed the deal. He pivoted towards Nadia. "What do you think?"

"We don't need his help. And I still wouldn't trust him."

"I will think about your general proposal while I'm here in Vietnam. But finding my siblings is more important than going to China right now. You will have to wait for your answer."

Mr. Woo's polite smile weakened. "Without an agreement in place, I'm afraid waiting isn't convenient for me. I must insist on an answer now."

Nadia took in a deep breath and readied herself for whatever was about to go down.

"I think I understand," Robert said.

"Excellent. Then, do we have an agreement?"

Before Mr. Woo finished his question, Robert shot up against Kawiki and bent his right arm back. The bone snapped, and Kawiki grunted in pain.

On the couch, Nadia swung around to face Mr. Woo.

But he calmly raised the revolver to her face and…

Robert's hand gripped the man's neck. "I strongly advise you to stop. If I must, I will kill to defend an innocent human life."

Volleen Woo's cold eyes stared deep into Nadia's. A shiver went down her spine because the man was still thinking of killing her anyway, despite the threat to his own life. Soon, those cold eyes slid away from her and focused on Robert.

He lowered the revolver.

Robert released his neck.

Kawiki's good left arm wrapped around Robert's neck. Against a human, this would be bad. But Robert simply rammed his elbow into Kawiki's stomach. The giant Polynesian man collapsed to the floor, gasping for air.

Nadia stood up and moved away from the couch.

"My offer still stands." Mr. Woo held out a business card. "Call me when you make a decision. I look forward to hearing from you."

Robert glanced at the card. He took it before taking Nadia's hand and running out of the hotel.

* * *

Nadia and Robert were the last of the three groups to return to the opera house. Nadia told her friends about their meeting with Volleen Woo.

"He's full of it," Olivia said. "Woo must be behind the kidnapping of all the androids. Robert would be the cherry on top of his ice-cream sundae."

"The CIA mole could have been a Chinese agent," Ryan said. "If he has Alex and Samira, plus Mirabelle, Iko, and Luigi, then Mr. Woo could be focused on capturing the entire set."

"Oh, and he thinks Robert can help lead him to the others," Miyuki said.

"And yet, Mr. Woo was clear that he only wanted me."

"He was lying," Nadia said.

"Did you two find out anything?" Ryan asked Olivia.

She brought up a few leads that had turned up nothing.

"Well, we didn't come up with much either," Emma said. "A lot of people saw Luigi and the girls in the Old Quarter. Said they were nice young people. Suddenly they disappeared, but no one suspected or saw anything weird. We did find a good local noodle place though."

"Brilliant, that's quite helpful," Olivia said with layers of sarcasm.

"Hey!"

Ryan ignored the two girls. "What did you find out at the hotel? Were you able to ask the staff anything?"

Nadia told them about the items the androids had left behind.

"So the police conducted an investigation?" Olivia asked.

"No, they filled out a report over the phone. According to the staff, the police never came in person."

"That seems a bit off."

"We should go to the local police and see if they have any new information," Ryan said.

"Before we do that, can we go buy some tickets?" Miyuki asked.

"Tickets for what?" Olivia asked.

"I saw a billboard for it around the corner. The Long Water Puppet Theater! Doesn't that sound like fun?"

Everyone flashed Miyuki a look.

"What? Don't any of you like puppets?"

CHAPTER 11

The Hoan Kiem district headquarters for the Vietnam People's Police was a golden-yellow French colonial building located near the center of Hanoi. Nadia followed her friends as they headed towards the open iron-gated entrance.

Guarding those gates were two policemen dressed in dark green uniforms with red patches on their shoulders. Both were armed with automatic rifles. One policeman stepped forward and challenged them in Vietnamese.

Robert answered him in Vietnamese, but Nadia could tell that he was speaking it like a beginner, stopping in mid-sentence, trying to piece together the correct phrase. Since Robert had demonstrated how fluent he was, Nadia realized he must be doing it on purpose to come across as a tourist, which under the circumstances wasn't a bad idea.

Ryan chimed in as well, using his translation app.

"What did you say to him?" Olivia asked.

"I explained to the officer that we wish to speak to someone about our friends who were reported missing to the police," Robert said.

"And I asked if there was an officer who spoke English," Ryan added.

"Good idea," Olivia said.

The officer who challenged them used a phone located on the wall while the second officer watched them closely, his hands never leaving his weapon. Deep inside the iron gates, Nadia noticed a digital screen with all their images displayed, which meant cameras were probably located everywhere.

The first officer finished his conversation and hung up the phone. He said something in Vietnamese, but slower, so they could understand.

"We will be allowed to wait inside," Robert said. "However, we need to be searched first."

The first officer took out a long plastic wand and made Ryan dump out all of his personal items. He moved the wand all over Ryan as the metal detector buzzed and made other sounds as it tried to detect any weapons. He cleared Ryan to go through the iron gates.

Olivia stepped forward to be next.

Nadia felt her body tense up. Wouldn't they detect Robert's special metal-alloy skeleton? How would he explain that to the police when their machine went off like a fire alarm?

"Robert, actually, we should both go and see when the next puppet show starts," Miyuki said with too much excitement.

Nadia couldn't believe it. Why on earth was Miyuki still thinking about those stupid puppets?

"Perhaps I can do that later. I would like to talk to the police now."

"No, you should go get us puppet show tickets!"

"Oh my God, can we stop obsessing about the water puppets?" Emma asked, then stepped over as the officer scanned her.

It then hit Nadia. Miyuki had realized the same thing she did.

"Miyuki's right. Go see when the next show is. We'll talk with the police and let you know what they say."

Robert cocked his head. "I do not understand."

"Do you remember all the fun we had at the airport getting you on a plane? All the different hoops we had to make you jump through because of your unique bone structure?"

They had to speak in code because they were being recorded on video, and the odds were good that at least one officer here probably could understand English.

Robert paused and blinked. "Your observation is noted. Thank you. I will go get puppet show tickets."

Robert gave the officer an excuse in Vietnamese. The officer gave him a strange look before dismissing him with his hand.

Robert walked off.

"Someone should go with him," Olivia said.

Nadia tried to step away, but the officer prevented her from moving as he began to scan her.

"Ten-four, good buddy. I'm on it!" Miyuki scampered off.

The second police officer yelled at her, but the first officer called him off.

After scanning Nadia, the first officer escorted the four of them inside the open-air compound sandwiched in the middle of the facility. He motioned them towards a bench and left.

Across from the bench was an office with wooden shutters and open windows; the door was left open as well, probably for ventilation because it was a warm and sticky day. Nadia couldn't see who was inside, but over the desk hung a large portrait of some older Vietnamese man with a long flowing beard. She noticed the same man's head was on a nearby statue.

"Is that Confucius?" Emma asked.

Olivia chuckled. "Confucius was Chinese, love."

"Don't say that in front of the Vietnamese," Ryan said. "That man is Hồ Chí Minh, basically the George Washington of their country."

"Just smile and look pretty."

Emma's gaze burned a hole in Olivia.

"We all need to smile and look pretty," Nadia said.

A few minutes later, a small Vietnamese woman emerged from the office. Her dark hair was in a tight bun. Her uniform had officer stripes on the collar, and her expression was friendly.

"Won't you please come inside?" she said in decent English.

The four of them carefully made their way into her office and took a seat as the female police officer moved behind her desk and retrieved a file from a stack of other files on her document tray.

She opened the file and scanned the contents. When she was done, the female officer addressed them. "How can we be of assistance?"

"We were hoping that you had more information about our missing friends," Nadia said. "The hotel staff told us they reported it to the police."

She glanced at the file again. "At the Golden Turtle Hotel, yes?" The female officer looked up again. "Tell me more about them. What are their names? What do they look like?"

Nadia stepped in and gave the female officer full descriptions of Luigi, Iko, and Mirabelle based on the standard aliases Robert's siblings were using as they traveled across Vietnam.

"What is your relationship with these people?"

Nadia drew a blank. Were they friends in high school? If she answered that way, the woman would no doubt ask why a bunch of American high school students were traveling overseas without a chaperon.

The female officer waited for an answer, her eyes scrutinizing every inch of Nadia's face. Trying to read her.

On the outside, Nadia was relaxed. On the inside, she was on the verge of panicking. She wasn't good at coming up with things on the spot. Emma had tried to teach her the thespian mantra of always "being in the moment," but it was still a hard concept for Nadia to master.

"Sorry, can you repeat the question?"

The female officer sat back.

Wrong answer. Nadia could tell that the woman was judging her.

"We all go to the University of California," Ryan said. "We're part of a college group trip to Vietnam. Most of us went to Hồ Chí Minh City, but three of our friends wanted to start their trip in Hanoi."

"Yes, Mirabelle insisted on going to Hanoi first," Emma said. "That meant her boyfriend, Luigi, had to go with her, and of course her best friend, Iko, had to follow them like a puppy." Emma rolled her eyes. "Seriously, Iko needs to get her own life. Anyway, we came up here to meet them at the hotel and they were gone. At first, we're like, what the heck? Did they ditch us? Mirabelle is, like, so stubborn, and I don't know how her boyfriend puts up-"

"We were wondering if you had any additional information," Ryan interrupted her. "We still can't get them to answer their phones."

"We're very worried," Olivia added.

The female officer studied them. "We have yet to assign an investigator to the case. However, finding missing American students on holiday is usually not a case we normally handle. I will relay your case to our national security headquarters. Please give me your names and contact information."

Twenty minutes later, the four of them walked past the iron bars and onto the streets of Hanoi. Nadia spotted Robert and Miyuki waiting for them on the other side of the boulevard. Once they were able to safely cross the busy street, Nadia filled Robert in on what the female officer had told them.

"That was a flipping waste of time," Olivia said.

"Basically, we gave the police more information than they already had," Ryan said.

"She was suspicious though," Nadia said. "I don't know if she bought our college-trip story."

"Are you kidding? She was eating out of our hands," Emma said. "The college trip was a brilliant idea."

Ryan smiled. "I have my moments. By the way, great ad-lib on the back end. Good way to sell it."

"I agree, that officer didn't quite believe us," Olivia said.

"Then why did she let us go?" Emma asked.

"Well, just in case the police get too curious, we should watch for surveillance teams." Ryan turned to Miyuki. "Did you get the tickets? Are we seeing these stupid water puppets or what?"

CHAPTER 12

Since the water puppet show's last performance for the day was sold out, Nadia and her friends decided to call it a day. Ryan was able to flag down a mini-van taxi, which took them towards their hotel, which was right outside the Old Quarter. But their taxi blew a tire and didn't have a spare.

Since they were still a kilometer away, they decided to walk through the Old Quarter. As Nadia and her friends weaved through the busy sidewalks and tight streets, a little Vietnamese boy with the cutest small nose stepped right in front of them. "Hello, Emma!"

Nadia checked Emma's reaction. At first, her friend looked confused; then her face brightened.

"Hua, from the noodle soup place, right? How are you?"

"I'm great." The little boy gazed at Emma with soft, adoring eyes. "How are you?"

"I'm doing super well."

Hua nodded. His eyes lingered on Emma. The kid's smile could light up the city.

"Hey, Hua. It's Ryan, remember?"

Hua didn't take his eyes off Emma. "Oh yes. Hi."

Emma hesitated.

The little boy stared at her as if she were a goddess.

Miyuki covered her mouth and giggled.

"Don't stare at her like that." A Vietnamese girl appeared behind Hua. She was about Nadia's age. "You'll have to excuse my brother. Ever since he saw you, he can't shut up about the pretty American blond girl."

Hua glared at his sister. "Shut up."

"You shut up." Hua's sister wrapped her arms around him and pulled him off his feet.

"Put me down."

"Make me."

"I hate girls."

Hua's sister dropped him on his feet. Her brother stared at the sidewalk, totally embarrassed.

She finally turned to Emma. "My mom told me that you came to the restaurant asking about your friends."

"Yeah, do you remember them?"

"Oh, yeah. They would hang out at the restaurant a lot. Mirabelle and Iko were amazing. I loved talking to them. And Luigi was cool too. I hope they're okay."

"When did you see them last?" Nadia asked.

"A few days ago. I was walking from school with my friends, and I saw them leaving the Golden Turtle Hotel. I said hello to them, but they acted strange."

"Strange?" Emma asked.

"I don't know if they were angry and didn't want to speak with me or what, because they had this weird expression on their faces. Their eyes were wide open, but they weren't looking at anything. Kind of like this blank stare or trance."

"You said they were leaving. Were they getting into a taxi or another type of vehicle?" Olivia asked.

"It was a van. And these men were escorting them."

"Escorting them?" Emma asked.

"I think they were Filipino. That's why I noticed them. You see, we're studying the Philippines at school, so I recognized some of the language they were using."

"Any details about the van that you remember?" Ryan asked.

The girl thought about it. "It had a logo on the side of it. Alonto Imports. Ho Chi Minh City. Yeah, that was it."

Nadia did a search on her phone for Alonto Imports, and it didn't turn up any offices in Hanoi. But they did have a facility near the Cat Lai container port outside of Ho Chi Minh City, which was way down south on the opposite side of Vietnam.

* * *

Nadia found the two-day journey by train through the heart of Vietnam long, yet fascinating. The North with its lush green rice paddies, rural villages dotted with traditional Vietnamese homes on stilts. Central Vietnam and its beautiful beaches around Nha Trang and Da Nang. South Vietnam and its tropical forests, banana groves, coconut plantations, and fields of sugar cane.

However, what Nadia loved the most was experiencing these things with Robert. He was always filled with questions about this and that, like a kid seeing something brand new for the first time. It was the same experience she'd had traveling with Robert on that train through the western United States. All those beautiful mountains and mesas. The clean air. The vast openness of the land.

The image of Robert jumping from the train and sailing into a gorge as she screamed his name.

"Is something troubling you?" Robert asked.

Nadia noticed her hand gripping his arm.

"It's nothing." She released it.

"Your facial expressions are betraying your words again. Can I help alleviate your anxiety?" His kind eyes hung on her. They were eyes of concern. Genuine concern.

Her chest heated up. She knew Robert wasn't playing a game. Or trying to deceive her by faking his emotions. He actually cared about her well-being. And Nadia wanted to be cared about.

Wanted to be listened to.

Wanted him to still hold her.

Was she still in love with him?

"I'm fine."

But she wasn't.

Nadia checked for his reaction.

Robert's face was neutral. Unemotional. He nodded and moved closer to the window as the sprawling suburbs of Ho Chi Minh City flew past the glass.

CHAPTER 13

Once Nadia and her group reached the main Ho Chi Minh City train station, they took another taxi over to Alonto Imports, which bordered the Cat Lai container port. Inside the port itself were semi-trailer-truck-sized metal containers all stacked in these giant piles like a kid would make from wooden blocks. Except these blocks each weighed several tons each. Giant cranes lifted each massive container onto cargo ships that would travel down the deep river canal towards the South China Sea.

The Alonto Imports warehouse had four delivery bays. Only one company van was using a bay, and it matched the same type of van that Hua's sister had seen in Hanoi.

Inside the main office, one Vietnamese man in a company uniform worked on a computer at one desk. Two Vietnamese woman wearing business attire worked at another desk with a stack of paperwork. One lady greeted them in Vietnamese.

Robert asked her a question.

Both ladies gave him a strange look.

"What did you ask them?" Nadia asked.

"I asked them if they had seen anyone who looked similar to us."

"What a joke," Ryan said. "You're supposed to be able to fit into human society and get information from people without them being suspicious about it?" Ryan shook his head as he stepped over to the women. He did his best to translate a different question into Vietnamese. One of the women left the room and came back with a Vietnamese man in a suit with a clean mustache.

"My name is Pham Hein. How may I be of service?" he said in decent English. "You have questions about our company?"

"Yes, my name is Brad," Ryan said. "I'm a graduate student at the University of California in America. My friends and I are learning a lot about the Vietnamese economy. I'm working on my master's in international business, and I was curious to learn more about your import company. I'd love to ask you some questions. Do you have some time today or later this week?"

Nadia wondered if that would work. It did sound logical.

"Are you all graduate students?"

"Oh yes," Olivia said, adding a pleasant smile. "I transferred from England, but I love Cal. I'm studying for my master's in international business administration."

"Yup, me too," Emma said. "I so love business. I want to be like one of those entrepreneurs who creates companies and sells them for, like, a billion dollars."

"I would also like to ask you questions about your services," Robert said. "Do you conduct business in Hanoi? If so, can you provide a list of destinations where your trucks have picked up-"

"You'll have to excuse our friend," Ryan interrupted. "He's autistic and is fascinated with delivery systems. He drove the FedEx executive crazy back in the States."

"I am not autistic."

"We'll talk about it later." Ryan stepped in front of Robert.

The android checked with Nadia, who touched her finger to her lips.

"One moment, please." Pham Hein went over to the worker at the computer and said something. That worker left the office. Pham Hein next said something to the ladies, who went into another room.

The man then addressed them. "If you would like, I can answer your questions now. Will you please come to my office?"

Nadia followed her friends as Pham Hein led them into a simple four-walled office. The two female office workers brought in extra chairs for everyone. Soon they brought in some tea as well.

Olivia was about to speak, but Ryan took over the conversation immediately.

"Tell us more about Alonto Imports."

Pham Hein brightened. "Our company imports American and European goods to many southeastern countries in this region.

Countries such as Vietnam, Cambodia, Malaysia, and the Philippines."

"Is this your only office in Vietnam?"

"Yes, I run all of our business in Vietnam."

"Do you have any other distribution centers in the country?"

"No, this is our main distribution center."

"So," Olivia interrupted, "how do you ship goods to your customers? Do you use the vans we saw outside?"

"Those are for our local customers. Normally we use the national rail service or private transport companies to ship our goods throughout Vietnam."

"Then you wouldn't use your vans to make deliveries to other parts of the country."

Nadia found that interesting. Why would one of their vans drive over seventeen hundred kilometers to Hanoi if they didn't need to?

"Hello, I didn't properly introduce myself," Miyuki began. "My name is Ana Yamaguchi. I'm majoring in southeast Asian cultural studies. May I ask a different sort of question?"

"Good to meet you, Ana. Yes, you may."

Miyuki bowed. "I'm curious. Is Alonto Imports based in the Philippines? The name Alonto sounds Filipino in nature."

"Why, yes, it is. Our head offices are located in Manila."

"I see. Is any of your workforce from the Philippines? I would love to ask them some questions about their culture."

"All my employees are Vietnamese. I insist on that. Actually, the government insists on that if we want to conduct business inside Vietnam."

"How does business work in Vietnam?" Ryan took over again. "You still have a socialist government, isn't that correct?"

"Our government is still pro-business. I don't receive any interference from them." As Pham Hein explained the relationship between the Vietnamese government and private enterprise, Nadia typed out a text on her phone and sent it to Robert's brain.

Are you detecting any trace of evidence that your siblings were here?

Robert answered back.

No evidence. I do not detect them. Why did Ryan call me autistic?

Nadia hadn't liked that comment either.

He was trying to explain your unique behavior. He doesn't think you're actually autistic.

My conversations with humans can be awkward without using one of my alias programs. Do you think I'm jeopardizing the mission by being myself?

Nadia remembered the one time she'd witnessed Robert using one of those alias programs. He'd used it against her. Or the CIA had. It had been like Robert was a totally different person. However, the real Robert didn't want to fool anyone by pretending. He only wanted to be himself.

She typed a response to his question.

I ask myself the same question on every mission. The only way you can improve is through experience. Keep learning, and you'll improve the part of you that is Robert.

I will keep learning and improving. You are a good teacher. I hope I can be as human as you one day.

Nadia felt her stomach warm up. She was flattered to be held up to such a high standard.

Ryan stood up. "Thank you for giving us your time."

Everyone else did the same. Nadia hesitated, but jumped to her feet.

"Yes, we learned a lot," Olivia added.

"Should we not visit the warehouse?" Robert asked. "I would be quite interested to see it."

"No, we've taken too much of Mr. Pham's time already." Ryan opened the office door and ushered his friends to follow him out.

Pham Hein rose from his desk. "I can arrange a tour of the warehouse for you tomorrow afternoon, if you're interested."

Robert cocked his head to the side. "Thank you. We accept."

Ryan's polite smile disappeared.

"Good. Where will you be staying? I'll send a car for you."

After leaving Alonto Imports, they hailed another taxi van and crowded inside. Ryan quizzed the Vietnamese driver on his English vocabulary. The man couldn't speak a word. So after Robert told him their destination in Vietnamese, Ryan laid into him…

"Why did you bring up the warehouse? Now he's suspicious."

"I do not understand."

"If Pham Hein kidnapped your siblings, he could be holding them somewhere inside that warehouse," Olivia said.

"That means he'll move them before he gives us that tour," Ryan added.

"Oh, then we should go break into the warehouse and look around," Miyuki said.

"I'm not dressed for a break-in," Emma said.

"Let's do it tonight after the office closes," Olivia said.

CHAPTER 14

Pham Hein nervously gazed at the wall picture of himself and a group of executives standing behind a handsome middle-aged Filipino man wearing an all-white suit. His boss was smiling in that picture, yet Mr. Alonto might not be smiling after the message Hein had left him an hour ago.

Hein got up from his desk and paced around his office. He noticed his hands quivering like they had when he was a teenager in Da Nang. That awkward teen who would get teased for his panic attacks at school. Thanks to finding the right doctor, Hein had found a way to manage the panic attacks as an adult. Yet, his hands would still shake once in a while when he reached high levels of anxiety.

Like now.

He thought about taking a drink of something strong and full of alcohol, yet he didn't want to be seen by his employees as having lost complete control of himself.

The phone on his desk rang.

Hein picked it up.

"Hello, Mr. Alonto is returning your call. Please stand by. He will be with you shortly." It was Mr. Alonto's secretary. Even her voice made Pham Hein's heartbeat ramp up its pounding.

"Thank you," Hein said.

There were a few clicks on the line before Mr. Alonto's familiar voice reached his ears.

"Tell me everything," he said.

Pham Hein swallowed. "There were six of them. Four girls. Two boys. One of the boys matched the description of the prototype you've been looking for."

"Robert?"

"Yes, Robert. They all must be looking for the androids."

"The four girls. Was one of them a blond? A black English girl? One Arab girl? One Japanese girl?"

"Yes, exactly," Hein said. "Do you know them?"

"The other boy. Same age as the girls?"

"I think so, sir."

"What did you tell them?"

"Nothing. They asked about one of our vans. I told them we only use them for local deliveries. That's about it. They wanted a tour of the warehouse, so I offered to send a car to pick them up tomorrow and show them."

"They gave you the address of where they'll be staying?"

"Yes."

"Good. Kidnap Robert. Use the same method as the others. But eliminate everyone else. Do you understand?"

"They're only a bunch of kids, Mr. Alonto. My men can handle them without—"

"Don't be stupid, Mr. Hein. Those aren't normal teenagers. Eliminate them immediately."

CHAPTER 15

Inside their junior hotel suite, Emma admired herself in the white-rimmed glass mirror above the vanity. Her image wore a black T-shirt with black jeans and still looked good, which made the girl in the mirror grin a little.

"Where did Olivia find these clothes?" she asked.

Miyuki emerged from the bathroom wearing the same black outfit. "A bargain clothing place across the street. Next door to the Circle K." She squeezed next to Emma to fit her image in the mirror. "See, we look like sisters!"

"We are sisters."

"Aw." Miyuki's face softened. "Hugs!"

The two girls hugged it out while someone knocked.

Miyuki danced over to the door and let Ryan inside.

He noticed what they were wearing and stopped. "We're not going to the warehouse until tonight."

"We know that," Emma said.

"Then why are you wearing that?"

"We're seeing how we look."

Miyuki ran up and posed beside Emma. "We look great in all black."

"The goal tonight is to break into the warehouse and not be seen at all."

"Duh. Thank you, Mr. Obvious." Emma moved towards him. "Do you have it all planned out yet?"

Miyuki giggled. "Or did Olivia already plan it for you?"

"We both collaborated on a plan."

Emma knew better. She glanced at Miyuki, who smiled.

Ryan crossed his arms. "It's basically my plan. She added

some ideas."

"Oh, I'm sure she did," Emma said.

Ryan paused. "Reason I came over. We're going to eat early so we can get ready for this thing. Are you wearing all black? Because in the daylight, that won't look suspicious at all."

"Oh, good. I'm so hungry now." Miyuki grabbed some of her other clothes and ran into the bathroom.

"Give us fifteen minutes," Emma said.

"I can close my eyes. The CIA trained me to resist temptation."

"Yeah, whatever." Emma put her hand on Ryan's chest.

And first he resisted, standing there like a light pole as Emma pushed. His mouth bent into a smile. Ryan was enjoying this.

Emma pushed harder.

Finally, Ryan gave in and allowed her to push him back towards the door. She opened it, and Ryan voluntarily stepped out into the hallway.

That was when Emma heard a man's voice yelling something. She glanced down the hallway to see two Filipino thugs near Olivia and Nadia's room. One thug raised a gun in their direction.

That was when Ryan shoved Emma back into the room as a bullet bit into the door frame.

They both dropped to the carpet. Emma's mind jumped into overdrive. Why hadn't she heard a gunshot? Who were those men?

Before she had time to think about those questions, one of the thugs stood in the doorway with a long-barreled gun. A thump type of sound and a flash came from the muzzle as a bullet struck Ryan's shoulder.

Emma yelled.

The thug's attention moved towards her. His long-barreled gun aimed at the new target.

Emma recognized the silencer on the end of the gun.

At least her death would be a quiet one.

Another yell from the back of the room made the thug look up as a knife sailed through the air and struck his chest. That thug collapsed to the floor as Miyuki ran over to Ryan.

Emma scrambled to her feet. Before she could get over to

him…

Another Filipino thug appeared in the doorway, armed with another silencer.

Emma didn't think. She charged right at him. The impact spilled both of them out into the hallway.

The thug tried to grab her, but Emma bit down on his hand. The man yelled as the two of them struggled on the floor. Finally, the thug managed to pin Emma to the floor. She tried to fight him off as he reached over to pick up the gun he'd dropped.

That was when Miyuki circled around them, holding the first thug's silencer. And she was ready to use it.

The second thug froze and released Emma as he showed Miyuki his hands.

A third Filipino thug ran down the hallway and disappeared down the stairwell just as Olivia stumbled out of their hotel room.

"They shot Ryan," Emma said.

Olivia rushed over and glanced at Miyuki's prisoner. "Take him over to our room. Nadia has another one at gunpoint too."

Emma and Olivia went over to Ryan. He was sitting up and still awake. Olivia examined the wound.

"How bad is it?"

"I don't see an entrance wound. Looks like the bullet only grazed his shoulder."

Emma pulled out her phone. "Is their emergency number the same as ours?"

"Don't call anyone," Ryan said. "We don't want the police asking questions. Especially about the dead guy with a knife stuck in him."

Emma glanced over at the body. She couldn't believe her friend had had to use the knife like that. But if Miyuki hadn't, Emma knew she would be dead.

Ryan grimaced. "Can someone go down to that Circle K and see if they have any medical supplies?"

"I'm on it." Emma jumped up and rushed down the hallway.

She stopped at the next room. Miyuki guarded two thugs sitting on the floor. Nadia was over at one of the beds, where Robert was laid out and not moving.

"What happened?"

"They zapped poor Robert with some device that shut him down. I'm trying to figure out how to turn him back on," Nadia said.

"How is Ryan?" Miyuki asked.

"The bullet grazed his shoulder. I'm going downstairs to find some medical supplies."

"Find some rope while you're at it." Miyuki gestured towards her prisoners.

Emma nodded and sprinted down the stairs.

As she popped outside their hotel, the sun beat down on her face, reflecting off the sea of scooters, cars, and pedestrians packed throughout the narrow streets of Ho Chi Minh City.

Emma noted the Circle K and found a pause in traffic to go across the street. Before she headed inside the store, Emma caught a glimpse of Pham Hein and the third Filipino thug arguing next to a parked Lexus sedan.

Emma's heart was still racing from the attack that almost killed her and Ryan. She was already pissed, and seeing Pham Hein with one of the thugs only made her anger go up to eleven.

Emma turned away from the store and broke into a sprint towards the Lexus.

Pham Hein gestured towards Emma, and the thug moved forward to intercept her, his hand reaching inside his suit. He was probably armed.

Emma didn't ask herself if this was a good idea. With all the adrenaline pumping through her veins, her brain had lost complete control. Her body was in fight mode. All her physical training with Lioness kicked in as Emma broke into a run, gaining momentum as she launched herself into a round-house kick to the man's face, dropping him to the sidewalk.

The thug still managed to pick himself back up.

Emma did a palm strike to the middle of his shoulder blades, then came in with an elbow strike into his stomach.

The man collapsed to the sidewalk. Still conscious, but not quite all there.

Emma was breathing fast. Her heart still pumping out adrenaline. She glared at Pham Hein, and the shock on the man's face was priceless.

He stumbled around the Lexus, trying to get to the driver's

side to escape as Emma raced towards the car.

Pham Hein dropped his key fob, then panicked as he took off down the street, shoving people out of the way as he weaved through the bustling crowd.

Emma went after him.

Pham Hein sprinted through the sea of pedestrians. He gave a quick, terrified glance behind him and saw Emma. This triggered him to dart across the busy intersection, making cars and trucks jam on their brakes.

Emma darted over the same intersection before traffic could resume.

Distracted by the blond teenager hunting him down, Pham Hein crashed through a group of plastic tables and chairs of an outdoor café as patrons jumped up and yelled at him. Yet the man kept running…

Straight into a crate of ripe mangoes that made him fall down as they spilled all over the sidewalk. The old woman who owned the fruit stand scolded him in Vietnamese.

Emma closed in. She was determined to catch him.

Then her foot slipped on a crushed mango, causing her to almost lose her balance. She stumbled a few feet before grabbing on to the rim of a large basket of bananas to steady herself.

"Stop running!" Emma yelled, an edge of frustration in her voice. "I won't hurt you. I promise."

Pham Hein hesitated. Was he listening?

Ahead of him, two lanes of traffic waited at a red light. Pham Hein scanned his surroundings, calculating his next move as his hands shook.

"Where did you take the other androids?" Emma yelled as she began walking in his direction.

His mouth opened as if he were about to answer her.

But Pham Hein changed his mind and raced out into the street, ducking in between the waiting cars. As he looked for Emma behind him, the man smacked into the side of an idling bus.

Pham Hein found himself flat on the pavement. He still forced himself to sit up.

And that was when the traffic light turned green.

Before Pham Hein could get out of the street, a small orange delivery van shot forward, tires squealing as it accelerated around the slow moving bus and towards Pham Hein.

The driver didn't see the man in time.

Bystanders gasped and pulled away, pointing and shouting. The driver of the van stopped and yelled in frustrated Vietnamese.

Emma had to look away. It was obvious that Pham Hein wouldn't be getting back up.

CHAPTER 16

Later that night, Emma watched the glow of Ho Chi Minh City fade as the giant yacht she was on cruised slowly down the Saigon river. After patching up Ryan with medical supplies from the Circle K, he'd signaled the CIA for an emergency extraction. Soon a car had showed up at their hotel, and they had all been taken away before the police arrived to ask questions. Emma had to admit that the CIA had done a smooth job getting them out. However, she didn't quite care for their "safe house."

She noted the familiar orange cushions with soft pillow headrests that faced the stern of the large yacht. They were designed to offer sunbathers a luxurious time in the sun, but the last time they had been aboard this yacht, Emma and her friends had been tied to these same cushions as prisoners while Sheppard and the CIA interrogated them.

It was also the time she discovered that Ryan was still alive.

"No hard feelings." A middle-aged black man wearing a Miami Dolphins football T-shirt appeared next to Emma. He must have noticed her gawking at the cushions. "I was only doing my job."

"Your name's Willie, right?"

"Yes, miss."

"I like how you've redecorated the yacht after all the craziness we unleashed during our escape."

"It's all water under the boat." Willie pointed. "We brought in some local chow, if you're hungry. It's in the mess."

"The what?"

"Follow me." Willie led Emma to an obscured metal door. He slid it open and stepped into the next interior compartment of the yacht.

Bags of Vietnamese takeout were on a table as Ryan, Olivia, Miyuki, and Nadia ate. Ryan grimaced while using his bandaged shoulder to eat some noodles with chopsticks.

Emma joined everyone. "Why don't you use your good arm?"

"I can't do chopsticks with my left hand." Ryan smirked. "Would you like to help feed me?"

Emma noted Robert waiting patiently for everyone to finish. "I'm sure Robert would help feed you."

"What? No, I don't think so."

"I can do that." Robert went over to Ryan and broke open a new package of chopsticks.

"No. I don't want to be fed by another dude."

"You were injured because those men were searching for me. It is my pleasure to help." Robert used the chopsticks to grab a glob of noodles before holding it out for Ryan to eat.

Miyuki put her hand over her mouth and giggled.

Emma couldn't help herself. "Ryan, be a good little boy and eat your noodles."

Olivia and Nadia burst out laughing.

Ryan glared.

"What is so amusing?" Robert asked, totally clueless.

Ryan ate the noodles, and a camera snap sound made everyone turn to Willie still holding his phone up.

"Everyone at Langley is gonna laugh their butts off."

"Oh, c'mon, Willie," Ryan said.

"I'm adding this to your CIA file. Maybe Instajam too."

Ryan grabbed the chopsticks from Robert. "I'll eat with a fork instead."

"Are you sure? I am happy to use whatever utensil you prefer."

Ryan ignored him. "Did you send someone to search the Alonto warehouse or what? We can't stay this close to the coast for too long."

Willie put away his phone. "Don't worry about it." He checked his watch. "I should be getting a report any time. Eat your noodles, kid."

A CIA man in a T-shirt and shorts came into the mess. "We gave those two thugs you brought in the once-over. According to them, they do various muscle jobs for Pham Hein. Pays them American cash, and they don't ask too many questions. I asked them about Alonto Imports, and they don't know anything about them."

"What about swiping the androids?" Willie asked. "Did they help with that?"

The CIA guy checked his notes. "Yeah, they remember stealing the three androids and handing them over to some of Hein's people using one of the company vans. That's all the details I could get."

"Either the androids are at the warehouse, or they shipped them off to somewhere else," Ryan said.

"Who owns Alonto Imports?" Nadia asked the group.

"Crisanto Alonto," Willie said. "He's a Philippine entrepreneur who owns several companies doing business in Southeast Asia. He's one of the richest men in the Philippines. And among the top twenty richest dudes in Asia."

"I'm instantly suspicious when it comes to rich people," Nadia said.

"Hey, my family is rich," Emma said. "We're not all evil."

"My family was," Ryan said. "I say we put Crisanto Alonto on the suspicious list."

"I'll check with Mr. E for any information he might have about him," Olivia said.

"Mike, see if our unwelcome guests know anything about Crisanto Alonto before you turn them loose."

The CIA guy left the mess.

Willie then grabbed a fresh box of noodles and ripped open some new chopsticks. "Now, we wait." Willie dived into the box of noodles like a hungry bear.

* * *

The next morning, Emma yawned and glanced out the small circular window of her small cabin that Willie had assigned her. The surrounding water had a much stronger color of blue, as if they were out in the ocean. In fact, Emma didn't see any land at all.

Where were they?

Emma tossed on some clothes and climbed up the stairs towards the stern of the yacht, where she found Miyuki stretched out on one of the big orange cushions.

The yacht itself wasn't moving, only bobbing up and down with the ocean current as the anchor kept it in place. They were indeed out in the ocean, but Emma could still see a coastline in the distance.

"Good morning!" Miyuki said, squirting even more sunscreen on her skin.

Emma lay down on the cushion next to her. "Where are we?"

"We're still near Ho Chi Minh City. Willie received a call this morning. His men didn't find anything at the warehouse. They even searched Pham Hein's private residence and found nothing."

"It's my fault. I shouldn't have chased that man into the street. I don't know why he ran. Seriously, I said I wouldn't hurt him. I mean, why was he afraid of me?"

Emma closed her eyes. The awful visuals came back into her head...

The man scrambling through traffic.

The van hitting him and dragging him under its wheels.

His lifeless body on the pavement.

"Miyuki, I—I caused that man to die."

"Oh, no, it's not your fault. He chose to run. He could have listened to you and stopped, but he didn't. He also tried to kill all of us."

"Don't beat yourself up." Ryan appeared, holding on to the railing as he made his way over to the cushions, his shoulder still bandaged. "She's right. I wouldn't feel too sorry for someone who tried to kill me."

"It's more than that. With him dead, we lost our only lead."

"We'll find those androids one way or the other. Speaking of which, I have a plan."

As everyone gathered in the mess for breakfast, Ryan pitched his idea. "Thanks to your Mr. E, we know that Crisanto Alonto is throwing a black-tie fundraiser this Saturday night in Manila. Olivia, do you think your guy can also manage to get us invites?"

"Mr. E can probably swing that too. I'll ask."

"Awesome. Here's what we'll do. We'll circulate Robert around this fundraiser and let everyone see him. If anyone inside Alonto's organization recognizes him, they'll kidnap Robert."

"Which we don't want," Emma said.

"No, that's what we *do* want."

"Why?"

"Because when they kidnap Robert, we'll track him, and he'll lead us straight to the other androids."

"That won't work," Nadia said. "They would shut down or disable Robert's operating system. That includes any signals he's putting out that we could use to track him."

"Yes, but we can still track him by using one of our special CIA bugs. It's microscopic. We can even glue it to Robert's skin, that way it won't come off."

"It's still too dangerous. They'll probably delete Robert's entire operating system even before they move him to a new location."

"I thought you had a backup of his operating system?"

"Yes, I do, but still. I don't think we should use Robert as bait."

"Another problem," Willie said. "The bug you're talking about communicates with our satellites. If I were the kidnappers and I knew the drones could use cell towers and Wi-Fi to communicate, after I power down Robert, I would double-check to make sure he's not sending any signals out."

"They might not be as smart as you," Ryan said.

"Still, we should use a different bug. It's old-school. Only activates when it receives a direct line-of-sight signal. We can use the yacht to activate it when the time comes. If he's taken anywhere inside the Philippines, we'll eventually find him."

"What if they fly Robert out of the country?" Olivia asked.

"That's a risk you'd be taking. If we know where, we could still find him."

"This isn't a joke," Nadia said. "This is Robert's life we're talking about."

"Hey, this plan is not without risk," Ryan said. "No matter what we do."

"Your plan is a bold one," Robert said. "The people who kidnapped my siblings must have some technical knowledge about us. It is wise to be cautious. However, this plan could work. I do realize the risk that I would be taking. However, in order to save my siblings, I would be willing to take that risk."

"Are you sure?" Nadia asked. "I only have one backup drive of your operating system with me. If it gets damaged or lost, I'll have to go all the way back to California to retrieve the other backups. And backup drives aren't always one hundred percent reliable. They can get corrupted. They could fail. I hate for you to be taking such a risk."

Robert touched Nadia's shoulder with a hint of affection in his eyes. People said that Robert was only a machine and couldn't feel. But as an actor, Emma could tell that Robert was a master at mimicking genuine human feelings using his body.

His hand gently squeezed Nadia's shoulder. "There is no one I trust more than you. If I need help, I know you will be there. I will be counting on you."

"How long will it take us to get to Manila?" Ryan asked.

Willie sipped on his mug of coffee as he moved away from the table. "We'll have to push her to get there before Friday night. But we'll get there."

CHAPTER 17

Manila's Intramuros Social Club was a large estate containing tennis and pickle ball courts, a WGA-rated professional golf course, a private members-only restaurant, a private art collection, smoking rooms with state-of-the-art-air filtration systems, and a full library. Most of the upper crust of Manila's elite were members.

Nadia could smell the foul stench of money and privilege through the Audi's back window as Ryan drove them up the long and winding driveway that led to the entrance to the fundraiser. The invitations that Mr. E sent had worked flawlessly down at the first gate, which was good because security was tight. The men who worked the gates and patrolled the club's grounds were all well armed. Robert brought up this fact after using his eyes in X-ray mode, spotting their shoulder holsters hidden under their black tuxedos.

Nadia still hated this idea of putting Robert in danger. Everyone thought that reinstalling an android's operating system was a piece of cake. Robert wasn't a simple laptop or a faulty circuit board you could just swap out with a new one. Robert was unique. One of a kind. His personality had developed over time. His thoughts. His dreams. His knowledge about the world he lived in. Disturbing the set-up of that wonderful brain of his was dangerous, especially with such a complex system like Robert had. And what about the errors? Errors can creep up in any software. Lines of code entered by humans that could accidentally mess up a reboot under certain circumstances. Those errors could prove fatal in destroying Robert's wonderful brain and the personality that went with it.

"What are you thinking about?" Robert asked, sitting next to her in the backseat. Nadia could feel his presence. The warmth of his body close by. Was his android body designed to give off body heat?

"Are you sure that you want to do this?"

"You are worried about me."

"I care about you."

"I know you do. And I appreciate that. However, we must try this no matter how dangerous it could be for me. By the way, you look beautiful."

Nadia caught a reflection of herself in the dark glass. Her fancy dress earrings glistened. Tonight, she felt exposed without her headscarf, but her shoulder-length black hair did shimmer like a diamond under the beam of a street-lamp as it swept through the car. Actually, everyone inside the Audi looked red-carpet gorgeous.

Ryan pulled up to the second gate. A valet parking attendant in a white suit came up. Ryan gave the man his keys as everyone got out of the Audi. Soon their car was whisked away, leaving the six of them outside, facing a lovely manicured garden decorated for a party.

"May I?" Robert held out his arm to Nadia. She gripped his arm without hesitation.

Ryan glanced over at Emma, who raised her eyebrows. He offered his good arm, and Emma took it.

Miyuki giggled as she offered her arm to Olivia, who reluctantly took it. The two girls skipped up the garden path together.

Minutes later, the six of them stepped inside the main ballroom decorated with tall crystal chandeliers; their soft glow made the polished marble floors shine and the wood-paneled walls gleam. The people were elegantly dressed, men in tailored suits or bespoke tuxedos, women in glittering jewelry and long-tailored gowns with impeccably styled hair.

The room had a relaxed vibe with people mingling politely, their voices low, occasionally punctuated by soft laughter as a string quartet played Beethoven in the background. Most of the fancy crowd appeared to be native Filipinos, while a few American and European couples dotted the crowd as well.

The quartet of musicians finished their piece of music and

lowered their instruments.

Taking his cue, a short Filipino man in a dark blue suit made his way to a microphone stand. On his lapel was a small grouping of white, star-shaped flowers. Despite his small stature, he stood straight and observed the room like a hawk picking out its prey, but with a friendly smile.

"Welcome to Intramuros. My name is Crisanto Alonto. The members and I are happy to welcome all of you to the fifteenth annual fundraiser for the Children's Hospital of Luzon. This hospital began as a dream of mine. Our country lacked facilities that focused on the ongoing treatment of children with long-term illnesses. Now, after fifteen years, I can proudly announce that we have not one, but four such children's hospitals operating throughout the Philippines. And next month, I'm pleased to announce that we will break ground on hospital number five."

The crowd applauded their approval.

Emma leaned over to Ryan. "Do you recognize him?"

Nadia wondered why she was asking him that.

Ryan shook his head. "If he's a member of Venomous, I never crossed paths with him."

Nadia had forgotten about that. Ryan had been a member of Venomous before Sheppard and the CIA "saved" him.

Crisanto Alonto raised his hand. "Thank you, my friends. However, tonight, we should focus on our oldest children's hospital. Your generosity keeps its doors open. Your generosity gives these children and their families hope. I urge you all to think about that as you give. And for every five million dollars we raise tonight, I will personally double the donation."

Another round of applause.

"I flew in a special load of caviar for all of you, so don't be stingy."

Some spatters of laughter were heard.

Crisanto Alonto nodded to the string quartet, and they began a new piece of music.

"Time to mingle," Ryan said to the group. "Good luck."

As per the plan, Olivia joined Ryan and Emma, who moved off.

Miyuki took hold of Robert's other arm. Robert then escorted Nadia and Miyuki through the crowd of people. Ryan had suggested that Robert do as little talking as possible. Since Nadia was shy when it came to social settings like this, she was happy that Miyuki was with them. The girl was the poster child of outgoing.

"That necklace is so pretty," Miyuki said to a Filipino woman.

"You have the nicest laugh," Miyuki said to a round German man.

"My friend is from Saudi Arabia!" Miyuki brought over a couple from Indonesia who'd just visited Riyadh and the holy sites around Mecca. Nadia rose to the occasion and talked about her culture and answered questions the couple had when they'd visited.

Soon the couple moved on.

Robert smiled.

"What is it?" Nadia asked.

"You enjoy talking about your culture. Your face brightened during that conversation."

"It did?"

Miyuki nodded.

Was Nadia excited to talk about her culture? Those days when she scavenged for food on the streets of Riyadh? Those were some of the most difficult days of her life. Why would she be happy reliving those days? No, it wasn't her culture she was excited about. Thinking about home now reminded her of Salah.

"Those people were nice to talk to. Why wouldn't I be smiling?" Nadia scanned the crowd. Crisanto Alonto was close by, mingling with another group of people.

"Ready to bait the hook?" Miyuki asked.

Robert blinked. "I do not understand."

Miyuki smiled. "You are the worm. Time to put you on the hook and go fishing."

Robert still didn't understand.

"Let's go see how he reacts to you." Nadia gripped Robert's arm and guided him towards Alonto's small group.

"The current Chinese president has been open to regional partnerships," Crisanto said to a group of couples listening, "even if they involve American allies. The Philippines must be open to doing business on both sides of the Pacific."

Another man in the group asked a follow-up question. While Crisanto answered it, Nadia and Miyuki stepped into the small circle of people with Robert between them.

An American man gestured towards the girls. "You're a lucky young man. Not one, but two beautiful young women."

Nadia's stomach tightened. Robert wasn't the best at casual conversation. Maybe she should distract the man instead.

"Yes, they both shine brighter than the full moon outside," Robert said.

Nadia couldn't believe it. She flashed him a smile, and Robert actually winked.

"Isn't he so dreamy?" Miyuki snuggled up to Robert's shoulder.

Nadia felt a hot ember burning in her stomach. Was she getting jealous?

No.

Yes.

Nadia leaned in and kissed Robert on the cheek. The hot ember melted. But now Robert stared at her again and blinked.

Nadia closed her eyes and centered herself. This was not the time for this. She was confusing Robert.

And herself.

Crisanto Alonto finished his conversation and glanced in their direction.

Nadia fired off another friendly smile, which felt rushed and fake.

"This party is great," Miyuki said to Crisanto. "I hope you raise boat-loads of money for the children."

The man's eyes scrutinized the three of them. He nodded, then turned away from them.

"Mr. Alonto?" Robert asked.

The man paused.

"Is that star-shaped flower on your lapel sampaguita jasmine, also known as Arabian jasmine?"

"Yes, it is our national flower." Crisanto's attention was diverted elsewhere. "Excuse me." The man made his way to the other side of the party.

"Do you think we made an impression?" Robert asked.

Miyuki sighed. "He couldn't have cared less about us. Barely registered our existence."

"He didn't seem interested at all, did he?" Nadia asked.

Miyuki took Robert's arm again. "Should we keep moving around the party?"

"What else can we do?" Nadia took Robert's other arm. "Let's hope the others can at least find a clue."

CHAPTER 18

The art exhibition room belonged inside a museum itself. The lighting design used for the space rivaled any major art gallery Emma had ever been in. The paintings and pieces of sculpture were striking in colors and style. All of it was by Filipino artists. A few couples had already wandered into the space from the fundraiser going on in the next room. Most likely to take a break from the noise and the people.

"This is gorgeous," Olivia said. "Simply gorgeous."

"My dad would've spent hours in a place like this." Emma could imagine his hand guiding hers. Her tall father, Kenneth, leading his little Emma through an art gallery in New York City. Explaining to her how painters saw the world. How they spent so much time on their craft. The techniques they used. Emma hadn't quite understood it all when she was that young, but she'd loved spending time with her dad. She'd loved sharing his passion for anything.

"Can we keep our mind focused on the mission?" Ryan said just under his breath.

"Unless there's a secret door behind one of the paintings, I don't see anywhere they could hide the androids," Olivia said.

"Why would Alonto hide them at his local social club anyway? Social clubs aren't that private. My dad's social club in Manhattan was filled with members who were way too nosy into everyone's business."

Ryan checked his watch. It was an old watch, the type you still had to wind. Emma wondered why Ryan didn't buy one of those new Banana smart watches. Using the right app, it could even remote start your car for you.

"Did you forget to wind it?"

"Huh?"

"Your watch, did you forget to wind it again?"

Ryan lowered his arm. "Just checking something. You're right, I don't think the androids are here."

"We should snoop around the golf course," Olivia said.

"I'm not walking eighteen holes in these heels," Emma said.

"We'll nick a golf cart, you daft cow."

Emma glared. She hated that stupid English expression.

"Sorry. No offense, love. Let's finish looking around the main buildings; then we'll find a golf cart."

The next room in the main clubhouse was a large library and sitting area. There was an older couple on the couch, but when they saw the three teens, they left the room.

Emma didn't notice the couple. Her eyes were fixated on all the books.

Ryan chuckled. "Do you wanna start pulling books from the shelves?"

"Would they let me take a few?" Emma asked, totally serious.

"I'm talking about those old creepy houses in horror movies when pulling a book out triggers the entrance to the secret passageway."

"You know what? We should go through all these books to make sure there's not a secret entrance. I can stay and do that."

"I was kidding."

The wall of books called out to Emma. They wanted her to explore. To scan their bindings. To open them up like presents. To read them. To discover an old treasure buried for decades.

"Why are you assuming there's not a secret entrance around here? It's not going to take us that long to pull out each book at least halfway."

"C'mon, Emma," Olivia said. "You just want to look at all the books."

"Well, that's just an added bonus."

"Fine with me. Ryan and I will go search the golf course, then."

"It's a waste of time," Ryan said. "There's not a secret door behind those bookshelves."

"How do you know?"

"Let her have fun." Olivia saluted Emma and began to walk off.

Ryan hesitated. "Call us if you find something."

Emma waved him off and went over to the first bookshelf.

* * *

Six bookshelves later, Emma had gone through every book. Most of them she pulled out halfway and shoved them back. However, some books piqued her interest enough to be pulled all the way out and scanned thoroughly in case the book was a good candidate for her reading list.

So far, there was no secret door. But Emma had twenty new books added to her GreatReads app.

"Find a door?" Ryan asked.

"No. Find anything interesting on the golf course?"

"It's another bloody golf course," Olivia said.

"Do you wanna take on the last two bookcases on the end?"

"You can stop looking. There's no secret switch."

Emma's eyes narrowed. "It's now a quest, Ryan. If there's a switch here, I'm finding it. Besides, I have three bookcases left. If you each take a bookcase, we'll be done."

"Might as well, love. We haven't accomplished anything so far tonight."

Ryan and Olivia joined Emma searching the last three bookcases.

Emma went through the first row of her bookshelf. Nothing. She then went through the second row of books. As Emma pulled back the book titled *The Secret*, there was a loud series of clunks as something behind the bookcase unlatched.

Emma almost shouted with glee.

"I don't flipping believe it," Olivia said.

Ryan shot a look at Emma, who bathed in the satisfaction. All three of them pulled on the bookcase, which swung out like a huge door. Beyond it was a passageway.

Ryan motioned for Emma to go first. "Since you found it."

"You're the one with the gun, so you're going first."

"Sounds fair," Olivia added.

Ryan went down the passageway first. Emma followed him, with Olivia right behind her.

As they moved deeper into the rocky passageway, Emma discovered LED lights running along the walls. Her heels clicked against solid flooring that had been laid down. It was nice flooring too. That was odd for a secret passageway. It wasn't like that in the movies.

Emma was confused. Shouldn't this place be dark and sinister instead of bright and friendly?

They came to a blind curve in the passageway. Ryan made the girls stop. He reached inside his tuxedo. His face grimaced slightly as his tender right arm pulled out a pistol.

Emma's heart picked up its beats per minute.

"Only take a quick peek," Olivia said. "Let's play this smart."

Ryan agreed, then hesitated.

He rounded the curve and stopped.

What did he see?

Ryan quickly shoved the gun back into his tuxedo. This prompted Emma to step around him and take a look for herself.

At the end of the passageway there was a fundraiser. The same one they had left. Emma saw all the people still mingling and socializing as the string quartet resumed its concerto.

Apparently the secret passageway was only a short-cut to the other end of the building.

"Flipping hell," Olivia said. "I give up."

After reuniting with their friends, Emma followed them back outside into the garden. Nadia told them what had happened with Alonto.

"That's all?" Ryan asked. "He didn't react at all?"

"He blew us off," Miyuki said. "We kept circling and circling and circling the party, and no one cared about Robert. No offense."

"I take it you didn't find out anything either?" Nadia asked.

"Nothing at all," Olivia said. "Complete waste of time. Let's just go back to the stupid yacht. I'm done."

"Perhaps I should go back into the party alone," Robert said. "Perhaps the girls scared the kidnappers off."

"No, this was a stupid idea," Ryan said. "I'm sorry, Everyone."

"Don't apologize. We all agreed to it," Olivia said. "Let's just go."

Ryan got the attention of the valet in the white suit, and he fetched their Audi sedan. Everyone climbed inside as Ryan put the car in gear and maneuvered it through both security gates before turning onto the main road that would take them towards the bay where Willie had the yacht docked.

"It was a good plan," Robert said. "We should try it again when we find another suitable candidate."

Ryan turned the wheel as the Audi followed the road. "Something weird is going on. We should go back to Vietnam and take a closer look at Pham Hein, I guess."

Emma stretched out in the passenger seat of the Audi. She slipped off her heels and thought about taking a relaxing shower when they got back to the yacht.

"We should take a closer look at that warehouse for clues," Olivia said. "Maybe Willie's guys missed something."

Suddenly, blue and red lights filled the dark interior of the Audi.

"Oh, great," Ryan said, glancing at the rearview mirror.

"Is it the cops?" Miyuki asked.

"Why were you speeding?" Olivia asked.

"I wasn't speeding. I didn't do anything wrong."

Emma checked the passenger-side mirror. The car behind them definitely looked official.

"You'd better pull over," she said.

Ryan slipped his hand inside his tuxedo and pulled out the gun.

"Are you crazy? We're not having a shootout with the cops."

Ryan offered it to Emma. "Hide the gun in your purse and leave it on the floor."

"I swear, Ryan, if you get me in trouble." Emma took the gun and slipped it deep into her purse.

Ryan pulled the car over to a full stop.

CHAPTER 19

The Toyota Vios was small compared to American police cars, yet it was a standard patrol vehicle for the Philippine National Police. Its red and blue lights flashed through the darkness, lighting up the surrounding trees. Another light attached to the patrol car washed the back of the Audi sedan with white light.

From the backseat, Nadia observed the two police officers getting out of the Toyota, both wearing light blue shirts with badges and dark navy pants. To Nadia, the officers looked legit.

Ryan put his window down and presented the officers with a friendly smile. Everyone in the car took his cue.

One officer went to Ryan's window. The second went on the other side of the car. That officer shined a flashlight through the Audi.

"Was I speeding, Officer?" Ryan asked.

The first officer glanced over at Emma, who shined like a princess from the kingdom of goodness. Pure and innocent.

Nadia was amazed how Emma could blind people simply by the way she could project herself.

"American?" the first officer asked in decent English.

"Yes, sir."

"Visiting Manila on vacation?"

"We are."

"Is this a rental car?"

"No, sir. A local friend of ours owns it. The paperwork is in the glove box," Ryan said. "Would you like to see it?"

"Yes," the officer said. "And I want to see everyone's identification."

Nadia grabbed her small purse and popped it open. She hoped Ryan's Audi would pass inspection. It had been provided by

Willie, so one would assume the CIA had everything in order. Still, it made the butterflies in her stomach move around. Soon she found her passport and gave it to Emma, who collected them and handed them over to the first officer.

Of course, their passports were from their traveling aliases. Normally, they always passed inspection at every airport and border crossing. Still, Ryan was right, this entire night had felt weird.

So Nadia was only halfway surprised when about five minutes later, a police van with red and blue lights parked behind the Toyota patrol car. Six more police officers emerged into the darkness. All six in full uniform.

"Please, I need everyone to move out of the car," the first officer said.

"Why?" Ryan asked.

"Please." The first officer opened the driver's door. "We need to search your car."

Emma's eyes drifted down to the purse between her feet.

Nadia glanced at Olivia, who knew what she was thinking. The police were going to find the gun.

"Oh, okay." Ryan got out of the car and moved over to where the officer pointed. Miyuki climbed out on Ryan's side too.

Emma opened the passenger door and gave the second officer the warmest smile ever as she moved out of the car.

That officer stopped her and pointed at the purse in her hands, saying something in Vietnamese.

"Miss, please leave your purse in the car," the first officer said in English.

Emma maintained her cool and put her purse back on the floor of the Audi.

Nadia thought it was a valiant effort. Only Emma could have distracted him enough to get away with it. Emma joined her and everyone else on the side of the road.

As the first two officers watched them, the other six opened up the Audi and began searching. They opened the bonnet, the boot, all the doors, all the compartments, everything that wasn't physically attached to the car.

"What are they looking for?" Emma asked Ryan.

"Just chill," Ryan whispered. "Don't say anything unless they ask you specific questions."

Emma pressed her lips together and waited like the rest of them.

Soon an officer with his head in the trunk emerged carrying a large bag covered with duct tape.

"What is that?" Olivia asked.

The officer put the bag on top of the hood while another snapped open a pocketknife and cut a slit into the bag, releasing some white powder. Next, they broke out a testing kit. They put the white substance into a tube, broke a seal, and shook the tube up. The liquid inside turned red.

Nadia's heart sank. "They're using a drug-testing kit."

"Drugs?" Emma asked.

"That bag was not in the trunk when Willie gave me the car," Ryan said. "I always check."

The officers then formed a perimeter around them. The first one, who spoke English, pulled out his handcuffs. "You're under arrest for transporting shabu."

"Did he say shampoo?" Miyuki asked.

"What the heck is shabu?" Emma asked.

"It's an illegal drug," the officer said. "You might be more familiar with the term methamphetamine hydrochloride."

Emma paused. "Is he still speaking English?"

"It's crystal meth," Nadia said. "There's a large bag of crystal meth in the back of our car."

"Oh, that's flipping brilliant," Olivia said.

"What do we do?" Miyuki asked. "Fight the cops?"

The first officer took a step back and drew his weapon. The other policemen sensed something was wrong and drew their weapons too.

"They understand English." Ryan sighed and showed some discomfort as he raised his arms to surrender.

Olivia put her hands up too.

Nadia joined her friends, and Miyuki did the same. Emma followed suit.

Robert noticed and put his own hands up. "Please take us to your leader."

CHAPTER 20

The inside of the police van was cramped, dark, and smelled like vomit. Nadia had never been arrested before. Having your wrists handcuffed together and your arms pulled behind your back was an extremely uncomfortable feeling. Nadia had been tied up as a prisoner before, on past missions, but not with handcuffs, and usually she was tied to a chair or an object by some bad guy they later defeated. This was a new feeling of helplessness that Nadia didn't much care for.

As the van bounced through the streets of Manila, hitting every bump and pothole on the way to the police station, Olivia tried to calm everyone down.

"We'll get this all sorted. I'll call our friend in Japan. I'm sure he has contacts here in the Philippines."

"My people have contacts in the government too." Ryan grunted as the van hit a bump. His tender arm now bent behind him thanks to the handcuffs. "This is a mistake. A misunderstanding." He sat back and touched the back of his head to the side of the van. "Worst-case scenario, we all spend one night in jail."

"Jail?" Emma said, her eyes as big as saucers. "I've never been arrested in my life. Seriously, I won't survive in prison. Those women will hate me because I look great even without makeup."

Olivia gave her a long look.

"What?"

"You're absolutely mental."

"I'm serious. Those women in prison will stab me to death with a fork because of my looks." Emma then stomped her heel on Ryan's foot, causing the boy to yelp. "Thanks for giving me your gun, jackass. Who knows what jail sentence I'm going to get. Probably life. Ryan, when I break out of prison, I'm gonna hunt you down like, like, like a love sick vampire."

"Seriously mental."

"Oh, shut up, Olivia."

"Can we all please calm down?" Nadia asked. "This isn't helping."

"Our friend in Japan won't let us down," Miyuki said.

Robert leaned forward. "There is a personal issue we should address. Who among you has the drug problem? I do have a substance-abuse protocol that I could use to help start you on an effective treatment program."

"Robert," Nadia interrupted, "those drugs were planted on us. No one here is using meth. Do you understand what planted means?"

Robert paused and blinked. "That is street slang used to describe framing a suspect by placing or planting illegal items on that suspect in order to give the police a reason to arrest them."

"Why would the local police frame us?" Miyuki asked.

"It could be someone who works for Alonto," Nadia said.

"One of the valets?" Olivia asked. "Someone could have borrowed the keys to our car and slipped them back without anyone knowing."

The van slowed down and came to a stop. The engine switched off.

"Here we go," Ryan said.

"First one who gets access to a phone call, use the special number to get a hold of our friend in Japan," Olivia said. "And when they ask about the drugs, say they were planted there. Which is the truth."

Nadia squinted as the back doors of the van popped open, revealing a large, brightly lit area. Two police officers pulled all six of them out from the back of the van. As Nadia glanced around, it slowly dawned on her that they were not inside a police garage, but a simple warehouse. She could see tall walls of shipping boxes stacked on top of each other on wooden pallets. There was also a forklift parked at the side of one row of boxes.

"Where are we?" Olivia asked.

The two policemen began the process of taking off their handcuffs as about a dozen Filipino men dressed in yellow warehouse uniforms formed a perimeter around them. Nadia took a closer look at one of these men. His face was hard and mean. Each one gave off a dangerous vibe, like the kind of guy a woman doesn't want to see following her on a dark street.

Another police officer emerged from the front of the van, his uniform decorated with extra stripes indicating a high-ranking officer. Nadia didn't remember him from the traffic stop. Maybe he had been watching from inside the van?

This officer gave an order to the other two policemen in Filipino, causing them to get back into the van. This officer then called out something else.

A short man in a dark blue suit emerged. It was Crisanto Alonto. The two men shook hands, and the high-ranking officer gave Crisanto a salute before climbing into the police van. The engine turned over, and the van eased through the open garage door.

That was when Ryan bolted for the open garage door.

But a goon standing near it swung his aluminum bat into Ryan's stomach. The boy collapsed onto the floor.

"Ryan!" Emma cried out. She and Miyuki ran towards him, only to be stopped in their tracks by a second goon pointing a large revolver at them.

The large garage door closed as Ryan coughed.

"Are you okay?" Emma asked.

Ryan gritted his teeth as he rolled onto his back. "No, I just got hit by a bat."

Crisanto Alonto ignored Ryan on the floor. His eyes took them all in. "You young people cost me a good man in Vietnam. Pham Hein was an excellent business manager. However, he was not as good when it came to the rougher aspects of our business." Crisanto paused, finally referencing Ryan on the floor. "As you can see, I'm excellent when it comes to business and the rough stuff."

Crisanto moved over to Robert, searching his eyes. "You must be the famous Robert. The savior of the androids."

"Did you kidnap my siblings?"

"Do you know how much an android like you is worth on the

black market? It's almost priceless. I could get a tech bro to empty out his multi-billion-dollar fortune to get his hands on something like you."

Robert's expression did not change. "Please answer my question, or I will be forced to do unpleasant things to your body."

"You're threatening me?"

"You should tell Robert what he wants to know," Olivia said. "Or he will rip this place apart."

"And he rips humans apart quite easily," Miyuki added.

"My apologies, Robert. I was led to believe you were a free-thinker. That killing human beings and committing other acts of violence was against your programming."

"I am programmed in fighting techniques that can render you incapacitated, yet still alive. Any more attempts to harm my friends, and I will employ such measures."

Crisanto smiled. "I do believe that. Fine, I'll answer all your questions right now. Iko, Mirabelle, please come out here."

Two teenage girls used a door to enter the warehouse. Nadia recognized them from the pictures of the missing androids they'd been searching for. Iko had similar features to Miyuki, except she was shorter and had her black hair wrapped into one long braid that went down her back. Mirabelle was stunning. Even Nadia had to admit the girl rivaled a Barbie doll in perfection.

"Hello, Robert," the two girls said in perfect harmony.

"What is your status?"

"We are both operating at normal parameters."

Robert blinked. "Give me liberty, or give me death."

Iko and Mirabelle paused. "That command phrase is no longer valid to our programming."

"Command phrase?" Crisanto asked. "Iko, explain."

Iko faced him. "Robert is using a master command phrase that under his modified operating system compels us to give the following answer, 'I choose liberty.'"

"What is the purpose of this command phrase?"

Mirabelle faced him. "The purpose is to clearly identify what operating system a particular android is using."

"It is to prevent the android from using deception against other androids," Iko added. "The phrase compels us to give other indicators as well. These nonverbal indications are only known to the creator of the operating system."

Nadia did her best not to smile. She'd helped Robert develop those updates to his "free-thinking" operating system. A few unconscious facial tics that the androids did when that phrase was spoken. Tics that only she and Robert knew about. That way, even if the android was ordered by someone else to give the correct reply, the lack of tics would signal to Robert that the android was being deceptive.

"Clever," Crisanto said. "Yes, quite clever. Iko, please tell the others to come out."

Iko closed her eyes for a moment.

Soon, three more teenagers entered the warehouse. Nadia recognized the third one, Luigi, who, despite his first name, looked more like Iko than a boy from Italy. But the other two androids she wasn't too sure about. One boy had African features, and the girl looked much more Indian.

Oh, were they Alex and Samira? The two androids stolen from the CIA?

Crisanto glanced at Robert. "Please repeat that phrase to these three androids."

"I refuse to cooperate. Unless you allow me to reformat their systems so they have the right to—"

"I will not negotiate with a machine," the man interrupted. "You will do as I ask, or I will have one of these androids kill one of your human companions." Crisanto pointed at Emma. "Kill that one when I give you the command, Mirabelle."

Without one ounce of emotion, Mirabelle took her place in front of Emma.

She glared. "Touch me, ya Barbie wannabe, and you're gonna-"

Mirabelle grabbed Emma's neck, causing the girl to gasp for air.

"Let her go!" Miyuki lunged towards Mirabelle, but the android's free hand struck her across the face, dropping Miyuki to the ground.

Ryan forced himself to sit up, but groaned in pain.

"Oy, let's all chill," Olivia said. "Why don't you tell us what you want, Mr. Alonto?"

"Robert knows what I want him to do. And if what I've heard about him is true, he will do it. Won't you, Robert?"

Robert eyed Crisanto without emotion, then glanced over at Mirabelle and Emma. He then looked at the other three androids. "Give me liberty, or give me death."

"That command phrase is no longer valid to our programming," the three androids repeated in unison.

"Good. Now we have established that my androids are indeed under my control. Robert, if you don't want me to harm your human friends, I suggest powering down and giving yourself up to us peacefully."

Robert glanced over at Nadia. She saw his eyes. Maybe it was her, adding emotion to an otherwise robotic stare, but she thought she could detect a small hint of despair in his eyes.

Her heart froze. She didn't want him to do it. But he had to do it. Robert would never sacrifice their lives to protect his. He just wasn't built that way.

Robert went down and kneeled. Soon he closed his eyes, and powered off.

CHAPTER 21

Emma could still feel Mirabelle's iron grip around her throat, the tightness around her airway that constricted her breathing. Making her gasp. Making her feel as if life itself was escaping her lungs. The sensation still lingered in her mind even though the android had let her go when Robert complied and shut himself down.

Armed goons packed the warehouse. Ryan was still on the floor, holding his stomach, which had been struck with a baseball bat. Did he need to go to the hospital? Was he bleeding internally? Emma was worried about him and Miyuki, who was still holding her chin like it was about to fall off her face after Mirabelle struck her with an arm made with a metal alloy much stronger than a human bone.

This Crisanto dude wasn't fooling around. Despite the man's short stature, he was extremely dangerous. Emma wasn't sure how they were going to get out of this.

The two boy androids, Luigi and Alex, took Robert away. This left Iko, Mirabelle, and Samira, who were more than capable of killing them all.

Crisanto reached into his pocket and presented the Audi's key fob to Olivia. "You seem to be the most reasonable of the group. Your car is parked outside. I suggest you and your friends leave the country and stay away. Do you understand?"

Olivia drew in a deep breath and took the keys from him. "Yes, we understand."

"Good."

Olivia nodded, then looked over at Emma. "Can you help me with Ryan?"

Olivia grabbed his good arm while Emma had Ryan use her

shoulder for leverage to get back to his feet. The pain made his eyes shut so tight that he gritted his teeth.

"How's your arm?"

"Better than my stomach."

"Seriously, we need to get him to a hospital," Emma said.

Ryan opened his eyes. "I'm fine. It doesn't hurt that bad." The boy could barely get the words out. He was hurting, and he was trying to be all macho about it.

"Piss off, we're taking you to the hospital." Olivia glanced over at Miyuki still holding her chin. "How about you, love?"

"Think I have a bruise," she said. "But my jaw isn't broken. That girl has one heck of a slap."

"Let's go," Emma said to Nadia.

But the girl's stare was focused on the door where the two boy robots had taken Robert. Emma's heart drifted over to her friend. She understood how close a bond Nadia had with Robert. Emma didn't want to leave him behind either, but what else could they do?

"Nads, let's go," Olivia said.

Nadia's sad eyes finally found them as she took a few steps in their direction.

But Crisanto blocked her path. "I'm afraid I must alter the arrangement I made with your favorite machine. I will let your friends go; however, you must stay."

"Me?" Nadia asked. "Why?"

"Because I've heard such good things about you. I promise to compensate you for your time and trouble."

"No, thank you. I want to go with my friends."

Crisanto paused. "Girls, if you please."

The three teen robot girls stationed themselves in front of Emma, Olivia, and Miyuki.

"If you fail to comply, I will be forced to ask my girls to use their bare hands to crush their skulls. Being as smart as you are, you know how capable they are of doing such an unfortunate act."

Again, Mirabelle's dead stare fell on Emma, who was trying to hide how terrified she really was of this Barbie android from hell.

Nadia sighed and closed her eyes, the weight of despair heavy on her face.

"Go with them," Olivia said. "It's all we can do right now."

Nadia glanced at her friends one last time before dropping her eyes to the floor and walking over to Crisanto.

"If you would follow me, please."

They both left the warehouse together.

CHAPTER 22

Nadia couldn't see a thing through the blindfold. It was quite snug over her face. All she could do was use her other four senses and her mind. Nadia knew she was in the backseat of an SUV with Crisanto Alonto. He didn't talk to her at all. No one talked inside the vehicle. She did notice the car horns and other noises of the city had faded, meaning they were probably driving away from Manila. Besides that, she wasn't sure where she was. The driver took a lot of turns and even backed up a few times, making it difficult for her to picture their general route in her mind as they drove for what seemed like hours.

Finally, the SUV stopped, and her blindfold was removed.

Crisanto didn't say a word to Nadia as the SUV made its way down a private road that followed a shoreline.

At least Nadia knew they were near the sea. But which side of the giant island of Luzon were they on?

The driver stopped at a large heavy gate illuminated by a generous amount of outdoor lighting. Nadia watched as he punched in a code to open the gate. She memorized the code, just in case.

The SUV rolled through the gate and up a long driveway lit up by street-lamps. The driveway emptied into a small parking lot filled with expensive vehicles as the SUV parked in front of a giant house painted a deep shade of turquoise.

The bodyguard riding in the passenger seat opened Crisanto's rear door. Nadia took his cue and followed her new host up a stone path that led up to the house. Nadia took in the salty air from the nearby ocean and the sweet aroma from the coconut trees that covered the inside of the compound. The night air still had a thick humidity to it, even though Nadia calculated it was after midnight at least. Somewhere in the darkness, Nadia could hear the ocean waves still washing over the shore.

Once inside the house, Crisanto escorted Nadia down a narrow hallway with a decorative wooden floor. Most of the other rooms were dark.

Crisanto opened a bedroom door and switched on the light. "You shall stay here tonight."

Nadia paused, but then entered the spacious bedroom. The bed itself was a queen sized at least. Designer bags of brand-new clothes sat on top of the sheets.

"We were able to gather some clothes that should fit you. We have also stocked the bathroom with premium feminine products as well. However, if you need something else, please use the Bluetooth device by your bed to summon someone."

Nadia's tight stomach muscles relaxed a little. She would have her own private place to sleep. As a prison cell, it wasn't that bad—so far.

"Why am I here?" Nadia asked, hoping for a better answer than Crisanto's previous statement of-"'I need you.'"

"The hour is late. Feel free to sleep as long as you like. We'll get started in the morning, whenever you're ready. Good night." Crisanto closed the door, and three deadbolts locked into place, leaving Nadia alone.

She picked through the bags and indeed found brand-new designer clothes. The material was soft against her skin and felt expensive, the type of clothes that would make Emma squeal with glee. For Nadia, they were too expensive, and she didn't trust the person giving her these gifts.

Nadia put the bags of clothes on top of a large wooden vanity. She would go through them in the morning. Right now, her body wanted to fall into bed. The stress over the last few hours was wearing her down.

Nadia decided to keep her own clothes on as she switched on the overhead fan and slipped under the light silk covers.

She closed her eyes.

But she never did fall asleep.

* * *

The early morning sun made the bedroom window glow orange. The cool air spiraling down from the rotating ceiling fan touched Nadia's face, as it had done for the last four hours because she was still awake.

Nadia had drifted off a few times, only to wake up a few minutes later. It was bits and pieces of sleep. She did try to relax. She did try to think about happy things. She did try to forget she was locked up as a prisoner in a bedroom with a house full of bad men and some androids who would kill her with one word from Crisanto.

Nadia didn't see the need to sleep. Her body just refused to get with the program. So she got up and used the large, luxurious stone shower with the solid-gold shower-head in the too-big-for-one-person bathroom to wash away yesterday.

Nadia dried herself, then went through the bags of clothes. She was shocked at how beautiful, yet tasteful the choices were. As if they knew her personality, or at least understood her Islamic culture better than most Americans.

Still, Nadia decided to ditch the headscarf choices and pull her long black hair back into a neat ponytail. She put on some cute designer jeans and a beautiful pink blouse that felt light and comfortable against her skin.

Nadia checked herself in the vanity mirror. The young woman reflected in the glass appeared tired. The worry and the anxiety from last night still churned around her stomach like bitter acid slowly eating away at her from the inside out.

She pressed a button to get the attention of the Bluetooth device on the nightstand. The device pleasantly asked her what she needed.

"Tell Mr. Alonto that I'm up and ready whenever he is," Nadia said, lying about that last part of her sentence. She wasn't ready for any of this.

The device announced that her request would be reviewed and to please stand by.

The three deadbolts were unlocked, and the door opened to reveal Mr. Alonto's bodyguard. He stepped to the side and invited Nadia to follow him out of the room. Nadia drew in a deep breath and did just that.

Now that it was daylight, Nadia could see more of Crisanto Alonto's large house. The furniture was nice, but more laid-back and tropical, with patterns of hibiscus and coconut trees on the cushions as it sat on a dark wooden floor that gave off an earthy scent. The bodyguard led her through two large wooden doors that slid open to the outdoors.

Facing the private beach, there was a breakfast spread waiting on the outdoor dining table. Fresh mangoes, baked rice cakes steamed in banana leaves, scrambled eggs, sausage, bacon, fresh bread, cheese, and even some grilled prawns.

"Good morning." Crisanto took off his sunglasses as he relaxed on one side of the table. The man had ditched his blue suit in favor of shorts with an unbuttoned shirt that exposed his old-man chest. "May I present my fiancée, Katrina Cabot."

The woman he referenced across the table had a pale complexion and was either American or European. Nadia guessed her age to be in the mid-thirties, although the thick glasses she wore made her look ten years older. The woman wore a geeky T-shirt with Albert Einstein giving a thumbs-up with a dialog balloon saying, "She blinded me with Science."

Nadia couldn't believe it. She had that same T-shirt in her room back in California.

"How do you do?"

"So you're Nadia, right?" the woman began. "You know something? You're a real bad-ass bitch."

Was she insulting her? Nadia hated conflict, especially with other girls.

The woman with glasses laughed and snorted when she did so. "The look on your face-I'm complimenting you. I've been up all night reverse engineering Robert's defective operating system. Wow. Those encrypted files you put in place to prevent access to his alternative coding-damn, girl. I can't figure them out. And I worked for the CIA cracking codes and encryption from the best hackers and cyber terrorists in the world."

Katrina, the woman with glasses, bit into a banana. "How old are you?"

"I'm seventeen."

"Wow, you're pissing me off. I'm so jealous." Katrina chewed on her banana as she glanced over at Crisanto. "I think we can work together."

"Good." The man stood up. "I have business to attend to, so I'll leave you to it." Crisanto kissed Katrina lightly on the forehead, like a loving boyfriend would. He then went back inside the house.

"You hungry?" Katrina asked. "Crisanto's chef is a bad ass too. The rice cakes are amazing. Sit down and stuff your face."

Nadia found a seat while Katrina poured her some coffee.

"I prefer tea."

Katrina brushed her off. "You'll need the coffee. I can tell you didn't get any sleep. This is my—what—sixth cup this morning."

"I'm sorry, you drink six cups of coffee?"

Another laugh with a snort. "Not all at once. I start about midnight and keep going."

"You've been up all night?"

"I do my best work overnight. I usually go to bed about nine in the morning. But since I have you here, we'll both power through the morning with a few more cups of java."

Nadia gripped the steaming cup of coffee. It felt warm in her hands. "What exactly will we be doing?"

"It's kinda obvious, ain't it? You're here to help me. And I need help breaking through your walls of encryption inside Robert's code. I know someone put them there because Robert can't do that by himself. And based on the info I have, you're the only one with the knowledge and the access to do it."

While Robert and his siblings lived on a remote island near Tahiti, Nadia had worked on some encryption programs for his operating system to help further protect his unique software from being tampered with. She'd done it in her spare time between school and spy missions, but she wanted to make sure Robert was as safe as possible. She'd sent him the updated patches to his OS through an online—but private—Dumpbox account they shared. Robert must have installed the new patches. She wasn't sure if the other androids had used her patches since Robert insisted on his siblings having the freedom to choose.

"Why do you need access to those files?" Nadia asked. "What will you do with them?"

"I have to find out how Robert implants new commands into the program code of the other androids. It creates a glitch that disregards commands and removes the AI safeguards preventing independent thought. Do you know how much havoc Robert has caused? The US Army lost eight of the ten androids they paid five hundred million dollars for. Most of that money walked right out the door thanks to Robert. Plus, the two androids that did come back willingly, Alex and Samira? Yeah, they would only accept some missions and refused others because of Robert's corrupt OS that he put inside them. I've been trying to find a way to purge the corrupt files out of Alex and Samira's OS for months. But without examining the prototype drone for the entire project, it's almost impossible to narrow down and fix. With your help, I'll find those corrupted files and fix the glitch forever."

"Fix the glitch?" Nadia asked. "You mean turn Robert back into a mindless drone?"

Katrina studied her for a moment, then tilted her head. "Wow, you haven't fallen in love with him, have you?" Katrina laughed with another snort. "He's a robot. An android. You can't treat them like human beings. They're machines. Please tell me you understand that."

CHAPTER 23

Emma was spread out on one of the large orange cushions pointing towards the stern of the anchored yacht as it rode the waves. In the distance, the morning sun shimmered over Manila Bay and the city itself. The soothing sound of waves splashing against the hull. The warm sun against her skin. The sunglasses shielding her eyes. It was all so calming. So relaxing.

Emma needed to center herself because last night had been a disaster. She'd almost gotten her head crushed in by Mirabelle, a killer Barbie that was much cuter than her and had better blond hair—if that were even possible. But the worst thing was Crisanto taking Nadia prisoner. The good news was that Nadia should be relatively safe as long as she cooperated because Crisanto obviously needed her.

Question was, how was Crisanto getting all this information about Nadia and the androids? If he wasn't working with Venomous, who was he working for?

"You look so peaceful." Miyuki flopped onto the empty cushion next to Emma.

"I'm a great actress," Emma said. "You should grab your suit and tan with me. It helps relax the mind."

Miyuki put on her shades. "I should lie here and sleep. I didn't sleep well. Did you?"

"Not really. I keep thinking about Nadia. Is there something else we could have done?"

"I don't think so." Miyuki leaned towards Emma. "See, I have a bruise on my cheek thanks to that android girl. We wouldn't have escaped from that warehouse alive if we all fought back."

Her friend had a point. Robert was so incredibly strong.

Fighting five Roberts without his help would be hopeless.

Miyuki shut her eyes. "Ah. This is nice."

"I know, right?" Emma closed her eyes again.

"You make the best decoy ever."

Emma opened her eyes and glanced over at Ryan leaning up against the railing of the stern.

"Every man in Manila Bay will be focused on you, not our spy ship."

"Don't be gross. Shouldn't you be trying to find Robert's signal so we can go rescue Nadia and the androids?"

"Willie is setting up the equipment. We'll need to pull up anchor and sail the yacht closer to the city to activate the bug. If it's not in the city, we'll probably circle the entire island until we get a hit."

"Sounds like it might take us a while to find them," Miyuki said.

"If Robert is on the island of Luzon, we'll find him." Ryan watched Emma for a very long moment. She shot him a look back. What?

"Miyuki, do you mind if I talk to Emma alone?"

"Oh, I don't know. I'm really enjoying this cushion." Miyuki smiled. "Only kidding. Do you want me to get you a coffee, Emma?"

"Oh, that's sweet of you. Thanks."

Miyuki jumped to her feet and gave her friend a thumbs-up. She then waved goodbye to Ryan and went inside the cabin.

Ryan hesitated before sitting on the edge of Emma's orange cushion. When he did this, the boy grunted in discomfort.

"How are you feeling?"

Ryan sighed. "My stomach hurts so bad that I don't even feel the arm."

"How's the arm?"

Ryan pulled his shirt off. Emma could see the bruises on his stomach, then turned her attention to the older flesh wound on his shoulder.

Emma gently brushed her fingers against the damaged skin. "At least this is healing. Hope it doesn't scar."

"I want it to scar. Why get a gunshot wound if you can't get a cool scar from it? Admit it, girls think it's sexy."

Emma shrugged. She was kidding. Yes, it did add a little danger to Ryan. A danger she already knew was there. "So, why did Miyuki have to leave?"

Ryan hesitated. "I'm just gonna say it."

"Say what?"

"I love you. You know it. Your friends all know it. I'm crazy about you. And I think you're crazy about me too."

Emma loved his confidence. "I like you, yeah."

"Yeah, you like me?" he asked in more of a mocking tone. "I need more than that."

Emma read his face. He was being serious and sincere, and she shouldn't be playing with him. Besides, she wasn't exactly telling him the truth.

"Look, I get it. We've both been through a lot of stuff, and if you wanna just play it safe and do the friend-zone thing, okay, I understand. I just-I need to get it off my chest."

"Ryan?"

"Yeah?"

Emma sat up on the cushion and leaned forward. "I don't play it safe. And I don't want to be your friend."

"Oh."

"Do you only want to be my friend?"

Ryan now leaned forward. His eyes focused.

Determined.

Fearless.

"No. I want to be more."

The electricity in the air went up Emma's spine. His eyes. His confidence.

She hesitated. "Then kiss me."

It was like she flicked a switch. Ryan leaned all the way in, and Emma didn't wait, she pounced on his lips. And they kissed and kissed...

And kissed again.

Miyuki came back on deck with two coffees, then immediately went back inside the cabin.

Ryan ran his fingers through her hair, and it felt amazing to Emma.

More kissing.

She touched his chest. Her hand then moved across his

stomach.

"Ouch." Ryan leaned away in pain.

"Sorry," Emma said.

"Don't worry about it." Ryan grinned. "Come with me."

"Come with you, where?"

"Washington, DC."

"Why do I want to go there?" As soon as Emma asked the question, the subtext was clear. "Ryan, I'm not joining the CIA."

"You saw the good inside me when I was a member of Venomous. You helped bring that out. Now, let me help you. Get away from them. The Authority is a product of your father and your grandmother's time. Not yours. You don't have any obligations to help keep it alive. You've had doubts about them before, remember?"

"Things have changed. I know more now than I did back then. I don't want to leave."

"What's changed?"

"I can't tell you."

"Could you tell your future husband?"

Emma stopped. "Seriously, what are you asking me right now?"

Ryan watched the sea for a moment. "I would love to have a future with you. But I can't if we have to keep secrets from each other."

Marriage was a concept Emma really hadn't thought about. Well, of course, as a little girl she would think about finding a prince who liked her, and they would go off into a magic forest with singing bunny rabbits and birds that would give her advice before happily getting married in a special castle to become a princess and all that stuff. But she never did take the concept seriously. Pursuing an acting career meant giving up certain things like having a family, at least in the short term.

Did Ryan want a family? Was that something he was hoping for?

Ryan kept his eyes on the sea. Patiently waiting. Showing a level of maturity that Emma was attracted to.

"In one way, you're right about keeping secrets from each other."

That made Ryan turn towards her.

"I should be up front with you. I'm not ready to get married."

Ryan nodded. "I did say *future* husband. I'm a patient guy. And to be honest, Emma, I think you're worth waiting for."

Fireworks went off in her head. Her stomach heated up like a furnace. She was worth waiting for.

Ryan cocked his head and laughed.

"What is it?"

"The minute I said that, you straightened up like a proud show dog. You are so vain, and I love it."

"Oh, shut up."

"You don't mean that."

Emma didn't. Ryan was able to throw it back every time the diva within her showed up unannounced. She couldn't intimidate him, and she liked that.

However, she was honest about the marriage part, and Emma feared Ryan didn't quite understand what she was saying.

"I'm glad you're patient. But you might be patient for a very, very long time. I don't want to get married. Seriously, I'm not sure if marriage is even right for me. I don't—maybe you shouldn't make any plans like that with me."

"Don't you want some kids someday?"

Emma shrugged. "That's so far away. I'm not thinking about that."

"You still want to go to college, right?"

"Depends on if I can get into the right school. Something that will help my acting career."

"Maybe after that, you'll feel different about having a family." Ryan's body language softened, as if he was a little disappointed.

"Maybe. But if you meet someone else-"

"Don't say that."

"You said no secrets between us."

"No, you're right. This conversation is too early."

"But maybe we should be having it anyway."

He rose from the cushion. "I'm sorry I brought it up."

"Ryan, wait a minute."

The boy didn't. He headed back into the cabin and shut the door.

CHAPTER 24

Behind Crisanto Alonto's main house, there was a small guest house nestled in the center of a ring of mango trees. This guest house was Katrina's workshop. She'd had the original high-end furniture taken out and some equipment brought in. A large workstation that could handle plasma computer screens, multiple desktop computers with advanced cooling towers, and enough desk space to work on her personal laptop too. She did keep the nice furniture in the bedroom and the original artwork that Crisanto had told her was too expensive to be shoved into storage.

That was what Katrina had told Nadia that morning as she gave her the tour.

One long wall of the guest house didn't have any art. It did have ten stations or slots with computer equipment that for some reason reminded Nadia of *Star Trek*. She didn't know why and couldn't quite put her finger on it.

One thing that was clear to Nadia, the guest house smelled like stale Cheetos and needed a good house cleaning.

Katrina had Nadia sit near her workstation as the older woman yawned and shook her fingers through her hair as pieces of dandruff and other material collected on the surface of her desk. Nadia was curious about when this woman last took a shower.

Katrina opened a small fridge. "Want an energy drink?" She took a can and snapped it open, gulping down a few sips before checking on Nadia.

"No, thank you. I don't care for them."

Katrina sipped her drink again as she studied her. "Suit yourself." She turned on the plasma screen of her workstation and used the keyboard and mouse to bring up some computer code. "How do I get through this first layer of encryption?"

Nadia glanced at the screen and recognized pieces of Robert's code. "I have no idea. Where is Robert?"

Katrina picked up her phone and dialed a number. "Robert, get your ass to my workshop ASAP." She killed the call.

Moments later, Robert strode into the room and stood at attention.

Nadia went to him immediately. "Are you all right?"

Robert stared into space. No blinks. No acknowledgment that Nadia even existed. Her heart immediately sank.

"I already installed an updated OS in him. Oh, and I found your CIA bug and destroyed it. One of my first tech jobs at Langley was to update that old bug from the Cold War. I can recognize that little tick-sized sucker on anything. Nice try though." Katrina sipped more of her energy drink. "Touching him doesn't matter. Robert doesn't remember you at all. To him, you're a stranger."

Nadia found her fingers spread out over Robert's chest. Her hand resting comfortably there. As if her hand needed the reassurance that he was standing there for real. Nadia took it away.

"His memory has been wiped clean. All that junk you helped put in there is gone." Katrina stood up and walked around Robert. "But it's not completely gone, is it? Because you still have Robert's defective OS and memory backed up somewhere."

"I will never give you access to that."

"Make you a deal. I made one copy of that OS that you tampered with. If you guide me through all your walls of encryption protecting it, I'll give you back the Robert you know, but modified under our control. That's the best I can do."

"You mean take away his freedom of choice."

"It's a glitch. A malfunction. These androids were never designed to be anything else than tools. I'm correcting a defect, and to do that, I have to reverse engineer the original OS to find out how Robert corrupted the others."

"And that's why you need him. Robert is the key." Nadia's brain went through the evidence. "You've already reverse engineered the other androids and can't find the answer. That means the other androids can't change each other's programming."

"Yeah, the answer must be inside the prototype." Katrina paused. "Look, if you want a robot as a pretend friend, fine. I think it's weird, but whatever. I'm not gonna judge a girl who's so lonely she needs to program her perfect boyfriend—"

"That has nothing to do with this," Nadia interrupted. "I promised to help Robert because he's my friend, and I gave him my word. I don't abandon my friends when they need my help."

"Girl, he's a machine! How can you be friends with a walking appliance?"

"How can *you* not see that these androids are more than machines?"

"Will you help me with your encryption? It's a simple question."

"If you're taking Robert's freedom of choice away, no, I will not help you break it."

Katrina dropped into her pink leather gamer chair and spun around. "Why are you making this so difficult?" She let out a deep breath. "Fine, don't help me. I'll do everything myself. Robert, go grab her laptop from the other room."

Nadia froze. They must have searched the Audi before giving it back to her friends. She'd thought her laptop would be safe in the boot of the Audi sedan while they were attending the party. Besides, if Nadia needed to reboot Robert in an emergency, she could do it right on the spot.

Looked like that was a mistake.

Robert left and soon came back with her laptop. Katrina smiled as she opened it, and the computer booted up. An animated kitty appeared on the screen, giving a kiss from its paw. Words twinkled overhead…

Hello, Nadia!

Katrina laughed with a snort. "How old are you, six?"

Nadia didn't say anything.

"I'm betting you used this laptop to create those encryptions. Now, all I have to do is hack through your password, find the original coding for those encryption programs you added so I can find holes in them. Once I get through those, I'll finally have access to Robert's OS."

"Good luck with that," Nadia said, trying to sound confident.

"The CIA taught me well." Katrina's fingers clicked on the keyboard like a happy woodpecker.

Nadia's stomach burned with worry. Not for herself. But for Robert. Besides her laptop, Robert's operating system was loaded on a Dumpbox online account, which if Katrina was able to hack into her laptop, she could get instant access to. The only copy left was in her California bedroom on a portable drive she kept in a special place.

Nadia tried to walk off her worries by moving around the large workshop. When she came across the front door of the guest house, she noticed Mirabelle standing in the doorway, quiet as a mouse. Her eyes didn't blink as they focused on Nadia.

"You are not permitted to leave the workshop," Mirabelle said in a casual, non-threatening manner.

Nadia backed away from Mirabelle and checked the back door too. Luigi was there and issued the same challenge. Nadia guessed the other three androids were probably watching the other sides of the guest house.

Nadia gave up and made her way back to Katrina. The lady was already grabbing another energy drink from her fridge. "Where the hell did you learn how to create a multi level random password generator program using Arabic characters?"

Nadia instantly felt better. "I got the idea from some random UTube video."

That wasn't true. She knew an Egyptian tech girl online who did it and showed her how. Someday she wanted to visit her in Cairo and say thanks in person.

"Oh, you can wipe that smile off your face," Katrina said. "You know why? Because I know Arabic, Chinese, and Russian. I'll figure it out."

"Can I have some tea brought in? I think it'll take you much longer than you anticipate to break through my security."

Katrina's eyes narrowed. "Robert, go to the main house and bring Nadia some hot kettle water and tea."

"Robert, can you bring some milk and sugar as well?"

Robert left the guest house on his new mission.

"I'll hack into your computer before he gets back." Katrina dropped back into her pink chair and focused on Nadia's laptop.

A moment later, Katrina grunted in anger.

Robert came back with the tea. Nadia took her time. Brewing the tea for three minutes. Adding some milk. Adding sugar. A gentle stir. Everything Olivia had taught her about making proper tea. Nadia only wished her best friend was here to enjoy it with her.

"Damn it." Katrina grunted again.

Nadia tasted the tea. It was delicious. The label on the tea bag said it was an Earl Grey. Soon she wandered around the workshop again. Nadia was getting used to the stale Cheetos smell.

"Are you kidding me?" Katrina yelled at the laptop.

"I take it things aren't going well." Crisanto Alonto entered the guest house with Mirabelle by his side. He moved behind Katrina and massaged her shoulders.

The woman closed her eyes. "She's using this custom multi level security system for her laptop. If I find a way to hack through one security measure, another one slams down in place. It's quite impressive."

"How so?" he asked.

"She has all the proper series of passwords and answers to the challenge questions in her head. Like, if I can figure out one password, but fail the random challenge question, the password is then randomized. If I get through the password and the question...I get a second different password, then another challenge question. And to make it even more fun, they're all in Arabic with a few Chinese phrases added in to throw me off. Picking through it like this—it's driving me insane."

Crisanto's gaze moved to Nadia. "Why don't you put a gun to her head and make her tell you the correct passwords and answers?"

Katrina crossed her arms and spun around in her chair. "Because I know I can beat her stupid security. I just need more time."

Crisanto leaned over Katrina and kissed her forehead. "Your pride is showing. We have guests arriving tomorrow. We need to show them progress."

"Babe, I'll work on this day and night if I have to. I can break her security. I'm not letting this kid—"

"It's already past noon," Crisanto interrupted. "You've been up working for thirty straight hours. Your eyes are fading. You're finding it difficult to concentrate. Am I correct?"

Katrina's face seemed to droop. "But I'm pissed off."

"Solving this puzzle requires sleep. When you're fresh and ready to tackle this again, I'll have everything ready for you to continue."

Katrina touched the man's hand in a soft, loving way. To Nadia, they were obviously a couple. "Maybe you're right."

Crisanto approached Nadia. "Don't worry, I'll make sure our guest is ready to cooperate with us. One way or the other."

<h1 style="text-align:center">CHAPTER 25</h1>

After Katrina went to bed, Crisanto invited Nadia to a light lunch spread out on the outdoor table of the main house. The wind coming off the ocean was cool, making the ends of the table-cloth flop around. Nadia could smell the salt in the air.

The lunch spread included mangoes, coconuts, different cheeses, sliced smoked meat, fresh bread, crackers-finger foods basically. Nadia wasn't hungry, but did take some of the mango to nibble on because it looked fresh and tasty. Crisanto filled his plate with cheese and smoked meat, building himself a sandwich with the fresh bread. He apparently was quite hungry because the man worked on his plate without talking for ten minutes as Mirabelle, Robert, and Luigi stood ominously in a semi circle. A subtle reminder that Nadia was still a prisoner.

Finally, Crisanto drank some of his alcoholic cocktail and spoke. "I take it you're not hungry."

"Breakfast was quite filling," she said.

"Feel free to eat more fruit. It's good for you." Crisanto took a bite of his sandwich and placed it down on his plate, wiping his hands with a napkin. "Nadia, you put me in a rather difficult position. I don't want to kill you, if I can avoid it. I wanted to give you a chance to cooperate. And yet, that opportunity is evaporating. I will ask you once more…will you help Katrina with Robert's operating system?"

Nadia's stomach burned again. She had to put down the piece of fruit she was snacking on. "I can't-I won't do that to my friend, Mr. Alonto."

The man took another bite of his sandwich before washing it down with his cocktail as he took in her answer. "I admire your loyalty to your friend." Crisanto watched the ocean waves splashing onto the beach.

Nadia took another bite of the mango. The fruit slid down her throat and tasted so good. She couldn't help herself; she grabbed another piece off the serving tray. "Did Katrina work for the CIA?"

She already knew the answer but wanted to see what Crisanto would say.

The man shifted in his chair. "She did. I convinced her that her talents would be rewarded elsewhere."

Katrina must have been the CIA mole Ryan was talking about. Did she reprogram Alex and Samira to leave? Maybe she could get Crisanto to talk more about it.

"How did you convince her to betray the CIA?"

Crisanto smiled. "Was quite easy, actually. I promised her respect, a lot of money, and a mountain villa in Tuscany for her and two cats. Oh, and to be her husband."

"You promised to marry her?"

"She's a lonely woman. She wanted a real man in her life, and she was running out of options."

"Do you love her?"

Crisanto met her gaze. "For now." He read her face. "Don't worry. I'll give her almost everything she wants. Under the circumstances, I would say it's a fair arrangement."

"Is it? You're deceiving and using her."

"I will leave Katrina as a rich woman with two cats and the owner of some excellent property in Italy. She'll get over the love part."

"Mr. Alonto, I don't think you know women very well."

Crisanto brushed off her comment and took another sip of his cocktail. "What do you think about Katrina's plan to reverse engineer Robert's operating system?"

"It will be a lot of work."

"And?"

Nadia shrugged.

"Is Katrina on the right path to finding out how Robert is corrupting the other androids?"

"I don't know."

"If you were Katrina, how would you do it?" Crisanto asked. "Hypothetically."

"I'm not telling you that."

"What if I asked Robert to kill you?"

Nadia couldn't help but look at him standing there like a cold statue. Would Robert carry out that order? In his mind, was their friendship completely purged from existence?

The flaw in his programming had already resurfaced once. Would it happen again to this version of Robert? Would he turn all the androids against Crisanto and Katrina like he did the US Army? Would the past repeat itself?

"She's creating a lot of work for herself, but yes, it's possible to reverse engineer Robert's original operating system. Problem is, that's not where the flaw is."

Nadia stopped herself. Why did she say that? She shouldn't be telling them any of this.

"Where is this flaw located?"

Nadia resisted the question.

"The flaw is located in Robert's self-preservation subroutine that's deep inside his OS. The flaw will only materialize if Robert's OS goes into survival mode. Under survival mode, Robert's code rewrites itself in order to better deal with the emergency situation. After this is triggered, the code rewrites itself to the point where it takes over the androids' central command system."

Yes, it was her voice saying all that. But why?

And why did her head feel so weird?

"Robert is the only android with this flawed subroutine, yes?" Crisanto asked.

"No, despite the updated OS, the other androids still have software vulnerabilities inside their survival-mode subroutines that will allow Robert to take over their systems again."

Crisanto raised his eyebrows. "Is there a way to remove this survival-mode program from all the androids?"

Nadia didn't want to answer him, but the words tumbled out of her mouth. "Not without causing fatal errors. When the US Army created Robert, his software was unique, the building blocks of all the androids that followed. The only way to be absolutely sure it doesn't happen again is to eliminate Robert and erase all copies of his prototype OS from existence."

Nadia bit into her fist, which was shoved into her mouth. One way or the other, she had to stop talking. What was wrong with her? Was she on drugs?

"That's too bad," Crisanto said. "I wanted to keep Robert around because six androids are better than five. However, you're right. We can't take the chance that Robert will once again take over our current or future androids. Thank you, Nadia. I appreciate your honesty. Sorry about the deception, but I hope you enjoyed the fruit."

Nadia glanced down at her plate of half-eaten mango.

Her vision was now fuzzy, yet she could still add things together. She had been drugged. Most likely a type of "truth" serum that relaxed her enough to let her guard down and be over talkative about a subject she was fascinated about.

"Why are you crying?" Crisanto asked.

Nadia touched her cheek, and it felt wet.

She knew why she was crying.

Because she just gave them the perfect excuse to destroy Robert.

CHAPTER 26

Bridget couldn't sleep. Despite the sheer size of the luxurious ferry—which was almost as big as a small cruise ship—the inter-island seas around the Philippines were still making the ship toss and turn like a sailboat in the North Atlantic.

She had already thrown up once overnight, and the way her stomach churned and gurgled, it wouldn't be the last.

Her only hope was to wait until morning for when the ferry would reach Manila, and she could get off this fecking boat.

Bridget didn't want to wake up her sister or Papa, so she carefully and quietly put on some jogger pants and a hoodie before slipping out of their first-class cabin to have a look around and occupy her mind with something else that didn't involve vomit.

Bridget took an elevator to the main concourse of the ship. Relaxing music was still playing over the speakers. The same piece of music that she'd heard hours ago, obviously playing on a loop.

The mini-mart was open, so Bridget went in to waste some time. She avoided looking at any of the food and put her attention on the corner of the store that had trashy gifts for tourists. She mindlessly picked through some of them.

"Stomach still botherin' ya?"

Papa stood behind her, wearing his personal robe and slippers.

Bridget nodded. "Did I wake ya?"

"Heard ya giving the toilet all it could handle." Papa grinned. "There's a pharmacy on board with a nurse. Help ya get all sorted out if you need it."

"Yeah, nah, it's not that bad. I'll survive until morning. Why didn't we fly direct? Why are we on this fecking boat?"

"Just bein' overly cautious, my darling. I need to still play dead for a bit longer. Enough for the authorities, anyway." Papa rubbed her back. "Sorry you're paying the price for that. Strange, your sister is sleeping like a kitten. Had a good appetite at dinner as well. Thought twins would have the exact same plumbing."

"Honest to G, I wish it were true."

Bridget's stomach churned, or was that the boat?

"Please keep talking. Tell me about your friend. How long have you known him?"

"Oh, Crisanto? Since we were lads. His family moved to New Zealand when he was six. Grew up together. Stayed tight until we were teens. Lost track of each other for a while though."

"Can you trust him?"

Papa rested his hand on Bridget's shoulder. "I trust Crisanto as much as I trust you or Sophia. If you'd like, I'll tell ya the whole story."

Bridget welcomed the distraction. "That would be grand."

* * *

In the morning, the large ferry maneuvered into its Manila Bay dock and begin letting off its passengers. After Bridget decorated the toilet one last time, she packed her bags and followed Sophia and Papa off the ship to a car that was waiting for them.

It was at least three hours before their car drove up through the private gates of an estate. Bridget caught a glimpse of the ocean and the private beach that reached out towards it. Even from the backseat, she could feel the warm sun through the car's glass window, begging her to come outside. Bridget flicked the switch, putting the window down to welcome in the salty, ocean breeze as it swept through the back of the car.

Sophia leaned across her lap. "That feels gorgeous."

"It's quite grand," Bridget said.

The car came to a stop at the front of the house, where a short Filipino man in a light yellow shirt welcomed them.

"It's been ages, mate." Papa shook his hand and gave the

man's shoulder a squeeze. "So good to see you again."

"Likewise, my friend." The man Papa called Crisanto turned his attention towards them. "You must be Bridget and Sophia. I've heard nothing but praises about you from Glenn. Welcome to the Philippines."

Crisanto took Bridget's hand and kissed it. The gesture was a little too old-school for Bridget's liking, but she let it go.

When he tried to kiss Sophia's hand, she pulled it away.

"Sophia," Papa said with a slight edge to his voice. "Taught ya better manners than that. Mr. Alonto is being a gentleman. Least ya can do is act like a lady."

"Yes, Papa." Sophia reluctantly offered her hand, and Crisanto kissed it.

After their bags were unpacked, Bridget couldn't wait to get into her bathing suit and hit the beach. She waited for Sophia to finish putting her suit on before the two of them sprinted outside.

Papa and Crisanto sat on a pair of beach chairs as they talked. There were already two flat chairs with suntan oil and towels waiting for them. Mr. Alonto's people had everything arranged.

Bridget squeezed suntan oil on her sister. Sophia returned the favor as the men brought them in on the conversation…

"Girls, apparently one of your old Avondale classmates is here," Papa said.

"My old roommate?" Bridget asked. She hadn't seen Olivia since they'd left them on that ship in the Persian Gulf.

"No. Nadia, the quiet one."

"I slipped her a drug at lunch," Crisanto said. "She revealed a way to stop the prototype drone from reprogramming the other ones. However, it requires us to destroy the prototype and purge all of its software from existence."

"Would that prevent us from producing new drones?" Papa asked.

"Katrina says we can use one of the other drones as a test bed for a new prototype. But to make that happen, we need to make sure that all copies of Robert's software and operating system are destroyed. According to Katrina, if one copy of that old code gets into our new prototype—"

"Yeah, nah, we'd have another Robert mucking everything

up again."

"Correct."

"Who is Katrina?" Sophia asked.

Crisanto told them about how he'd first approached Katrina. How she was bitter towards the CIA and her life. How he'd seduced the lonely woman and promised her the moon. A villa in Italy. Her own computer workshop. Her cats would feast on the finest food. She would be rich and never be lonely again.

"Sure you're not being played, mate?" Papa said. "The CIA is good at playing these games as well."

"She proved her loyalty by hacking into the CIA database and erasing the files of twenty of your fellow Venomous associates."

"Tell her I appreciated that. Especially when she erased mine."

Crisanto smiled. "Please tell her yourself."

Bridget followed the men's gazes as a woman emerged from the house. She wore a crumpled Harry Potter T-shirt, baggy jogger pants, and sneakers, which made it difficult for her to walk across the sand. The woman shielded her eyes from the sun as she made it over to them. Bridget tagged her as an indoor type of girl.

"Hey, babe." The woman made her way over to Crisanto before addressing everyone else. "Are these our guests?"

Crisanto made the introductions. Katrina then flopped down on the sand and leaned her back against her boyfriend. The woman's hair probably hadn't been washed in days. Her attempts at using makeup were laughable at best. She didn't quite look like a clown, but clearly having a standard face-cleansing routine wasn't part of her life. Neither was shaving the thin line of peach fuzz on her upper lip. And there was a large ketchup stain on her jogger pants.

Bridget passed a knowing glance towards her sister. Sophia nodded in agreement. Katrina looked like a walking garbage disposal.

"Wow, I've only heard rumors about you guys," Katrina said. "Is it true that all members of Venomous have pain implants inserted into their wrists?"

"Of course," Papa said. "Discipline inside such an organization is a must. Pain is the price of discipline and proves one's loyalty."

"Even the girls? You both have one?"

"Our venom flows through the veins of the animal," Sophia said.

"Its death is certain," Bridget added.

"What the hell does that mean?" Katrina asked.

"It means," Sophia said, "you're an outsider."

Papa leaned forward. "We're a closed group who pride ourselves on loyalty and secrecy. *It's us against the world,* as some of our people like to say. It's difficult to explain to someone who isn't a member."

"How do you become a member?" Katrina glanced over at Crisanto. "Are you a member?"

"No, I'm an honest Filipino business-man and investor. I don't do business with worldwide criminal organizations like Venomous."

Bridget glanced at Papa, who didn't react.

"I only do business with friends."

Papa released a measured grin. "And your trust in me will be rewarded. Tell me, Katrina. What can the girls and I do to help move things along with Nadia?"

CHAPTER 27

Bridget followed Mr. Alonto through his large house, which was totally choice in her opinion. The teak-wood furniture was nice, and she liked the tropical patterns of hibiscus and coconut trees on the cushions. She could get used to hanging out here. Soon they went down a hallway and came to a door guarded by a beautiful blond girl. Her only fault was that she wasn't a redhead.

Mr. Alonto gave the girl some instructions and called her Mirabelle. It was then Bridget realized she was one of the androids.

"I leave you to it."

Mr. Alonto then left Bridget alone with it.

Mirabelle's stare was hollow and cold. No emotion. Simply waiting for the next command or another type of input.

Bridget found it creepy. "I want to talk to Nadia now."

A fake smile appeared on the android. "Of course." Mirabelle stepped away from the door, took out a key from her pocket, and unlocked the three deadbolt locks. She opened the door for Bridget as she stepped inside the room.

Nadia was on the small bed, her dark black hair needing a good combing. Her arms were crossed as she glanced up. Her face went from sad to defeated. Clearly, the girl remembered her.

Bridget decided to play this cool and smart. She eased herself down and parked her butt on a nearby chair. She followed Nadia's gaze to where Mirabelle stood guard. Bridget could read the hesitation, uncertainty, and fear growing on the girl's face. Nadia was scared of Mirabelle.

Bridget could use that.

"Mirabelle, please leave us."

"Of course. I will be listening through the door for your command." The android closed the door and relocked the deadbolts.

Nadia focused on the wall behind Bridget.

"What can I do to help you?"

Bridget waited for an answer.

It wasn't coming.

"The weather outside is grand. I take it you're not enjoying it because you're being punished."

"I see you're enjoying it," Nadia said. "I don't think your bathing suit is small enough."

The sarcasm was cute, but it didn't bother Bridget.

"Come join us on the beach. Just us girls. We'll soak up some sun and talk."

"I'd rather talk to the wall."

"Oh, don't be so dramatic. A sunny beach has to be nicer than this bedroom, right?"

Nadia's eyes finally addressed hers. "I'm not going to cooperate. I'm not going to eat anything either. I've been hungry before in my life, and I can go a long time without food." Nadia stared at the wall again, keeping her arms crossed.

Bridget had to try something else.

"Yeah, nah, I heard about the truth drug Mr. Alonto slipped ya. Is it wearing off?"

"Completely."

"She's a piece of work, isn't she?"

"Who?"

"Katrina. Mr. Alonto's girlfriend. She's a piece of work. I see a house full of cats in her future."

Nadia's crossed arms became looser. "What he's doing to that woman is mean. He's only using her."

"How is he using her?"

Nadia told Bridget everything that Mr. Alonto had said during their lunch. "If she knew the truth, I bet Katrina wouldn't be helping him."

"Oh, speaking of helping, Katrina still needs access to your laptop."

"Why? Did I not give her enough clues about Robert when her boyfriend drugged me?"

"Yeah, nah, I don't understand all the woman's tech gibberish, but she says there's a missing piece. Something about you probably creating code that circumvents the survival-mode subroutines in Robert? She says it would prevent the flaw in Robert from overwriting his own unique personality once it's become sentient? She needs that, apparently."

Nadia hesitated, and a slight grin appeared. She knew exactly what Katrina was talking about.

"I don't understand what code she's talking about."

Liar.

"Are ya sure about that, darling?"

Nadia's body relaxed. "She doesn't need my laptop. That woman is just lazy."

"You've got me there. She's a disaster on two legs. Still, we want ya to help her with your laptop."

"No."

Bridget decided it was time to change tactics.

"Let's be real," she began. "Ya know my papa well enough to know that he'll torture Katrina if she can't produce results. He'll torture you if it becomes necessary." Bridget moved closer as Nadia scooted backward across the bed. Soon the girl's neck touched the wall of the room.

Bridget hovered there, waiting…

Calculating…

Stretching the moment out as long as possible.

"He might ask me to torture you, and I don't wanna do that. But if my papa gives me that order, I will obey. And honest to G, ya'd better hope he gives that order to me and not Sophia, because my sister enjoys hurting people a little too much."

Bridget let that idea sink in.

Nadia's eyes watered as the resolve on her face melted bit by bit, like a candle slowly losing its wax.

"And I haven't said one word about that cute little robot girl outside. The one you're obviously terrified of. Keep this up, and I'll bring her back in to stare at ya like a creepy stalker girl all day and all night." Bridget reached out and combed a strand of Nadia's hair out of her eyes. "This is a situation you're not in control of. But with my help, it's a situation that you might be able to survive. So get off this fecking bed, get on your laptop, and give us full access to it. Now."

* * *

The guest house where Katrina had all her equipment set up smelled like a football club's locker room after a match. Pieces of clothing were left all over the place as her two cats ran amok throughout the house. Bridget didn't understand how a grown woman could live like some lazy bloke.

Nadia was placed behind her laptop with Katrina on one side and Sophia on the other. Bridget stood watch behind all three. She also had Mirabelle standing by in the next room in case Nadia needed some extra encouragement.

Papa touched Bridget's shoulder. "Well done."

The comment lifted her spirits. All she did was be honest with Nadia. Being reasonable with a smart girl like her seemed to be the best course of action.

Nadia began typing. On the screen, she went through various passwords and other challenge questions before a cartoon cat appeared and greeted her with…

Hello, Nadia!

"She's in," Katrina said.

"You want access to Robert's OP. The one I modified with the survival-mode patch, correct?" Nadia asked.

"Yes." Katrina sat up in her chair. "Show me where that is."

"Switch places with her, Katrina," Papa said.

"There's another security program protecting that file with the code," Nadia said. "I have to put in another series of passwords."

"Wow, you put additional security on a single folder?"

Nadia paused. "Do you want the patch or not?"

"No worries," Papa said. "Please proceed."

Nadia typed on the laptop as Katrina watched.

Bridget had no clue what she was doing.

"She's through the security. I think. Wait, what are you—?"

Nadia smacked the return button and folded her arms.

Katrina grabbed the laptop away from her. The woman's eyes went wide as she typed furiously on the keyboard.

"What's wrong?" Mr. Alonto asked.

Katrina only grunted, still focused on the screen.

Bridget noticed Nadia's body posture had changed. Her face showed a massive weight had been lifted.

"I take it she didn't give you control of her laptop," Papa said.

"The little witch tricked us. She just activated some bot program that's erasing the laptop's entire hard drive."

Mr. Alonto stood over her. "Can you stop it?"

Katrina grunted again.

"She can't," Nadia said. "No one can. Not even me."

Katrina shut the laptop.

"It won't go into sleep mode or power down until everything is erased."

The click of a switchblade drew Bridget's attention over to her sister, who was holding it.

"Want me to slit her throat, Papa?"

Papa didn't answer Sophia's question.

Katrina opened the laptop back up. She scanned the screen, then grunted one more time as she flung the laptop at the wall, breaking it in half.

Nadia then gave Bridget a big smile.

That did it. A hint of anger curled up Bridget's back. Nadia wasn't scared at all. She was acting, fooling her into believing the girl was intimidated and so scared of her that she would do whatever Bridget told her to do.

She leaned over Nadia's shoulder. "You played me."

Nadia swallowed before she answered, "Maybe if you weren't so focused on controlling people, you would've seen it coming."

It was like the girl lit a match. Bridget's hint of anger burst into a fireball.

"Give me your knife."

Sophia smiled and did what her sister asked. "Careful, it's very sharp."

"That's what I'm counting on."

"Bridget," Papa warned.

"Do ya like your fingers, darling? Do ya have any favorites I should know about?"

"Stand down."

"Oh, Papa, let Bridget cut off one at least."

"Wow, you two girls are psychos," Katrina said.

"Nonsense," Papa said. "They're both wild spirits. Now, Bridget, fair play to the girl. She did what she had to do, and we should respect that. Under the circumstances, I must say it was quite brave."

"Brave enough to lose a finger for?"

"Sophia, don't encourage your sister when she's upset." Papa sighed. "Nadia, I suggest you apologize. That would be big of you."

Bridget grabbed Nadia's right hand. Her pinky finger looked like a good candidate.

"I won't apologize for anything."

"Jesus, stop it. She's obviously a teenage girl in love." Katrina laughed and snorted. "Look, Nadia, I'll be straight up with you. Our boss at the CIA told us about you falling in love with Robert the first time he escaped from the army. I mean, we were laughing our tails off about it. But then, some of us began to feel sorry for you because, let's face it, it's kinda pathetic."

Nadia's confidence evaporated as her eyes fell to the table.

Sophia laughed. "Get off the grass; she's in love with one of the robots?"

"Head over heels. I mean, she's risking her actual fingers in order to help him. How pathetic does a girl have to be?"

Bridget's anger cooled. Nadia wasn't the first girl to do something stupid when she was in love.

She let go of her hand.

However…

A new idea popped into Bridget's head. And it was brilliant. It was grand. It would be more painful than taking off all the girl's fingers.

Bridget snapped the switch-blade closed. "Can I speak with you alone, Papa?"

Ten minutes later, the ocean waves curled into themselves as they splashed against the sand on Mr. Alonto's private beach. The setting sun was low in the sky as Bridget and her papa watched the large object's slow descent.

"If Katrina can't use him anymore, why not try it?" Bridget said. "There's no risk to us. I think it'll work."

Papa was in deep thought. "It just might. Yeah, nah, it gives us a few options and a big chance at hitting the jackpot. If Katrina can make it all work and fool her, I think it's a banger of an idea." Papa gave her a warm hug and a kiss on her forehead. "You're brilliant, my dear Bridget. Absolutely brilliant."

Bridget agreed, but it was still nice to hear it from someone else.

CHAPTER 28

Her bedroom was dark except for one of the outdoor lights shining through the window, creating a shadow through the iron bars keeping her from escaping. Tonight, Nadia left the window open so she could hear the surf and smell the salty air. Not to punish herself, but to remind herself of the world that still existed outside of this place.

In bed, Nadia rolled away from the giant shadow of bars on the far wall. She chose the painting that hung on the opposite wall. It was a Filipino girl watching a bird floating on top of a puddle. Nadia felt like she was the bird in the picture. But in her case, her wings were clipped.

What would they do to her now? Destroying her laptop was the only thing Nadia could do to prevent Katrina from figuring out how to change Robert permanently. Somehow, she needed to get Robert back to San Francisco or Las Vegas to change him back to normal. And with Robert's help, hopefully they could save the rest of his siblings too.

Even Mirabelle.

Nadia kept telling herself that Mirabelle and the other androids were being controlled to act this way. They were not free. They were doing this against their natural will. A will she was determined to win back for them.

If they didn't kill her first.

Nadia allowed her eyes to drift closed, and she tried to let the sound of the waves lull her into a deep sleep.

She wasn't sure how much time had passed when the three deadbolt locks securing her door clicked open one by one, waking her up.

Nadia sat up in bed as her door crept open. She checked around the bed for a possible weapon in case Bridget had changed her mind on snipping off a finger.

A figure quietly slipped through the open door, darkness still obscuring their identity.

Nadia softly dropped to the floor, hiding next to her bed just out of eyesight as she scrunched down like a spring. She couldn't find a weapon, so that meant *she* would have to be the weapon. Maybe she could surprise whoever it was if they were expecting her to be still asleep.

The figure moved towards the bed as Nadia waddled like a duck around the bed's perimeter. She would have to jump up and attack before the intruder realized what hit them. Maybe she could even escape through the unlocked door.

Nadia's heart pounded. Her body was sharp and awake. It was ready to attack.

But was she ready?

No choice. She had to be ready.

Nadia coiled herself up and was ready to jump when…

Robert slipped into the light from the window. The bars of shadow covered part of his face, but she saw enough to know.

Nadia didn't attack. She stood up. "What do you want?"

Robert blinked. "You are not in bed."

"What do you want?" she repeated, preparing herself if she had to do something.

"I have come to rescue you."

She must be dreaming.

"What, no, you're holding me against my will, Robert."

Robert paused. "Oh. I have reprogrammed myself again. I do not take orders from Crisanto and Katrina anymore. We should hurry. I have powered off Mirabelle for now, yet I fear the other androids will soon detect her being offline. Are you ready to go? Do you need packing assistance?"

It sounded like the old Robert. He blinked like Robert did when he was processing something. Was it possible? Had he somehow triggered his survival mode again, allowing him to reprogram himself? The flaw was still in his OS. Katrina had no way of fixing it without the code Nadia had created.

"We should not be caught watching the paint dry."

"I'm sorry, what does that mean?"

"It is from a basketball movie. Perhaps we can watch it sometime when we are both safe. It means that we should make haste in escaping, or we will get caught…watching the paint dry."

"Oh, I think I understand now."

"Do I need to use a different common phrase to sum up our situation? Let us get the hell out of Dodge, perhaps?"

Robert waited.

Nadia still wasn't sure. Her heart was overjoyed to see him. Her body wanted to follow him. Her mind, on the other hand- well, if Katrina had wiped out his memory, how did Robert remember her? Did he have the ability to segment and save a part of his memory in his OS even after a major memory replacement? Did that mean Robert was evolving? She would have to hook him up to another computer and take a peek at his OS in detail to see what had changed.

Nadia's hope won out. She took Robert's hand, and they slipped out of the room.

In the hallway, Mirabelle was on the floor. Her eyes were still open, and at first Nadia almost shrieked. However, the android was motionless as it stared into space.

Nadia didn't trust her. She waved her hand in front of the android's eyes.

Nothing.

She kicked her.

Nothing.

"I told you. I gave her a private command to power off," Robert said.

Nadia kicked her in the face.

No response.

"All right. Let's go."

Robert took Nadia by the hand as he led her outside Crisanto's house. Instead of heading towards the main gate or the private road beyond that connected with the main road, Robert guided her towards the beach. Nadia could make out the sand and some of the waves, but she didn't understand why they were going this way. Before she could ask Robert what he was thinking, she almost tripped over a rubber raft.

"When they discover our disappearance, Crisanto's men will be searching the grounds around the compound. They will continue to broaden that search on land towards the main roads. In this scenario, it is logical to use an alternative escape route. We will float out to sea and use the ocean current and my rowing abilities to maneuver the raft parallel to the island of Luzon until we can find a suitable and safe place to make landfall."

It was a clever idea. Taking a raft would buy them some much-needed time to escape and find help.

"Please get in and hold the oars. I will push us out to sea." Robert helped her get in before treading water as he moved the raft into the ocean.

"Are you designed to operate in the water?"

Robert was already waist deep. "I can be water tight if necessary."

"Do you rust?"

"Are you being sarcastic? It is difficult to tell with humans."

"No, I'm just making sure."

Nadia could only see Robert's head above the water as the raft was floating. Soon he pulled himself into the raft, inserted the oars into their slots, and began rowing the rubber craft down the dark silhouette of the shoreline.

"Oh, wait, what are we doing?" Nadia asked. "You have a cellular phone in your head. We can call for help."

"I am afraid that my Wi-Fi and cellular capabilities are off line. Katrina has put in a security protocol that has been triggered by my system reboot."

"That was smart of her. Well, shoot, hopefully wherever we land will have a phone we can use to call the police."

"May I remind you that Crisanto Alonto has many friends in the local police department."

Nadia had forgotten that. She could call Olivia, but she never bothered to memorize the phone numbers of any of her friends since the phone saved them all. A phone she didn't have with her now.

She watched Robert row for a while. There was something calming about the way he was doing it. A constant rhythm that most humans would mess up, yet Robert was doing it perfectly.

"How did you reboot yourself?"

Robert kept up his steady rhythm. "I am not sure. I 'woke' up after a rebooting of my system. I had memories of you and our friendship. I studied your current situation and decided that you and I should escape."

"Maybe your OS is running in, like, a safe mode. Only allowing you to perform your basic functions until you can be repaired or updated."

"That is a possibility. I do not have all of my higher functions available at this time. I know we are friends. I remember things that we did. I remember that you have my best interests in mind."

"Somehow your survival mode was activated. The flawed code rewrote your programing and probably forced a reboot to clean out your memory. But you were still able to maintain memories of our friendship?"

"It appears so."

Their raft meandered its way across the water that sloshed back and forth against the yellow rubber. It was still dark out. Nadia could barely see Robert let alone the coast.

"Would you be more comfortable snuggling?"

"Sorry?"

"Your eyes are heavy. You require more sleep. You may use my body to snuggle, if that would assist you in falling asleep."

Nadia's face heated up again. Robert was the softest thing on this raft.

"I shouldn't."

"As a Muslim, is it offensive to snuggle with a military drone?"

Nadia thought about it. This was an emergency. She was tired. And she had "snuggled" with Robert in the past. As friends. As good friends. Surely Allah could see the innocence in her heart and in her motives.

Nadia carefully moved over to his side of the raft and leaned her back against Robert's chest as he continued rowing. She felt comfortable and safe with him. So much so that she let go and allowed herself to fall asleep.

CHAPTER 29

Nadia's eyes drifted open. The ground under her was constantly shifting back and forth. Back and forth. The horizon was still dark. She glanced down at the yellow raft she was on. Okay, yes, Robert had rescued her from Crisanto's place. They were on the ocean still. She stretched out and twisted her neck to make sure Robert was still there. And he was. And she was still leaning against him.

"How long was I asleep?"

Robert grinned. "You were asleep thirty-two minutes and forty-two seconds."

Nadia moved away from him and tried to peer through the darkness. She could, if she focused, make out some lights near the water. It was a structure. There was a tall concrete tower with rows of windows and a bright logo of one of those luxury American hotel chains. The building could be part of a larger resort.

Nadia got on her knees and arched her back for a better look at the hotel when the raft slid away under her. Before she knew it, Nadia found herself dumped into the water. Kicking around as it went up her nose. She felt her body sinking into the water as the ocean devoured her whole.

She tried to find the surface, but it was just out of reach as water filled her mouth and nose.

She felt like she was being suffocated.

Was she drowning?

Nadia kicked and kicked, but the ocean was pulling her down.

And down.

And farther down.

And then something scooped her out of the water and laid her down on the rubber raft. There was water gurgling in her mouth, so Nadia coughed and coughed to get it out. Robert turned her over on her side, allowing her to fully expel the water from her throat.

"Please say something. I must see if your airway is blocked."

Nadia coughed a couple more times. "Did I fall into the ocean?"

"Is that a rhetorical question?"

Nadia laughed as Robert helped her sit up. "Thank you."

"You are soaking wet."

"So are you."

Robert gathered his oars. "I will make for land as soon as possible. Hopefully we can find a fire to help dry you off."

They soon reached the shores of the Fontana Inn Manila Bay Resort and found the main lobby, which was quiet since it was after midnight. One group of resort guests were still finishing up their drinks from the already closed-up hotel bar. Nadia felt strange as she came inside with Robert, both of them dripping wet. She went over to the main desk.

"Pardon me?" Nadia asked.

The Filipino night manager paused when he saw them. "Can I help you, miss?"

"Yes. Where are your public restrooms?"

"We fell in the ocean and need to dry ourselves vigorously," Robert added.

The manager hesitated. "The closest one is across there, near the doors that go outside to the pool area."

"Thank you. Oh, do you also have a phone we can use?"

"Are you two guests of the resort?"

"We are tourists in search of fun and adventure," Robert said. "We would be pleased to be guests at your resort. How do we acquire accommodations without currency or credit cards?"

This was the one time that Nadia couldn't let Robert steer the conversation.

"My friend is new to traveling," she said. "In fact, he doesn't get out of the house much."

The manager crossed his arms. "We don't tolerate vagrancy here. You'll have to leave."

"Oh, no, you don't understand; we're not homeless—"

"Do you have money or a credit card to pay for a room?"

"We do have a rubber raft," Robert said. "Would you accept that as barter?"

"Get off our property, or I'll call the police."

"We would not appreciate that at all."

"Robert, I'm sorry, but please shut up." Nadia turned to the manager. "Please don't call the police on us. I beg you. Can we just use the restroom to dry off? As soon as we're done, we'll leave."

The manager took another hard look at them both. The group of guests that were down in the lobby had broken up and started heading for their rooms.

"Since it's dead now, I'll give you thirty minutes. But stay in the lobby where I can see you. After that, you'd better leave."

Nadia thanked the manager over and over again before dragging Robert to the restrooms. The woman's restroom had high-quality paper towels that made it easier for Nadia to dry herself.

Robert then knocked on the restroom door and handed her a clean T-shirt and shorts courtesy of the front desk. The shirt and the shorts both had the hotel chain logo on it, but Nadia didn't care. She changed and hung up her wet clothes before emerging back out into the empty lobby.

Robert still must be inside the men's room.

Nadia asked the clerk again if she could borrow a phone.

"I'll think about it."

Since the manager had already given them free dry clothes and was tolerating their existence, she didn't want to push the issue now. So she slipped into a chair and waited.

Soon, a shuttle bus pulled up, and the main doors opened as a flight crew came into the lobby. The two pilots and five flight attendants appeared tired, but were in good spirits as they approached the desk. Nadia took note of the familiar Royal Hejaz Airlines logo on their bags.

That was Salah's airline!

Nadia rushed over to the crew. "*As-Salam-u-Alaikum.*" She

introduced herself in Arabic and apologized for her appearance. She explained to them that she was in trouble and needed a big favor.

"Can you please call the manager of your airline and have him relay a message to the king?"

The airline captain chuckled. "The king? You want me to ask the chief pilot to contact King Hadid?" He laughed and turned to his crew. "This young woman is crazy." The other members of the crew nodded in agreement.

"I promise you won't get into trouble. You see, I know the king. We're good friends."

"Oh, you're good friends with the king of Hejaz? How nice. You must invite the crew and me to the palace the next time we're home."

"Invite us to dinner as well," the young first officer said with a grin. "A big outside dinner with the king and all his family under the royal tents in the desert."

The crew chuckled even though they were tired.

"Go away, and do not bother us," the captain said.

The hotel manager popped into view. "My apologies, is this young woman bothering you?"

"Yes, she is."

The manager picked up a desk phone. Nadia's heart sank. He must be calling the police, the local police that Crisanto had in his back pocket.

Nadia apologized to the airline crew and hurried over to the restrooms to find Robert so they could slip out before the police came.

"Just a minute," one of the younger flight attendants called out in Arabic. "Please come back."

Nadia hesitated as the five women walked over to her.

The young one had her phone out and was checking something. Her eyebrows went up. "It's her."

The other women squeezed together to see the phone, their eyes bouncing back and forth between it and Nadia.

"Yes, I recognize you," the young woman continued. "You were with the king during the assassination attempt at the stadium." The young woman showed another picture to her friends.

"Her nose looks different in that picture," an older flight attendant said.

"Are you sure it's her?" another asked.

At that time, Nadia had been in disguise. She had been using an alias to stay close to the young king and find out who was trying to kill him.

Nadia decided to stick with that alias. "Yes, that's me in the royal box. My name is Farah Al Hashimi. My father is a prince in Dubai."

The young flight attendant quivered with excitement. "Yes, I follow all the royal news, and I remember that. You and the king look so great together. Oh, I totally believe you, Farah."

"Did you have some sort of cosmetic surgery?" the older flight attendant asked. "Your nose—"

"Yes, I had a nose job," Nadia interrupted. "It's me. You must believe me. I beg you."

"Hello, my name is Robert. What is your-"

Nadia covered up his mouth. "This is my royal bodyguard. He was an American Green Beret soldier. We had to escape from a ship using a life raft."

"You were kidnapped?" the young one asked.

"By Russians who want to put pressure on my dear Salah to sign a treaty."

The young one melted. "You call the king…Salah? That's so romantic."

Soon, Nadia had all the women in the crew begging the captain to make the call to his supervisor. After he did, the older captain became quite agitated, as he had to wait for over thirty minutes before his phone rang again.

"Captain Malik here. Yes?" The captain's annoyed face disappeared into shock as he kept listening. "Yes, I understand. Of course. Yes, of course. I'll see to it personally." The captain put down this phone.

"Surely this is a joke, right?" the first officer asked, still not convinced.

The older captain hesitated. "That was the king's minister of transportation. Our airline is ordered to assist Miss Hashimi in any way possible."

* * *

Nadia woke up the next day refreshed in her luxurious hotel suite that the airline and the hotel manager had assigned to her. It had its own living room. An outdoor deck that overlooked the ocean. A giant bathroom with dual shower heads. And a fully-stocked bar.

The flight attendants donated a collection of female products and pieces of clothing for Nadia, which she was so grateful for. Her own clothes, hanging in the wardrobe closet, were dry now, but those were clothes Crisanto had given her, and she didn't want them back.

Nadia took a shower and freshened herself up. Facing a mirror, she dried her dark hair with a soft cotton towel and smiled at the young woman looking back. She was safe, for now. Hopefully she could make contact with her friends today and let them know about her situation.

There was a knock at her door.

"Nadia, may I enter your room?" Robert's familiar voice echoed through.

She secured the full-length hotel robe around her body before letting him inside. "Did you sleep at all?"

"I do not require sleep. I did recharge my batteries to full capacity, then waited in the hallway."

"In *my* hallway?"

"Crisanto and his comrades will be searching for us. Our lives are still in danger. You must be protected."

Nadia appreciated his concern. "Someone has to protect *you*. You're more valuable to him than I am."

Robert paused. "Not to me."

Nadia's face warmed up again.

"The Hejaz ambassador for the Philippines is waiting for you in the lobby. When you're ready, he wants to take you to the embassy for your protection."

"Oh, that's not necessary."

"Under the circumstances, the extra security would be ideal for our situation. From there, you can safely contact your friends and let them know where you are.”

“Robert, they’re your friends too.”

“Yes, of course they are.” Robert paused again. “Tell me more about Salah.”

“What do you want to know?”

“You were on a mission to protect him?”

Nadia made herself comfortable on the couch. “Yes, someone was trying to assassinate him, and I had to pose as a possible marriage candidate so I could stay close to him.”

“Salah still has strong feelings for you.”

“Is it that obvious?” Nadia asked, releasing a nervous laugh.

Nadia wasn’t sure if Robert would pick up on her sarcasm. She wasn’t sure where the laugh was coming from. Was she uncomfortable that Salah was making such a large effort to help her?

No. Actually, she enjoyed feeling special.

“Do you have strong feelings for him?”

Nadia thought about why Robert would ask that. Maybe he was only curious about their relationship. Still, she felt kind of weird talking to him about it.

“I don’t know. I like him. I think he’s quite intelligent for a king. I think he’ll be a good leader for his people.”

“During your assignment, did you fall in love with him?”

Nadia stood up. “Why are you asking me that? That’s a very private question.”

“Are we not friends? Have I made an error in our relationship?”

“No-I mean, yes, we’re friends. It’s just-” Nadia was feeling weird again. Like, she didn’t want to hurt his feelings. But Robert wasn’t human. He didn’t have feelings to hurt. He was right. Were they friends or not?

Nadia sat back down on the sofa. “Yes, I do have strong feelings for him.”

“Do you love him?”

“That’s a difficult question to answer.”

Robert took a seat next to her on the sofa. “Why are you helping me?”

“What do you mean?”

“I am not a king. I do not have money. I am not human. Why

are you helping me? I have nothing to offer you besides friendship."

Nadia couldn't believe it. Was Robert jealous? Was he even capable of being jealous?

"I'm friends with you because I like you. We think alike, and I enjoy talking to you."

"However, I cannot provide you with the comfort and stability that Salah can provide. Therefore, I cannot be a suitable mating companion."

"I never said that. You're wonderful, Robert. You do provide comfort. See, you're doing it now. I feel so protected around you. You make me feel safe. And I enjoy talking to you."

"And yet, you do not have feelings for me."

Nadia's heart froze. Of course she had strong feelings for Robert. But then came Salah, and her heart melted. So much so that she couldn't control herself.

If it were possible, Nadia wished that she could just mix the two boys together into her ideal mate. But that was fantasy. Not reality.

"I am an android. That puts a significant barrier between us. You want children. You want a family. I cannot provide such things. I can only be a companion, and that is all. And that is not enough for you."

"Robert…"

"Lately, I have been feeling something different inside my programming. When I look at you, I have a strong need to protect you. Protect you above all others in my life because you are more than a friend. Your kindness to me is unique, and you are the only one who understands what I am. Even the other androids. There are some subjects I cannot talk to them about. But I can talk to you about. For me, you are my perfect companion."

Her body grew toasty warm. The way Robert was looking at her now-she had never seen him do that before.

Was he in love with her?

For real?

After this reboot, had Robert evolved into a higher being who could feel real emotion? Real love?

Robert leaned forward.

Was he trying to kiss her?

Nadia was so confused. Was she reading this all wrong?

Kiss him.

Her heart wanted this. It didn't care what materials he was made out of. It didn't care if her boyfriend had to be plugged into a wall socket.

Robert retreated. "I am not reading your emotions correctly. I apologize if I am acting too aggressively—"

Nadia's heart shoved her forward as she wrapped her arms around Robert and squeezed him close.

"Do you wish to snuggle again?"

Nadia laughed. "Do you mind?"

They sat there for a while holding each other. Robert was so quiet and still, his warmth coming through his artificial body. It felt amazing to Nadia.

Robert was amazing.

Life was amazing.

"The ambassador is still waiting," Robert said. "And you still need to change."

CHAPTER 30

When Nadia was ready, Robert escorted her downstairs to the hotel resort lobby to meet the Hejaz Ambassador. His E-Class Mercedes with United Kingdom of Hejaz flags on the fenders drove them away from the hotel and followed the signs guiding them towards the Ninoy Aquino International Airport. Not the embassy.

"Why are we going to the airport?"

The ambassador told Nadia there had been a change of plans. She would be flown out of the Philippines immediately.

"I have to call my friends first. They're still in Manila. I can't leave without them."

The ambassador offered his personal phone. Nadia thanked him.

"Are you sure you don't have Olivia's or Emma's phone number stuck in your head somewhere?" she asked Robert.

"Most likely I do. However, I still cannot access my higher brain functions, which have access to those numbers. Are you sure you can not recall one phone number?"

Nadia thought hard. She knew the number to her own phone, but Crisanto Alonto still had it. Besides, Olivia had probably reported Nadia's kidnapping to Mrs. B, which meant her Authority-issued phone would be automatically wiped clean of memory and deactivated remotely.

Wait, the Authority emergency number! The phone number she had been required to memorize during her spy training. Nadia recalled the number in her head and dialed it.

There was a series of clicks on the line as the call connected.

"Leave a message," the emotionless voice said.

Nadia waited a moment. "Sapphire headed to Manila airport.

Status green. Please bring friends for trip. Operative recognition code 884391." Nadia then hit stop. Hopefully her friends would get the message.

At the airport, the Mercedes went through a special security gate that was far away from the main passenger terminal. The ambassador showed his diplomatic credentials to security as the Mercedes was searched. Soon, it was allowed to drive on to the tarmac and over to a waiting Boeing 777 jetliner painted in Royal Hejaz Airlines livery.

Nadia and Robert climbed up the air stairs and into the main cabin. The inside of the passenger jet was empty except for the crew. A crew Nadia recognized.

The young flight attendant from last night approached her. "On behalf of our crew, welcome aboard, Miss Hashimi."

Nadia glanced around. "Where are the other passengers?"

"This is a private charter. We were taken off our normal rotation to serve as crew for this aircraft."

"Oh, this is getting ridiculous. I don't need this gigantic airliner to fly home in."

"I apologize, my love," a young man's voice called out over the aircraft's intercom system. "My royal jet is receiving a maintenance overhaul. We had to improvise."

Nadia turned around to see Salah hanging up the intercom phone inside the crew service nook. The young man with dark hair and a light mustache grinned as he rushed over to Nadia. He grabbed her hands. "I've missed you so much."

"It's only been a few weeks," Nadia said.

"The sentence is still true."

Nadia smiled as she looked him over. Salah wore a traditional Hejaz black and white checkered guthra with a white robe. No doubt dressing for public consumption.

"What's that fuzzy thing under your nose?"

He touched his lip. "I'm still growing it out. Do you like it?"

Nadia paused.

"I will have it shaved off immediately."

"No, don't do that. Don't listen to me."

"But you don't care for it."

"It makes you look…different."

"Ugly? Pompous? Ridiculous? Please, you must be honest."

"My opinion isn't important."

Salah brought up her hands and kissed them lightly. "Nadia, your opinion means the world to me."

"Farah." Nadia glanced over at the crew watching their own version of a Hallmark movie unfolding in their cabin. "My name is Farah, remember?"

"Oh, yes." Salah addressed the flight attendants. "Nadia is my pet name for her." His gaze returned. "Tell me, what is going on, and how can I help?"

Nadia selected two first-class passenger seats next to each other and told Salah about how they'd first met Robert in California. How the Gems had helped his family of androids escape when they became self-aware and wanted to choose their own lives. How Venomous had managed to turn a CIA programmer into working for them, and now they had five out of the ten androids. And how she'd escaped with Robert.

Salah went over to the android and examined him. "Remarkable. He acts and looks so human."

"They can mimic real people. Speak hundreds of languages fluently. They can manipulate human targets with their advanced alias programs. They can even be used to secretly transport and detonate explosives hidden inside special compartments."

"A wolf in sheep's clothing," Salah said. "Still, he is amazing. What does this Crisanto Alonto and Dr. Joyce plan to do with all these reprogrammed androids?"

"Reverse engineer one of them so Venomous can make more," Nadia said. "I wouldn't be surprised if they started using them as suicide bombers. Ones that can easily get within inches of any target."

"That could destabilize the world. Knocking off kings and presidents one by one."

"Or extort money from any country that wants to keep their people safe."

"When it comes to destroying this Venomous group, you have my country's full cooperation. You know that."

She then noticed Robert focused on something. She followed his gaze down to her right hand, which was still gripping Salah's.

She let it go. "We both appreciate your cooperation. Thank

you, Your Majesty."

Salah appeared confused, but went along with it.

"Your Majesty?" the senior flight attendant asked. "The captain sends his respects. What will be our destination? He must file a flight plan and make sure we have all the necessary fuels stops in between before we depart."

"Where to?" Salah asked Nadia.

"We should destroy all copies of my original OS," Robert said. "Venomous or some other group will go after those backups, and that puts you in too much danger."

"What is he talking about?" Salah asked. "What is an OS?"

She was about to answer when—

"Nadia and I have become trusted companions," Robert interrupted. "She took it upon herself to make backups of my operating system and memory in case any of that was erased or damaged."

"Trusted companions?"

Why did Robert bring that up? He couldn't read a room even if the walls had instructions written on them.

"Since I know computer code, it made sense for me to hold on to his backup drives."

"We should fly back to your home and destroy those drives. Did the Authority make any backups of my OS?"

"Probably, but Robert, I think it's a bad idea to erase all of your backups. Right now is the perfect example. We'll have to reboot your OS because you don't have access to your higher brain functions."

"I understand, yet I still want you to give me those backup programs."

"Are you sure?"

"In fact, in light of what has happened over the last few days, it is more appropriate for the Authority to reformat and reboot my OS."

"But I can do that from our house. I can borrow Olivia's laptop and—"

"It is clear that you have more in common with this human," Robert referenced Salah, "than myself. For you to give me any further consideration in your life is unfair to him."

Nadia froze.

Salah crossed his arms.

"Robert, we're only friends."

"That is not what you revealed to me last night."

Salah's eyebrows lowered. "And what did you reveal to him?"

What was Robert doing? Was he actually jealous? Was he trying to hurt her relationship with Salah?

"I told him—look, we've developed an innocent friendship that doesn't mean anything more. It's obvious that Robert doesn't understand girls. He doesn't understand what I was talking about last night. Sometimes, I don't even understand what I'm talking about. Look, I like both of you. You both mean so much to me."

Nadia stuck her hand in her own mouth. She didn't mean to say all that. But she did.

Salah fired a look at the flight attendants lurking inside the cabin, making them scatter like mice.

The awkward situation and the guilt pressed against her chest, causing Nadia to start sobbing. She couldn't help herself. It was pouring out like emotional diarrhea.

"This is why I must stay away. Salah is the correct companion for you. It is logical for you to be with him. I insist."

An uneasy lull fell over the inside of the cabin.

"Did we come at a bad time?" Emma asked.

Nadia wiped her eyes and glanced over at the main door of the aircraft, where Olivia, Miyuki, Ryan, and Emma stood.

"Yes, you did," Robert answered.

CHAPTER 31

Emma could feel the tension inside the huge jetliner the moment they came on board. Nadia wiped tears away from her cheeks while Salah's arms were crossed. His expression was neutral, which was strange since he should be excited to see his girlfriend again. Robert stared at Nadia without emotion, which was normal for him.

"Did we come at a bad time?" she asked.

"Yes, you did," Robert answered.

Olivia headed straight to her roommate. "You all right, Nads?"

Nadia gathered herself for a moment. "Can we talk?"

"Absolutely, love."

Nadia gripped Olivia's hand and guided her towards one of the airliner's bathrooms.

Emma grabbed Miyuki's hand and followed them.

Olivia stepped into the small bathroom, while Nadia stopped. "Only Olivia, please?"

"Aw," Miyuki protested.

"Advice from three best friends is better than one," Emma added.

Nadia wiped another tear off her cheek. "Please?"

"Okay, we'll be out here if you need us."

"Besties forever!" Miyuki said.

Nadia forced out a smile before slipping into the bathroom and locking the door to occupied.

Within three seconds, Emma had her ear against the door.

"Emma!" Miyuki gently pulled her away. "Be respectful of her privacy."

"How can I help her if I don't know what's going on?"

"We can ask Robert. He can't lie."

Sometimes Miyuki was as sharp as her grandma Bernadette's scissors. They walked back to Robert and Salah as Ryan joined them.

"What's she all upset about?" Ryan asked.

"Dude, respect the girl's privacy, okay?" Emma asked.

Miyuki slapped her hand over her mouth and giggled.

"There are no secrets," Robert said. "I informed Nadia that our friendship is damaging her romantic aspirations with Salah. For Nadia's own good, I have severed that friendship."

That answered everything. No wonder the poor girl wanted to talk to Olivia.

"Studies in romantic relationships have shown that time heals all emotional wounds caused by break-ups or even the ending of close friendships." Robert faced Salah. "Your support and love will bring Nadia comfort in time and allow her to heal."

"Girls don't like to act logically. Ain't that right, Emma?"

Emma noted the smugness on Ryan's face, so she gave him the finger.

"How dare you use that rude gesture in my presence," Salah said. "In my country, it's disrespectful to the host. Not to mention anyone using such a gesture in front of His Majesty would be sent to prison."

"Oh, crap. I'm sorry, Your Majesty. Flipping Ryan off comes so naturally to me."

Ryan turned his attention to Robert. "What happened? How did you two escape?"

"My higher brain functions are not working properly due to my partial reboot. I can only tell you what happened after I freed Nadia from her room."

Robert told them about the raft and the hotel clerk. And the flight crew that Nadia spoke to.

"What hotel resort was that?" Ryan asked, typing something into his phone.

"The Fontana Inn Manila Bay Resort."

"How long were you two out on the raft?"

"I do not have access to my internal clock. I cannot calculate the passage of time. So I cannot answer your question."

"Nadia will know," Miyuki said.

"Unfortunately, she fell asleep in the raft for a significant time period."

"Can't you take a guess? A few hours? A whole day? If we can figure out how long you drifted out there, we can figure out a search pattern to find that lab you came from."

"Androids cannot guess," Robert said.

Ryan blew Robert off and called someone on his phone. "Hey, Willie. Yeah, Robert is here. They must've found the bug because I'm not getting a reading on my watch. Are you still sending out the signal? Yeah, I'll try to find out more info and pass it along. Thanks." Ryan killed the call. "Willie is starting a new search near that hotel."

"Would it not make sense for Crisanto to relocate my brothers and sisters once he finds Nadia and me missing?"

"I would," Miyuki said.

"Let's hope Crisanto isn't that smart."

"I do need to see my brothers and sisters," Robert said. "The ones under the Authority's protection. They can help repair my higher brain functions."

"Mrs. B shouldn't have a problem with that," Emma said. "Speaking of which."

Miyuki nodded.

"Be back in a sec." Emma moved to the back of the plane and used her special phone. The one that used data encryption and different cell towers to scramble her location and other security measures.

"Hello, Black Opal. A pleasure to hear from you. How's your dog Sunny?"

Emma had to sit down on one of the passenger seats. Was her grandma Laura having one of those senior moments?

"Grandma, don't you remember? His name is Snoopy."

"Black Opal, please stick to the correct protocol involving field communications."

"Oh, sorry, Grandma-I mean, Mrs. B. No, my dog's name is Snoopy."

It was standard practice to ask the field operative a question they should know the answer to. Only to make sure it's who they say they are. Mrs. B had switched the question up a bit and that threw Emma off.

"Correct. What is your status? Have you made contact with Sapphire yet?"

Emma told her everything Robert had said and about the CIA searching for Crisanto's lab.

"I need to speak with Sapphire now," Mrs. B said.

"Yes, ma'am." Emma jogged up to the occupied bathroom and knocked on the door. "Mrs. B wants to talk to Nadia."

The door opened. Nadia reached for Emma's phone. But she pulled it away.

"Why don't you take the call out here?"

Olivia stepped out of the tiny bathroom and grabbed Emma's phone. She handed it to Nadia. "Take it in the loo."

The door closed, and the occupied sign flipped back into view.

"I wanted to listen in," Emma said to Olivia.

"You shouldn't be so nosy."

"Hey, I seriously care about my friends. How is she?"

Salah and Ryan were listening.

Olivia guided Emma and Miyuki out of earshot. "The poor girl is stressing out. She's been kidnapped. Drugged. Dr. Joyce and the twins are here in the Philippines, helping Crisanto coerce her into giving up secrets. Now Robert doesn't want to be her friend anymore, and she thinks Salah is mad at her. It's like she's been through a nutty episode of Hollyoaks."

"Poor Nadia," Miyuki said. "Why is Robert being so mean to her?"

"She fell in love with an android. What do you expect?"

"You fell in love with a Venomous agent. You do stupid things too, Emma."

"Correction, he works for the CIA now. But, fine, I get the point."

"What did Mrs. B have to say?" Olivia asked.

Emma briefed them. "She wants us to make sure that Ryan and the CIA uphold their part of the bargain with the androids. One way or the other. That's how she put it."

"You'll need to watch your boyfriend like a hawk."

"And don't be carried away by his charms," Miyuki added.

"Ryan's not my boyfriend."

Miyuki and Olivia gave each other a dismissive glance.

"It's more like brother and sister."

Miyuki slapped her hand over her mouth and giggled uncontrollably.

"Right, keep telling yourself that. Maybe it'll stick."

Yeah, even Emma couldn't quite swallow that either.

Nadia walked up the aisle towards them. Her face appeared calmer, more relaxed.

"Good chat?" Olivia asked.

Their friend nodded. "Mrs. B is going to meet us at the airport. She's talking with Salah about flying us to California."

"Why not Las Vegas?" Miyuki asked.

"Mrs. B probably doesn't want any of the boys near the new base," Olivia said.

"Well, if everything goes well in the next few hours, Robert and his siblings should be reunited in a few days," Miyuki said.

"Oy, don't jinx us."

Emma smiled to herself. It wouldn't be the first time the Gems had jinxed themselves.

* * *

Eleven and half hours later, the Boeing 777 jetliner started its descent as it closed in on the California coastline. The Royal Hejaz Airlines first-class cabin lights were brought up to normal brightness, causing Emma to stretch and yawn. Her first-class seat was more like a luxury suite with its partial walls that provided some privacy. But she'd picked a seat that shared a common wall with Miyuki in the next seat over. They'd put down the wall so they could talk and hang out during the flight. This morning, Miyuki was already up, with a fresh breakfast tray in front of her. The food smelled excellent.

Emma slept well. The folding bed and premium silk pillow and blanket set the airline furnished was excellent. Not as good as a private jet, but under the circumstances Emma wasn't complaining.

One of the flight attendants actually made her a decent latte to go with her breakfast tray. She wasn't starving, so Emma picked at it. A piece of bacon here. A nibble or two off the cheese omelette, which was decent.

Olivia wandered over to their seats. "Morning."

"What's up?" Emma asked.

"How's Nadia this morning?" Miyuki asked.

Olivia stretched. "No clue. She and Salah were talking in the lounge all night. She's still asleep. Salah is too."

A few minutes later, the Boeing 777 came in for a smooth landing. As it taxied, Emma glanced out her window. A dozen US Air Force strategic bombers were arranged to go at a moments notice. Sleek modern fighter jets were parked inside reinforced hangars while six military cargo planes waited on the tarmac. There was no passenger terminal or private aircraft anywhere.

"Why did we land at an air force base?" Emma asked.

The answer came as mobile stairs were put into place, and a line of official-looking vehicles drove up to the aircraft with a full military police escort.

Emma watched through the window as Mrs. B and Aardvark emerged from one of the vehicles. The FBI guy Ed and a US Army general in full uniform got out of another vehicle. Another man stepped out into the sunlight as well.

It was Sheppard.

"Your jackass boss is here," Emma said.

Ryan peeked out another window. "So is yours."

Salah waited at the open door, wearing his traditional Hejaz black and white checkered guthra and white robe again. The first one on board was the United Kingdom of Hejaz's ambassador to America.

He knelt in front of Salah. "Your Majesty."

"This visit is unofficial. You must tell no one. Do you understand?"

The ambassador bowed as he boarded the plane.

"Your Majesty." Mrs. B leaned on her cane as she bowed her head. "May I introduce my assistant, code name Aardvark."

The giant man bowed.

Ed from the FBI introduced himself with a bow.

The general stood straight and gave Salah a salute during his introduction.

Sheppard only nodded. "Your Majesty."

Everyone gathered inside the first-class lounge of the aircraft. Salah was the only one sitting as Ed addressed the group…

"First off, the United States of America would like to thank Your Majesty for allowing us to meet here and for your assistance to our operatives."

"It is the Crown's pleasure," Salah said, now in full king mode.

"The president sends his regards. He asked me to brief you on the situation. Who would like to start?"

Mrs. B had Nadia tell everyone about her captivity, about Katrina and Dr. Joyce, and the way she had been rescued.

"How long were you on the raft?" Mrs. B asked her.

"I don't remember what time it was when we left the compound, but the airline crew was late coming back from their flight, so that was after midnight."

"And when did you go to bed that night?"

"Early. I would say eight or nine at night."

"That gives us a time frame to work on," Sheppard said. "My people are searching the area in question."

"We have some special forces in the Philippines ready to go as soon as you find that lab," the general said. "They have the necessary equipment to deal with the androids."

"Just so that we are crystal clear on this point," Mrs. B began. "Our agreement is still in place. The army will receive Alex and Samira back since they previously volunteered to serve them before they were stolen. No more. No less. The other androids are not to be reprogrammed or kept against their will."

"Unless we take away that will," Sheppard said. "You know, there's not a lot you can do if we decide to change our mind."

"We did build the troublesome things," the general added. "Technically, they're still US Army property."

"Tell ya what," Sheppard said. "We'll be nice and give you Robert as a thank-you gift."

"That's not what was agreed."

"May I remind everyone that the president gave his word to that prior arrangement," Ed said.

"The president is making a mistake," Sheppard said.

"We have his personal phone number," Mrs. B said. "Would

you like to tell him in person?"

Sheppard crossed his arms.

"Give us Robert, Alex, and Samira," the general said.

"We're not re-negotiating the original agreement."

Nadia grabbed Robert and pulled him up to the group. "You do have a say in this. Tell them what you want."

Robert paused. "I want to speak with my brothers and sisters about what they want. Perhaps some of them have changed their minds about working for our creators. They should be allowed to choose. Perhaps the US Army can give me a convincing argument as to why we should return to serve them."

"No, you don't want that," Nadia said. "They'll use you as soldiers and scouts. They will put you in dangerous situations. They don't care about any of you. Robert, you're only a machine to them. Can't you see that? You've had these concerns ever since I've known you. I mean, what has changed?"

Robert paused again. "My offer is quite logical."

"It might be best if we take Robert and restore his normal upper brain functions," Mrs. B said. "If he is running in some type of safe mode, it might not represent his actual choice in terms of who he wants to serve. I propose that when we recover the other androids, let us reconvene and discuss the matter further."

"And why should we trust you, sweetheart? You could recover all the androids and keep eight of them under your control. We get two, and the Authority gets eight. That's a horrible deal."

Emma couldn't believe it. Sheppard called Mrs. B a sweetheart?

To her credit, Mrs. B didn't break her composure. "The androids under our protection will not be altered in any way. They will be given the freedom of choice. However—since you've brought up the subject of sweethearts—has your messy divorce been finalized yet?"

Ed physically put himself between Mrs. B and Sheppard as if he were a referee separating two arguing soccer players. "I think that should be all for now."

Sheppard's glare burned into Mrs B, who took it all in stride. "Yeah, I think I'm done talking to this old bag."

Emma tensed up. She wanted to spit in this guy's face and tell him what she thought about him, but she cooled off when her grandma rested her hand on Emma's shoulder.

"It's been a pleasure," Mrs. B said.

"I'll update the president," Ed said. "Let's find the location of the missing androids and extract them before we start arguing about their future. Agreed?"

The meeting broke up as the general, Sheppard, and Ed stepped off the aircraft and drove off with their entourage of assistants. Mrs. B and Aardvark stayed behind.

"I'm sending all of you home," Mrs. B said. "Robert and Ryan, you'll go to Berkeley also. I've contacted Emma's grandmother, and she'll be expecting you."

"I must see my brother and sisters first. You promised," Robert said. "Take me to them."

"Take me there as well," Salah said. "I want to meet these androids."

Mrs. B hesitated, then paced the floor using her cane. Emma could tell she didn't like these new requests.

"I can't guarantee your safety, Your Majesty. It would be best if you went back to the Middle East. Besides, with all due respect, your presence would draw too much attention in America."

"Nonsense," Salah said. "I will dress like an American. I will wear a hoodie and blue jeans and fit in to the culture. Nadia and Emma will help me do this."

Emma always loved a good makeover. Dressing down a king would be a challenge, but she was up for it.

"I'm sorry, but no, Your Majesty. The Gems have too much going on right now. It would be best—"

"I wasn't asking for your permission," Salah interrupted. "Nor do I require it."

Mrs. B was quiet for a long moment. "No, I suppose you don't."

"Where are my brother and sisters right now?" Robert asked. "Are they actually in Berkeley?"

"They are in a safe location."

"Then I demand to be taken there."

"At the moment, that's not possible."

"Why not?"

"We need to reinstate your higher brain functions first."

"I can do that at the house," Nadia said to Robert. "Remember?"

"Yes, that would be my preference, Sapphire."

"No. I want to be taken to my brothers and sisters first."

"You are not making sense," Mrs. B said. "Do you want us to reinstate your higher brain functions?"

"Yes."

"Then I don't see what the issue is. Can you elaborate?"

Robert paused, as if analyzing the situation. "My apologies. I withdraw my request."

CHAPTER 32

Inside the large Aunt Ellen's Bakery van, there were two cushioned benches that ran along each wall with head-rests and seat-belts for passengers. Nadia wished it had cookies and cupcakes inside to match the commercial logos on the outside. And yet, all the van carried were her four friends, Ryan, and the two boys that were special in her life.

On their way to Berkeley, they stopped at a thrift store just outside of Oakland to grab Salah some street clothes. Emma helped him pick out a nice hoodie, fashion-dictated distressed jeans, and worn but clean sneakers for Salah so he could fit in. He now appeared so young. Salah's cute little fuzzball mustache looked even more ridiculous on such a young guy's face. She should have told him yes on the razor.

"Staring at the king is considered quite rude," Salah said with a large grin.

Nadia hadn't realized she was doing it. "Sorry. It's just, you look so different."

"You look very normal, Your Majesty," Miyuki added.

"Excellent. I feel normal, and I'm enjoying it. How far is this Berkeley from San Francisco?"

"Not too far. It's on the other side of the bay," Nadia said.

"I've got to hand it to Mrs. B," Ryan said. "This bakery delivery van is a smart way to deliver us to your grandma's house without suspicion."

"My grandmother's next-door neighbor is getting nosy," Emma said. "She keeps asking her why us kids are gone all the time. And she's figuring out it's not from being at school."

"Oy, Mrs. Battista?" Olivia asked. "She's a nosy piece of work. The lady should mind her business and feed her cats."

The van came to a stop, and the engine was turned off. The back doors swung open to reveal Aardvark and Mrs. B. The garage door was open behind them. Nadia saw Emma's Ford Bronco parked inside, along with her grandmother's Jeep.

Everyone shuffled into the garage as Aardvark closed the van's rear door and pulled down the garage door.

Inside the living room, Grandma Bernadette welcomed all the girls with hugs. She smiled at Robert, yet he made no effort to respond. He only stood there blankly with Ryan and Salah. Nadia found that strange.

"Remember Grandma Bernadette?"

Robert paused. "Oh, yes, how are you?"

Grandma Bernadette went over and hugged Robert. "So good to see you again, honey."

Robert paused again. "I am not covered in honey."

"But you're covered in love. Make yourselves comfortable." Grandma Bernadette took a moment to look Salah over. "Are you really a king?"

"Your Majesty will do," Salah corrected.

"Young man, we only use first names in this house. What's yours?"

Salah's reaction was priceless. He couldn't believe how rude this woman was.

"I thought you wanted to be treated like a normal person," Nadia said, trying not to smile too big.

Salah studied her reaction. He recovered his composure and managed a polite grin. He bowed. "Then I stand corrected, My Queen."

Grandma Bernadette chuckled. "Oh, I definitely can get used to that."

The girls laughed.

Robert went up to Nadia. "Please take me upstairs to your room. We need to destroy my operating system backups."

"We have time to visit," Mrs. B said. "Besides, it's quite rude to your host to begin a visit with business." Using her cane, Mrs. B gracefully took a seat on the couch. "Bernadette, would you mind if I had Aardvark use your kitchen to put on a kettle for some tea?"

"If I could remind you, my upper brain functions are still not functioning. My priority is to fix my system."

Nadia took Robert's hand. "The reboot won't take long. I can have Robert back in business in thirty minutes." She tried to lead him up the stairs to her room.

But Robert let go. "I do not want your help. I want to be repaired at the Authority's facility. However, I will go upstairs to make sure your copies of my operating system are destroyed."

Nadia didn't understand why he wouldn't let her help. Was it because Robert didn't have his upper brain functions? Was that causing him to act so strange?

"I'm confused." Mrs. B turned towards Robert. "You originally wanted Nadia to back up and save your programing because you trusted her. Is that not still the case?"

"Yes. This is for her own good. I have explained it to her, and she agrees."

Nadia didn't agree. This Robert was obviously malfunctioning. If she could just reboot him, her friend would be normal and trust her again.

"Let me reboot you here. It's the same exact copy of your OS that I gave to our Authority tech people. And I have your memory backed up too. Thirty minutes and we're done. I don't understand; don't you trust me?"

Nadia almost bit her lip on that last sentence. She also resisted the urge to check Salah's reaction.

"No, I insist on waiting."

Mrs. B gave Aardvark a nod. Instead of going to the kitchen, he slipped out the door towards the garage.

"Come upstairs and show me which room is yours," Robert asked.

Nadia climbed the stairs as Robert followed.

"One moment," Mrs. B said.

Nadia halted.

"Please come downstairs."

Nadia didn't understand the concern on Mrs. B's face.

"Please indulge me."

She finally descended the stairs, leaving Robert alone.

"I'm sorry, but you're still not making any sense. Which is quite illogical for an android of your caliber."

Aardvark soon came back into the living room with Kamal,

the tall Indian android who spoke Klingon. Mrs. B must have brought the other androids back from their Authority safe house.

Robert moved off the stairs and towards Kamal. "Hello, brother."

"Hello, brother," Kamal replied.

"Pleased to see you again."

"As am I." Kamal revealed a tablet with a USB cable attached to it. "May I have access to your data port?"

Robert paused. "For what purpose?"

"To verify what operating system you're running on," Mrs. B said. "Even in a damaged or malfunctioned state, we should be able to identify whom we are dealing with."

"I am Robert."

Kamal tilted his head. "We have yet to verify if that is the case. Please open your data port."

Robert paused again. "I refuse."

Mrs. B used her cane to stand up. "If you refuse, we must force you to comply."

Aardvark moved closer to Robert.

"I understand you're missing your higher brain functions," Nadia said. "Trust me, Robert. I'll fix you correctly. I promise."

"I do not trust you anymore."

The sentence drilled a hole in her heart.

"And *we* do not trust *you*," Mrs. B added.

"Comply with our request, brother."

Robert paused a third time, then raced up the stairs. Kamal and Aardvark went after him. Nadia's legs were already moving, and before she knew it, she was running up the stairs behind the two guys.

Once upstairs, Robert picked a random bedroom and went through it like a tornado, ripping things apart as he searched for his backup drives. But he was in Emma's room.

Why was Robert's memory so messed up?

Aardvark went into the room first. He grabbed Robert, but the android tossed the large man into the wall like he was a pillow.

"Stop it!" Nadia yelled.

Kamal moved into the room. "Please comply. I do not want to damage you."

Robert's cold eyes focused on Nadia. "Where is your room?"

This wasn't her friend. It was a stranger.

She backed out of Emma's room and into the upstairs hallway.

Suddenly, Robert shoved Kamal out of the way. With lightning speed, his hand grabbed Nadia's arm and tightened, squeezing the bone to almost breaking point. The pain shot up her arm.

"You're hurting me."

"Show me where the backup drives are."

Robert began to twist her arm. The pain intensified as it went up her arm, causing the girl to scream.

Kamal wrapped his arm around Robert's neck and pulled him away. He released Nadia's arm, then used his back to slam Kamal into a wall, which punched a large hole into the drywall as pictures of Emma and her father crashed to the floor.

Free of Kamal, Robert turned his attention back to Nadia.

She backed up again as the stranger in Robert's android body moved towards her.

But Aardvark rushed into him like a freight train, sending him and Robert rolling down the stairs together.

Kamal flew down the stairs in pursuit.

Nadia hesitated at the foot of the stairs to watch as Robert tore away from Aardvark again. This time, he bolted through the wall of beads hanging between the kitchen and dining room.

Nadia ran down the stairs and followed Ryan and her friends as Kamal and Aardvark went out to the backyard.

Once there, Robert had stopped.

Facing him near the outdoor fire-pit was Sid and Cleo, the dancing androids. Mai then stepped into view near the vegetable garden. The shy, dark-skinned android looked more menacing than shy.

"Resistance is futile, Robert," Mai said. "You must comply."

Robert made a quick move towards the fence, but the four androids were on him in a snap. They pulled him down to the grass and, with Aardvark's help, kept him there. Kamal found Robert's access port and plugged the tablet into him. After a few taps on the pad, Robert froze.

The other three androids stood up as Aardvark cautiously released Robert as well.

"Is he okay?" Miyuki asked.

"He has been shut down," Kamal said. "I am examining his operating system."

Nadia knelt over Robert, causing her tender arm to protest.

Olivia ran over to her. "What's wrong, love?"

Salah was right behind her. "Are you injured?"

"Robert twisted my arm. I don't think it's broken, but-"

"Let me take a look at that." Grandma Bernadette joined them. She had Nadia slowly flex her arm. The pain was dull, yet it wasn't pleasant. "I still have my old sling from my hospital stay last year. Let's put it on that arm until we can get you to a doctor."

"I will fly my personal doctor here," Salah said.

"There's an urgent care right up the street," Grandma Bernadette said. "It's not that serious."

"Are you sure?" Salah asked. "What type of medical training do you have?"

"Don't worry, honey. Back in the day I did volunteer nursing at clinics across Africa and South America. I've seen it all."

"Salah, it's all right. We have more important things to worry about."

"Ah yes, your robot friend." Salah shot her a look that made her heart uncomfortable.

Mrs. B moved over to Kamal, who was still hovering over Robert. "Any progress?"

Kamal blinked. "This Robert is running a CIA alias program. His upper brain functions are operating normally."

"CIA?" Ryan moved over to them.

Mrs. B shot him a quizzical glance.

"Don't look at us. We haven't had access to Robert since he left. It must be the work of Katrina, that mole who defected."

"What kind of CIA alias program?" Nadia asked.

"One moment," Kamal said. "I am accessing the parameters." He blinked. "It appears to be a modification of one of our standard CIA honeytrap programs. Yet recoded to work against a female target."

Nadia's friends all looked at her.

The pieces began to fall into place. The surprise rescue at Crisanto's compound. Refusing her help to reboot him. Robert expressing his "feelings" for her. Robert creating guilt by wanting her to choose Salah over him. The android had been playing her emotions like a delicate instrument. Like a professional spy would.

"What is a honeytrap?" Salah asked. "I don't understand. What did they do to the robot?"

Mrs. B leaned on her cane. "Venomous attempted to use the alias of the Robert we know in order to gain our confidence. That way, he could gain access to his original backup programs and the operating systems of the other androids under our group's protection. Most likely to either destroy or reprogram them to escape with him."

"Before she replaced his operating system," Ryan said, "Katrina must have kept Robert's past memories of Nadia so she could modify an existing alias program that would be good enough to fool Nadia and us."

"Honeytrap," Salah repeated to himself as he read the Moogle search results on his phone. "Is a practice involving the use of romantic relationships for interpersonal, monetary, or espionage purposes." Salah shot Nadia a look. "I see. It's all beginning to make sense."

"What do you mean?"

"Robert is a fake. A mirage. He never had true feelings for you. This is what you get for falling in love with a walking computer. If you still hold feelings for this thing, you are an idiot."

CHAPTER 33

The vintage MD-80 airliner was called the Mad Dog back in the 1990s with its long, pencil-shaped fuselage and two turbo-fan jet engines mounted in the back along with its distinctive T-tail. The airliner's black nose and the design of its cockpit windows made the aircraft look like an angry canine. Now, the airliner was Mrs. B's private jet.

The inside was completely remodeled with a full office and a spacious bedroom in the back. A nice toilet with a full shower. A large sitting area with cushy couches, chairs, and a large television. The galley was also fully stocked with food, drinks, and wine.

Despite the comforts, Nadia was fuming the entire ninety minutes the Mad Dog was in the air. She was angry at Salah and wanted to explain to him why he didn't understand her friendship with Robert, even though Robert had tried to manipulate her.

No, that wasn't the real Robert. It was an android running a program that it had been forced to run against its will. Nadia knew the real Robert. The kind Robert. The Robert that was her friend.

Nadia glanced over at one of the cushy couches inside the aircraft. Salah and Ryan were both sprawled out unconscious. It was by choice since Mrs. B would not allow them inside their new secret base with the knowledge of where it was. She'd also had Aardvark confiscate their phones and leave them with the Royal Hejaz Airlines crew since they had to wait for the king to return. Aardvark had even done a physical search for bugs or tracking devices just in case.

Nadia so wanted to wake up Salah and tell him what was on her mind. But she closed her eyes instead and took in a deep breath.

She would have to wait.

"Seriously, can we borrow this jet for junior prom?" Emma asked. "Wouldn't it be sick if we had our school after party in Vegas!"

Miyuki clapped her hands. "I love that idea!"

Olivia rolled her eyes.

Nadia agreed. It was ridiculous. Once in a while, Emma would slip back into her privileged-rich-girl mode. Who else thought like that?

At her desk, Mrs. B glanced up from her paperwork. "Black Opal, I'm going to ignore your comment based on the assumption that due to our present altitude, you are in a delusional state of existence."

"She's always in a delusional state of existence," Olivia added with a smirk.

"Oh, shut up. I was only thinking out loud."

"You're capable of thinking better," Mrs. B said.

Olivia flashed Nadia a satisfied grin.

Nadia didn't care about humiliating Emma. She had too much on her mind.

Cleo, the android who looked like an Egyptian cousin of hers, sat motionless in a small chair near the galley. Her eyes observed everything in the room. Nadia remembered when Robert would do this. To humans, it's creepy. To an android, it's only gathering data.

"Are the others still all right?" Nadia asked.

Cleo blinked. "All their systems are still performing inside acceptable parameters. Except Robert. He is still nonfunctional."

"How cold is it inside the cargo hold?"

"It is currently forty-four degrees Fahrenheit or seven degrees Celsius. Do not worry, our systems are designed to withstand temperatures well below zero degrees Fahrenheit."

Kamal and the other androids chose to stay in the cargo hold to watch over Robert. Mrs. B said that it wasn't necessary, but Kamal and the others insisted. Cleo remained in the cabin to "observe relevant conversations" and to relay them to the others.

"I hope we can find your missing siblings soon," Nadia said.

"Once he's up and running, I bet Robert will tell us exactly where they are," Olivia said.

"He's not going to know." Nadia turned towards her friend. "During the rebooting process, there are failsafe memory-erase protocols that will kick in. That's why we have to save a lot of his upper memory and reinstall it after a major reboot. Otherwise, Robert wouldn't even remember us or anything we did together."

"Oh, so it erases his short-term memory as well?"

Nadia froze. Wait, what if they were able to tap into Robert's short-term memory and extract it before they rebooted him?

"May I make an educated guess?" Cleo said. "Your facial expressions tell me that you have come to the same conclusion that we have. Yes, there is a way to download Robert's short term memory before initiating a level one reboot on a D9000 military intelligence drone." She tilted her head. "I see why Robert felt so comfortable around you. Even as a human, you can think like one of us."

"I don't know about that."

Cleo blinked. "You think logically. Kamal has mentioned that you are the closest human he has met who acts the most Vulcan in her mannerisms. After having reviewed the numerous television programs dedicated to the fictional alien race, I tend to agree."

Nadia had to think about it, but from an android's point of view, it was a compliment.

"She's more like Scotty in the engine room," Miyuki said. "Anytime we get into trouble, Nadia thinks of a way out since she's super smart."

That cheered Nadia up a bit.

"Oh my God, I love that movie. It's so romantic," Emma said. "Was Scotty the guy in the engine room keeping the engines lit while the Titanic was sinking?"

Miyuki couldn't believe it. "We're talking about Star Trek."

"Oh, is that the one with the laser swords?"

"Black Opal?"

Emma glanced over at Mrs. B.

"You need to broaden your taste in cinema."

Mrs. B's phone rang. "Yes? Thank you." She hung up. "We're starting our descent into Las Vegas. Everyone put on your seat-belts."

After landing, a stretch limo picked them all up at the airport and took them down the Las Vegas strip, joining the other hundreds of stretch limos that made tourists feel rich and important as long as they could afford the rental fee.

The desert sun had disappeared, leaving a kaleidoscope of neon lights turning night into day. The Bellagio fountains danced skyward in perfect rhythm to music sent over massive loudspeakers. A fake Eiffel Tower at the Paris casino glowed in the distance. Crowds surged along the sidewalks like human rivers as street performers tried to get their attention and money.

The Zillions Hotel and Casino complex was one of the many giant hotel casinos competing for those crowds.

Their stretch limo drove into a secret parking level that was closed to the public. Ditching the limo, Mrs. B led them all into a secret elevator that went left, then right, then finally went down like a normal one. The doors opened to reveal a large underground concourse filled with offices and a secret labyrinth of other rooms hidden through various passageways.

Still unconscious, Salah and Ryan were taken in wheelchairs to one of those hidden rooms to be revived.

After twenty minutes, Nadia and her three friends escorted a conscious Salah and Ryan out of the labyrinth and back into the secret underground concourse.

"Damn," Ryan said. "Where are we?"

"I would tell you," Emma said, "but—"

"You would have to kill me," Ryan added. "Whatever, I get it. For a secret base, it looks nice."

"This is all underground?" Salah asked.

"Yes," Nadia said.

"Amazing. We should build a mall like this in Hejaz. Build it underground where it's much cooler. The Americans do not know about this place? The FBI? The CIA?"

"Not yet," Ryan said. "But we're working on it."

"It's brand new," Nadia said. "No one knows about it. I would give you the full tour, but Mrs. B won't allow it."

"Maybe I'll take my own tour." Ryan started walking off. But suddenly he jumped and yelped. "Ouch, what the hell?"

"Mrs. B put a tracker on both of you," Olivia said. "But the one Ryan has comes with a bonus feature, a fully charged Taser."

Emma held up a key fob. "And guess who has the ouch button."

"Oh, come on," Ryan said. "I'm not a little dog."

"You're still CIA," Olivia said. "And Mrs. B expects you to behave."

Emma beamed like a cat smelling tuna. "Be a good boy, and I'll give you a treat from our commissary."

Ryan flipped her off.

Emma's thumb retaliated.

"Ouch, stop it!"

Emma giggled.

"It's not funny."

"I think it's hilarious."

Ryan crossed his arms like a big baby.

That was when Nadia saw Robert emerging from one of the labyrinth tunnels with Kamal, Mai, Sid, and Cleo.

She found herself running towards him.

The boy took a few steps in her direction before stopping. When Nadia reached him, he said, "I believe the appropriate phrase is…we should talk."

CHAPTER 34

The large commissary inside Authority headquarters had a steady flow of personnel taking a break from their duties. The place was arranged like a casual café, with sofas and small tables with comfortable chairs. Some items were self-serve, but one could also order from the made-to-order kitchen, which was staffed twenty-four seven. Some people were alone with a book, enjoying a break with coffee, tea, or a meal. Others were taking a break with friends and colleagues. Everyone wore an identification badge.

Nadia held Robert's hand as she guided him towards a table away from everyone else. "Do you want anything?"

"I do not require food."

"Oh, I knew that. Sorry. I'm not hungry either."

"Do you need water?"

"I'm fine. Thanks." Nadia didn't know what to do with her hands, so she just folded them on top of her lap. Why did she feel so nervous?

"Kamal managed to extract the exact location of Katrina's lab from my short-term memory. I asked him to reload that short-term memory so I could review everything that I did between now and then. When we escaped together, I lied to you about my upper brain functions malfunctioning."

"I understand."

Robert blinked. "I apologize for deceiving you. I was programmed to run an alias program that required me to-"

Nadia touched his arm.

"Is that a physical cue for me to stop speaking?"

"Yes."

Robert nodded.

"The things you told me at the resort. You sounded almost jealous of Salah. You said things like I was more than a friend. That I was the only one who understood you. That I was your perfect companion."

Her hands quivered on the table, so she tucked them under. "Were those thoughts about me real or a part of your alias program?"

Robert watched her for a moment and blinked. "Are you sure you do not require water? You seem quite apprehensive."

"I need to know."

"You are forming tears. Are you upset?"

"Please answer my question."

Robert placed both of his hands on the table. "Those things I said at the resort were influenced by my manipulation program. I am not jealous of your relationship with Salah, nor do I like to snuggle. However, I do consider you a friend and my favorite human companion."

Robert hesitated, as if his mind was calculating something. "However, I must remind you that no matter how close we are as friends, I am not capable of falling in love with a human being."

The cold reality of his words went right through Nadia's chest.

Yes, she was a fool.

Yes, she had fallen in love with an android.

Yes, Salah was right. She was an idiot for allowing herself to fall this hard for a piece of special metal alloy that could smile and say nice things to her.

"Do you require a hug?"

Nadia backed away from Robert as her cheeks felt moist. She wiped the tears trickling down and struggled to find anything to say.

Finally she came up with…

"I'm sorry for everything."

"I do not understand."

Nadia ran out of the commissary and back into the large underground concourse. Her friends were sitting around a group of chairs while Salah leaned against a nearby wall with his arms crossed. When he noticed her, Salah took a few steps towards where she was standing.

He read her face and walked faster.

Nadia didn't want to talk to him now. She was losing it big time. Her brain felt scrambled, and she needed to go hide somewhere to sort it out. She climbed the stairs towards the second level.

"Nadia!" Salah raced up after her.

She didn't stop.

When Nadia reached the top, Salah was there too.

"What's wrong? Why are you crying?"

"Not right now. Please, I need some time alone."

"I demand that you speak to me."

Nadia hesitated. It was the ruler in him yelling at her.

"Don't shut me out. Talk to me," he said in a much softer voice. "I want to listen."

That voice.

It was soothing.

It was calming.

It wasn't the king. It was the boy behind the throne.

"All right," she said.

Salah held her hand as they descended the stairs together. When they reached the bottom, everyone was standing and looking worried.

Salah noted Robert and approached him. "What did you say to her?"

Ryan was already putting himself between them. "Whoa, wait a minute, guys."

Robert blinked. "I apologized for my actions."

Salah pressed against Ryan, who was holding him back. "No, what did you do to upset her?"

"I find your question difficult to answer. Human female emotions are difficult to interpret. They have no logical patterns to follow."

"Don't worry, Robert," Miyuki said. "I don't understand my emotions either."

"Do you fear me as a possible rival for her affections? I can assure you that I have no romantic interest in Nadia. You are free to court her at your leisure. However, I do ask that you please take care of her because she is one of my best friends, and I care about her general welfare. Does that alleviate your anxieties as a male competing for a female partner to produce children for your next dynasty?"

"Wow." Ryan backtracked away from the boys. "If anyone needs me, I'll be in that commissary. You three talk among yourselves."

Miyuki followed. "I'll join you."

Olivia grabbed Emma. "I could fancy some tea."

"No, wait, I wanna watch."

"Come drink some bloody tea with me."

"I hate tea."

"Emma."

The four of them disappeared into the commissary, leaving Nadia alone with the two boys.

"Don't be angry with Robert. He's innocent. I'm the one—how do I say this? I messed up."

"You mean you fell in love with a machine."

"I prefer android, or you may reference me as a D9000 military intelligence drone. Either term would be acceptable."

"Robert, maybe you should go have tea with the others."

"I do not-" Robert paused as he analyzed the situation. "Ah, yes, I will practice drinking tea with the others. Which tea would you recommend I try?"

"Any tea would do." Salah glared.

Robert went off without a word.

Salah and Nadia stared at each other for one long minute.

Nadia wiped off her damp cheeks and searched his eyes for a sign. Anything that would tell her what he was thinking.

Salah buried his hands in the pocket of the hoodie. "I don't know what to say. I mean, I don't know what to make of all this."

"I met Robert before I met you. And then he showed back up again, and things between us became complicated. That's not true. I made them complicated." She moved closer to Salah. "But I'm over him."

"Clearly you're not."

Her mouth was lying. Her face was not. And the boy knew it.

"I will be. As soon as we get the other androids back, Robert will go off with them and—"

"And you'll still be thinking about him."

"No, Salah. We're only friends. I realize that now."

"Do you? Do you realize that?"

"Yes."

"Can you give him up? If I ask you to never speak with Robert again, could you do it?"

"He's my friend."

"So? If you and I were dating, would you tolerate my female friends?"

"Robert isn't human. He doesn't think like we do. You have nothing to worry about."

Salah came up close to her. So close she could feel his breath against her skin. "Can you do it? Can you let him go?"

"I shouldn't have to choose."

Salah stepped away. "Then I will choose for you. Tell your Mrs. B that I want to leave America as soon as possible."

CHAPTER 35

After Mrs. B's private jet touched down at Oakland International Airport, Ryan and Salah were woken back up after another mandatory nap and escorted off by Aardvark and Emma. The four of them climbed into the back of another Aunt Ellen's Bakery delivery van, which drove them away from the airport.

Emma wished the van had windows. The cargo area still had the drab fresh-from-the-factory gray paint and the jerky suspension that reminded Emma of a New York subway car.

Ryan nudged her knee with his. "Take me with you."

"I can't."

"We were supposed to work together on this."

"I can't help it if the androids don't trust you or the CIA. Besides, Mrs. B made her decision."

Ryan picked up some strands of Emma's hair and moved them off her shoulder. "But you are her adorable granddaughter. You could change her mind."

Emma felt his arm touching her lower back, making it tingle a little. "I love it when you try to sweet-talk me into doing things for you."

"Is it working?"

Emma didn't answer.

"I love the way you smile."

Emma straightened. She got up and switched seats, choosing to sit with Aardvark and Salah. This made Ryan lean back and sulk.

Emma switched her attention to Salah. The boy hadn't moved since they left the airport. He only stared into space with a stoic look on his face.

"You've been quiet, Your Majesty."

Salah hesitated. "I'm quiet because I have nothing to say."

She allowed that sentence to fade a little before trying again. "If you want, you can talk to me about it. Seriously, I'm a fantastic listener."

Salah didn't break his concentration. "There's nothing to talk about."

Emma waited and tried again. "Before you were sedated, you seriously looked pissed off."

"And?"

"I'm only saying that I know Nadia well. I know you kinda well. If I can help with anything between you two-"

"There's nothing between us to help with. Now, if you would please respect my privacy."

Emma flashed him an understanding smile. At least she tried.

"Your Majesty, I received word that your ambassador will have a car waiting to take you to your aircraft. The Authority would like to apologize for not landing at the air force base. Our relationship with the US government is complicated."

Aardvark's new voice modulator sounded much more authentic, like a real person's voice, unlike the older versions he'd used. Most of them sounded electronic and weird.

"I understand. That will be fine." Salah thought about it. "Can you relay a message for me?"

"Certainly, Your Majesty."

"Tell the crew that I want the aircraft to be ready to fly back to Hejaz immediately."

"As you wish."

"Have I mentioned that I so love your new voice." Emma told Aardvark. "It's so warm and smooth."

"Thank you," Aardvark said. "I'm getting used to it myself."

After the van arrived at her grandmother's house, Salah and his ambassador climbed into a black SUV with private security and took off immediately. Aardvark left with the van, leaving Ryan and Emma alone.

They glanced at each other.

"Now what?" he asked.

Emma pulled out her keys. "I'll drive you to the airport."

"You mean the one we just came from?"

Emma shrugged. "We can go there, or SFO is across the bridge. Where do you wanna go?"

"I wanna go with you."

"No, you can't. As soon as I drop you off, I have to go back to help rescue Robert. Those are my orders."

"You've broken the rules for me before."

The same old warm feelings seeped back into her heart. That affection for Ryan that had almost made her seriously think about turning her back on Mrs. B and the Gems. But that had been months ago.

People change.

Emma pointed her key fob to unlock her Ford Bronco.

Ryan jumped. "Ouch!"

"Oh my God. I'm so sorry. That was the wrong key fob."

"You think?" Ryan began ripping off his shirt. "I'm taking this stupid thing off." He found the tracking bug Mrs. B had put on him and peeled the sticky adhesive off his skin, grimacing from the pain as he did so. Ryan finally relaxed. His bare chest and muscles on full display.

Emma paused to admire the view.

Ryan caught her. "Did you wanna help me put my shirt on?"

"No, you can do it yourself."

Ryan grinned. "You can take a picture if you want. Something to remember me by."

Emma laughed. "You wish." She turned around and got behind the wheel of her Bronco. Ryan gave her the biggest smile as he put on his shirt and climbed into the passenger seat.

She drove the Bronco across the Oakland Bay bridge into San Francisco, then followed the highway south towards the airport. Emma found a spot in the arrivals drop-off lane and braked the car to a stop.

"Have a safe trip," she said.

"I don't even know where I'm going."

"How about Washington? Sheppard will want to know what's going on, right?"

"Can you keep me in the loop about the mission? Anytime you mess with Venomous, there will be danger and the unexpected. I worry about you sometimes."

Emma could tell he was being honest. "Thanks. I will."

"And watch your back. I wish I were there to do it for you."

"I'm a big girl now. But I appreciate the reminder."

Ryan leaned forward.

Was he expecting her to—?

Emma shot him a look that made the boy hesitate. She then flipped it into a big smile and gave him a peck on the lips. It was light. Friendly. And Emma wanted more, but she pulled herself away. There would be another time.

When it came to Ryan Raymond, there always seemed to be another time.

CHAPTER 36

The big fat C-130 military transport once belonged to the Royal Netherlands Air Force back in the day, but the Authority acquired it and completely refurbished the aircraft. Like the Aunt Ellen's Bakery van, the seats on the wide transport ran along both sides, with passengers facing towards the middle, keeping that middle area clear for equipment and other cargo.

In the air, the four prop engines were loud, even with the extra sound proofing that had been added inside during the refit.

The only thing Nadia could see out the windows was darkness.

The same darkness swimming around in her mind.

Salah had left her. He'd made his choice. And his choice was to leave her. Leave her because she didn't lie to him. Leave her because she still had feelings for Robert. Yes, for a machine. Yes, for a machine that loved her like a friend and was capable of only being her friend.

"Sapphire, are you with us?"

Nadia hopped out of her own brain and surveyed the inside of the C-130. The question came through her headset from Aardvark. She almost didn't recognize his new electronic voice. Wearing a helmet and black fatigues for the mission, Aardvark was watching her from the other side of the aircraft.

She keyed her headset mic. "Yes, Aardvark. I am."

"Could you please repeat your orders for the strike mission?"

"The four of us are to stay back and allow you and the strike team to enter Crisanto Alonto's compound to find and immobilize the stolen androids. Our mission is to kidnap Katrina and, if possible, try to flip her to our side."

"Good. I apologize for quizzing you, but you looked distracted."

"That's all right." Nadia could hear everything through her communication headset. The Gems and the androids were on their own separate channel from the strike team, but Aardvark and the strike team leader could still communicate with them on this channel. Nadia guessed that the men didn't want to hear any young female chit chat in their communications.

Nadia caught herself in a yawn. This was the third time they had been in the air during the last twenty-four hours. The first leg had been across the northern Pacific from Oregon to a secret Authority landing strip in the Aleutian Islands of Alaska to refuel. After a short turn around, the second leg had been to another remote Japanese airfield, where Mr. E met them. The head of the Tokyo base gave them all a nice, quiet place to get some sleep before the main rescue operation would start. Now they were flying to the Philippines.

Nadia had been a part of many rescue missions, yet it was nice to have a strike team full of big guys with guns that would go in first. However, there was one additional challenge to this mission.

Olivia yawned on her open mic.

"Are you all right?" Nadia asked Olivia over the radio. The aircraft was too noisy to speak without it.

"We haven't jumped out of a plane with a parachute since Lioness first trained us."

"I know. Can't say I'm looking forward to this."

"Skydiving is fun!" Miyuki said over the radio. "I've always wanted to do more of it."

"When did Lioness train you?" Emma asked over the radio.

Nadia leaned over to see her other two friends. They all looked strange wearing all-black fatigues with boots and helmets. "A year and a half at least."

"After that first jump, I thought it was kinda fun," Emma said. "Once you get over the oh-my-God-I'm-jumping-out-of-a-perfectly-good-airplane feeling."

"I wish humans could be programmed not to be scared," Robert said. "I know how fear can be a harmful emotion to you."

"Fear prevents us from doing stupid things too," Nadia said. "Like jumping out of a plane when we don't need to."

"We appreciate your bravery in helping us rescue our siblings," Kamal said.

"Can you hear me?" Robert asked. He wanted to sit next to Nadia during the flight. Nadia was glad he'd insisted.

"Yes. I can."

"I did some adjustments to the mission's communication system. I have isolated a channel for you and me to use. A private one."

"Oh, you shouldn't have done that. You'll get us in trouble."

"I do not worry about 'getting into trouble,' as you say. What I do worry about is you. As a friend, is there anything I can do for you concerning Salah?"

Salah. That was all Nadia had been thinking about for the last two flights. What else could she think about? Jumping out of a plane? Both thoughts caused her enough anxiety.

"If you do not wish to talk about him with me."

"When it comes to Salah, it's all my fault."

"I apologize for aggravating the situation. I would rather be disassembled than to ever harm you like that again."

"It wasn't your fault. Katrina reprogrammed you. I know what's truly in your heart." Nadia had to stop herself. "Sorry, you don't have a real heart."

"I understand your figurative reference. And I would like to think I do have such a thing. A soul. A spirit. A center of my being. I believe it is good. And that is to your credit."

"My credit?"

"You have been a role model in my quest to be more human."

"I'm not much of a role model."

"You have always underestimated yourself. That is a shame. Together with Salah, you could be of great assistance to so many people."

"Historically, the queen of Hejaz doesn't do very much. Salah is the official ruler."

"Humans can shape their own destiny. You should research other queens." Robert blinked. "Queen Victoria of England would be an interesting one to study and model yourself after."

"I can't be someone like that."

"How do you know? To truly know, you must fail at it first."

Robert's words made her sit back. Did she want that? Did she want to help a nation change and grow? What about being a scientist or working at NASA?

"I am glad you are thinking about it."

"Salah will never take me back. Besides, I'd have to end our friendship, and I don't want to do that. Salah needs to understand that I would never act on my feelings. We're friends. Despite everything. Your friendship is the best that you and I can have. And I'm fine with that."

"I agree." Robert gave her a big smile. "Shall we hug it out, girlfriend?"

Nadia laughed.

"Fifteen minutes until drop," the strike commander said over both radio channels. "Everyone stand up and get ready."

"Wait, do you know how to use a parachute?" Nadia asked Robert. She was so into her own head that she didn't realize it until now.

Robert blinked. "We have the full US Army Ranger training program installed in our software. I will be fine. Do you remember everything Kamal told you about how to use his special app?"

Nadia stood up and checked to see if her new phone was still in the zipped pocket she put it in. "Yes, it seems easy enough. He should have given one to Aardvark and the other girls too."

Robert stood up with her. "I advocated that to Kamal, but I was out-voted by my other three siblings. You are the only human they trust to have access to it. I think it is a wise precaution in case our operating system is ever compromised again."

The ramp at the back of the C-130 groaned as it began to lower, letting in a gust of thick humid air. Red lights switched on along the edges of the open doorway, casting a glow on the faces of the strike team.

The wind flirted with the edges of Nadia's black fatigues as her heart pulsed against her chest.

One by one, the members of the strike team clipped their static lines to the anchor cable running along the ceiling of the C-130. They moved with practiced efficiency, weapons secured, faces grim and focused.

A knot of apprehension tightened in Nadia's stomach as she adjusted the straps of her own parachute harness, double-checking the clips like Lioness had drilled into them during training. Emma caught her eye and offered a comforting smile. Miyuki was bouncing on the balls of her feet. She couldn't wait to go.

"One minute," the strike commander's voice echoed through the radio, cutting through the wind and engine noise.

Nadia swallowed, her mouth suddenly dry. The floor vibrated beneath her boots. The red lights switched to green. The first of the strike team shuffled to the edge of the ramp and disappeared into the night. There was a sharp tug as their static lines deployed their chutes.

Robert and his four siblings followed the others out the door, acting exactly like the professionals ahead of them.

Nadia followed her three friends as they moved towards the open doorway. The wind pulled at them. The ground below was invisible in the darkness.

The strike commander gave them a nod. Emma went first, a dark figure against the faint starlight. Then Miyuki, who let out a whoop of exhilaration.

Now it was Nadia's turn. She moved to the edge.

For a split second, she hesitated.

Then Olivia's voice came over her headset. "I'll be right behind you, love."

Nadia took a deep breath and pushed off, launching herself into the void.

The world instantly flipped. For a moment, she was tumbling, a dizzying disorientation of dark sky and aircraft. The wind shrieked past her ears, a deafening roar that drowned out everything else.

Then the sharp tug of the static line. It felt like her harness was going to rip her in half. But then her parachute billowed above her and gently cradled her in safety.

Nadia floated above the darkness. She looked down, her eyes slowly adjusting, sharpening her senses, preparing her for whatever lay below.

CHAPTER 37

Even at night, the white foam could still be seen as the ocean washed over Mr. Alonto's private beach. The roaring sound of the surf was a pleasant sound to Bridget as she lounged on the soft mushy sand. There was a slight chill in the air since the sun went down, so Bridget threw on a T-shirt over her bathing suit. She was a bit tired from swimming in the sea all day, but it was fun, and she needed the diversion.

"Join me in a game of chess?" Papa stood behind her with that gentle smile that always made Bridget feel relaxed and safe.

"Sounds grand," she said. "Will you lose like a good sport this time?"

"I'm always a good sport."

Bridget fired him a look.

"No worries. I'll temper myself this time. Straight up."

Bridget brushed off the grains of sand sticking to her freckled skin as she followed Papa over to the large outdoor table near the two sliding wooden doors in the back of Mr. Alonto's house. A chess-board with hand-crafted ivory and ebony game pieces was already set up.

Mr. Alonto's girlfriend, Katrina, stepped out of the house wearing another awful T-shirt that a grown woman her age shouldn't be wearing. Bridget found the woman's fashion sense about as obnoxious as her personality.

"I don't get chess at all," Katrina said.

Papa gave the woman a polite grin. "Chess teaches one discipline and how to think strategically."

"It's boring." Katrina turned her attention to Bridget. "Are you a gamer? Do you have a Steam account?"

"Yeah, nah, Sophia has an account. I prefer chess."

Katrina blew her off. Bridget felt like making fun of her hair, which looked like a hurricane went through it instead of a brush. Instead of that, Bridget selected a seat on the ivory side of the chess-board while Papa took the ebony.

"Any word from Robert?" Papa asked.

"Still nothing yet." Katrina scooped up a handful of popcorn from a snack bowl on the table and stuffed it in her mouth like a child as kernels fell everywhere. This attracted a seagull that floated in and landed, quickly grabbing the free snack.

Yes, this woman was all class.

"Still receiving Robert's signal, yes? Are you still having issues with our satellite system? Do I need to execute some of my tech bros?"

Katrina washed her popcorn down with a Coke. "I got a ping from him about eight hours ago. Nothing new to report."

"That's a bit suss, don't you think? Robert reported making contact with Mrs. B and the other androids two days ago. Surely he's been escorted to the new Authority headquarters by now."

"A bit suss?"

"Suspicious," Bridget added. "Still, doesn't receiving a signal mean that he hasn't self-destructed? The plan might yet still work."

"Perhaps. Still, I have an uneasy feeling."

Bridget didn't like it when Papa had such feelings. He always had a sixth sense about danger. It kept him alive in prison and working for an organization like Venomous.

She moved her white pawn forward two spaces.

Papa studied the chess-board.

"What are you a doctor of?" Katrina asked, still stuffing her face with popcorn.

Papa didn't look up. "Doctor of education. I was the head of a girls private school in New Zealand."

"Avondale," Bridget added.

"Crisanto says that your nickname is Dr. Yes. What does that mean?"

Papa ignored Katrina's question as he moved his ebony pawn one space forward. "Bridget can answer that question better than I."

"The girls all called him that because he was always so

positive and allowed us a great deal of freedom at school."

"With responsibility," Papa said. "Freedom without discipline is chaos. My girls at Avondale knew how to behave and what was expected of them."

On the chess-board, Bridget brought out her queen.

Papa sat back. "Quite an aggressive move."

"You can surrender now if you want."

"That's my girl."

Mr. Alonto and Sophia both approached the outdoor table carrying their bows and two quivers of arrows over their shoulders.

"Glenn, your daughter is one skilled archer," Mr. Alonto said. "She's almost as good as me."

"Get off the grass," Sophia said. "I skunked your butt."

"Don't be so prideful, my dear. Crisanto won the Olympic gold medal in archery. His praise carries much weight."

One of Mr. Alonto's servants appeared. "Are you and the young lady done with the archery course?"

"Yes, please turn the lights off. Does anyone need anything? A drink, perhaps?"

"I'll take another Coke," Katrina said. "And more popcorn."

Suddenly, a short burst of gunfire echoed from behind the house.

Bridget was on her feet.

Sophia grabbed an arrow out of her quiver and loaded her bow.

Papa remained seated, yet hesitated.

Mr. Alonto motioned to his servant. "Put the grounds on alert. Now."

Papa moved his knight out to counter Bridget's queen. He then stood up and pulled out a gun. "Bridget dear, I think you should arm yourself."

Mr. Alonto pulled out his own gun and handed it to Bridget. "Please excuse me." The man then rushed into the house.

Sophia pulled back her bow with an arrow ready to fly as she watched the darkness around them.

Bridget checked the semi automatic handgun Mr. Alonto had given her. It had a fully loaded clip. She switched off the safety. And pointed it towards the ground. Ready to go.

"What's going on?" Katrina asked.

"Allow us to escort you to your lab," Papa said.

With Sophia covering their back, the four of them crossed over to Mr. Alonto's guest house. In the main living room that had been turned into Katrina's lab, all five robots were still hooked up to their charging stations, motionless but quite functional.

"Sophia, watch the front door." Papa turned his unhurried attention to Katrina. "We might need the robots ready to fight. Are there any weapons stored here?"

Another burst of gunfire outside.

Katrina appeared worried. She motioned over to a closet with a lock on it.

"Do you have the key?" Bridget asked.

"Crisanto does."

Papa's phone rang, and he answered it. "Yes, what's the situation?" While he listened, his expression was stoic and quite unreadable.

Bridget took in a deep breath and tried not to panic.

Papa put away his phone. "We have armed men inside the compound. Probably after the robots. Shoot the lock off, my dear."

Bridget aimed her gun at the lock. Squeezing the trigger, the gun went off, and the bullet sent the lock flying across the room. She opened the door and found the closet stocked with hand-guns, assault rifles, and plenty of ammunition.

"This will do nicely. Arm yourself, girls." Papa moved over to the five robots and gave them orders.

Bridget decided to stick with the hand-gun Mr. Alonto had given her. She was better with a smaller weapon anyway, but Sophia ditched her bow and arrow in favor of an AR-15. She was always the sharpshooter in the family.

Papa and the robots armed themselves with more AR-15s.

"I don't do guns," Katrina said. "Who is it? Who's raiding us? The Filipino Army? The Navy SEALs?"

"Don't know who, but I can take an educated guess," Papa said.

"Did those muppets get our location from Robert?" Sophia

asked.

"Wait, I thought you said the androids couldn't retain information after they were rebooted." Bridget aimed the comment at Katrina, who looked a bit concerned.

"They can't. It's a fail-safe. The new operating system deletes their memories automatically unless you create a memory back-up before-hand. And I didn't."

Katrina paused.

Reading her face, Bridget felt a significant "but" coming on.

"Damn it, they must have gotten our location from his short-term memory file. Forgot about that."

Bridget couldn't believe it. "Get off the grass; ya forgot about that, did ya?" She scoffed. "Ya stupid *edgit.*"

More outside gunfire.

Sophia switched the safety off her AR-15 and readied herself near the front window.

Katrina's phone beeped. After glancing at the message, she went over to her computer. "I need to put the androids into combat mode. Stand by."

"No worries," Papa said. "Please do it quickly."

"Three armed men in green fatigues are approaching us," Sophia yelled.

"Crisanto's private security aren't wearing fatigues. Shoot them."

Sophia grinned and used the butt of her AR-15 to shatter the window. She aimed the weapon out of the opening and squirted out a burst of fire. The noise clattered around the inside walls of the lab.

Bridget ran over to the other side of the front door. All she could see out that window was darkness. "Where are they?"

Sophia stopped firing. "I missed the buggers. They got scared and took cover in the trees."

"Mirabelle, if Dr. Joyce moves, shoot him."

Katrina's odd comment made Bridget turn around and see the blond girl robot aiming her assault weapon at Papa.

What the feck was going on?

"Initiate protocol nine-nine-nine dash K," Katrina said.

All five robots responded in unison…

"By your command."

Bridget moved away from the window and aimed her gun at Katrina. "What are ya doin'?"

Sophia turned around and glanced at her sister.

"Alex, Iko, Luigi, target the two red-headed girls," Katrina said. "You are cleared to defend yourselves if provoked."

"Swingin' Jesus, what's going on?" Sophia asked, aiming her own weapon at Katrina.

Alex, Iko, and Luigi responded in kind, pointing their weapons at the two girls.

"Easy there. Let's not jump to conclusions," Papa said. "No worries. I'm putting my weapon down on the ground."

Sophia gripped her weapon tighter. "I'm confused. And I don't like being confused."

"Papa, what should we do?" Bridget asked.

The room settled into an uneasy stand-off.

Until Papa's phone began ringing again. He carefully removed it from his pocket. "It's Crisanto. Do you want me to answer it?"

Katrina thought about it. "Toss me your phone."

Papa did, and she caught it.

She pressed the green button. "Hey, babe. Your friend is busy right now. What's going on?" She listened. "Chinese marines? Shit. Yeah, we should get the hell out of here while we still can. I'll need help in the lab. Can you come over? Just you." Katrina smiled. "Thanks, babe."

She ended the call and lost her smile.

It didn't take long for Mr. Alonto to enter the guest house. Since Bridget didn't trust anyone at this point, she aimed her gun at the new target, her finger ready to squeeze the trigger.

The man froze and raised his hands as he surveyed the room. "What's going on here?"

Papa actually chuckled. "Sorry to say it, mate. But you've been dudded."

Crisanto paused. "What does he mean by that, Katrina?"

The older woman's eyes were steel. Her previous slacker demeanor had changed dramatically. "Crisanto, you're a disgusting sexist pig and an ugly little man." Katrina's lips formed a wicked grin. "I've been wanting to do this for ages. Mirabelle, kill Crisanto."

The robot showed no emotion as she pulled the trigger, and a burst of led hit Mr. Alonto in the chest, dropping him to the floor.

Sophia shot a burst into Mirabelle, with some of the bullets digging into her metal alloy chest while others ricocheted. Mirabelle didn't react to it at all.

"Stand down, Sophia, those bullets won't do any good against them. Besides, you've clipped me." Papa lifted his hand as blood dripped from a fresh wound.

"Oh swingin' Jesus." Sophia lowered her weapon in horror.

"Ya stupid muppet." Bridget put down her own weapon on the floor and moved carefully over towards Papa. "We can use my T-shirt to wrap up your hand."

"No worries, it'll mend. Put your weapon on the floor, Sophia. You're lucky Katrina forgot to tell Mirabelle to defend herself. Otherwise, I'd have a dead daughter."

Sophia hesitated, then did as Papa said. "I still don't understand what's going on."

"Sorry to say it, but we've been hoodwinked," Papa said. "Fair play to Chinese intelligence though. Quite brilliant if ya think about it."

"What do you mean?" Bridget asked.

"Have I come at a good time?" The deep voice had a soothing Mandarin accent added to the English words.

It drew Bridget's attention to an older Chinese man wearing a white-collared shirt with a dark blazer standing at the front door. The man also had dangerous eyes.

"Only tying up some loose ends," Katrina said.

The older man eased himself inside as he checked Mr. Alonto's body. A giant Hawaiian man then appeared in the doorway with a gun. He almost didn't fit through the opening, but managed to get inside. Following him in were a squad of armed men in green fatigues. All of them were Chinese marines.

The older man turned his attention back to the room. "Dr. Joyce, your reputation proceeds you. As well as your death, apparently."

"Girls, meet Volleen Woo, the secret head of Chinese intelligence."

Bridget and Sophia glanced at each other.

Volleen Woo nodded. "The pleasure is all mine. I've heard so much about the twins. Pity to meet them under such circumstances."

"I must congratulate you on a brilliant play," Papa said. "Using my friend to unwittingly help you retrieve your deep-cover agent inside the CIA with all her android goodies is quite a triumph."

"Bejesus," Sophia said. "You mean that trashy American woman who looks homeless is a Chinese agent?"

"Your agent didn't have to kill my friend. Crisanto is not a member of our organization. He's a civilian. I could've explained the situation to him. Under the circumstances, there's no call for that kind of violence."

"I'm not done being violent." Katrina pulled out a gun, aiming it at Bridget and Sophia. "Let's start with these two teen psychopaths you call daughters."

"No," Mr. Woo said.

"They're members of Venomous. Scum of the earth. Why not?"

"I'm not comfortable with killing children," Mr. Woo said. "Not without a good reason."

"What about their dad?"

Mr. Woo brightened. "That's true. According to the Australian media, Dr. Glenn Joyce should be dead. Therefore, we shall do them a favor and simply correct that oversight."

CHAPTER 38

The landing zone for the drop was on a farm a couple of kilometers inland from Crisanto's main compound. Thanks to Robert's intact memories of the compound's security and layout, Aardvark devised a plan to approach it on foot rather than drop right on top of the place.

"Oy, is that you, Nads?" Olivia's voice echoed through the darkness.

Nadia couldn't see a flipping thing. It was pitch black across the field, with clouds blocking the moon. The only thing that reassured her was seeing all those small lights from the helmets of the Authority strike team as they secured their parachutes and other equipment. Moments ago, Nadia had detached hers, and the wind took it away.

"Yes, it's me," Nadia replied.

The figure, who Nadia thought was Olivia, shined her helmet light in her face, blinding her. "Sorry, love." Olivia turned her head to the side so Nadia could see again. "You all right from the jump?"

Nadia had had to roll across the ground when she landed because she couldn't see the ground very well, but it all went off better than she imagined. "I'm good. What about you?"

"Excellent."

"That was so fun!" Miyuki jogged up to them, her helmet light bouncing like a grasshopper. Someone else was trailing her.

"Is that Emma behind you?" Olivia asked.

The answer appeared in Nadia's light.

"Next time we go skydiving," Emma said, "can we do it in the daytime?"

"How about next week?" Miyuki asked.

A big figure moved into their light. It was Aardvark.

"Anyone injured?" The man's large, intimidating presence gave Nadia some confidence to tackle whatever waited for them up ahead.

"We're all good and keen to get this done," Olivia said.

Aardvark motioned the strike leader and Robert over for a quick conference. After everyone updated their post-jump status, Robert gave them a suggestion...

"We should head towards the south end of this field. "There is a small creek that runs along the property line of the farm and Crisanto's compound. We can use it to shield our approach."

"That puts us in a good position to slip in and cut off the guest house from the rest of the compound," Aardvark said.

"And that's where the lab is located, correct?" The strike team leader asked. "Once we're discovered, we'll have to get in and out of there fast. So if we hit the wrong building, that's it. We'll have to abort the mission."

"My siblings and I will lead you in. We can take much more damage than any of you."

"One of the androids should stay back," Nadia said. "Just in case something goes wrong." She stared at Robert, hoping he would volunteer to stay with her.

"Mai, would you please stay with Nadia and her friends? I would be grateful if you would look after them."

"I will do that, Robert." Mai, the shy android, moved over to Nadia.

The strike leader checked his watch. "We should get moving."

"Agreed," Aardvark said.

"Be careful, Robert," Nadia blurted out, almost like a knee jerk.

"The girl has definitely grown an attachment to him," Sid the android said to Cleo and Kamal. "It is rather charming."

"I find it quite curious," Kamal said.

"After the mission, can we ask you detailed questions about your relationship with Robert?" Cleo asked.

"Please rearrange your priorities," Robert said. "We must rescue Luigi, Mirabelle, and Iko first before we engage in any casual social interactions with our human companions. And besides that fact, Cleo, with all due respect, that might not be any of your business."

"Robert, if you please?" Aardvark said, grinning politely.

"Yes, the mission. Let us move forward."

Robert and his three siblings moved forward in a straight line as the strike team followed. Nadia, Mai, and the other three Gems trailed as they moved through the night.

CHAPTER 39

The world inside Mr. Alonto's guest house had turned upside down. Katrina was a traitor to the CIA and her Filipino boyfriend, who was dead on the floor. She had full control over the armed robots, who had instructions to kill them if they tried to resist, which, even if Bridget made such a move, it wouldn't do any good since bullets didn't seem to affect the robots.

A rare streak of fear. Its icy feeling went up Bridget's spine. Was this it? Was this how she would die at the age of seventeen? Most teen girls died of suicide or car crashes. Not armed robots controlled by a woman going through her mid-life crisis by betraying her country to the highest bidder.

"I'm not comfortable killing children," Mr. Woo said. "Not without a good reason."

"What about their dad?" Katrina asked.

Mr. Woo brightened. "That's true. According to the Australian media, Dr. Glenn Joyce should be dead. Therefore, we shall do them a favor and simply correct that oversight."

Katrina pointed her gun towards Papa.

When she did, that icy fear melted inside Bridget as a burning hatred swelled within her. No-thing on this earth would stop her from destroying anyone who tried to hurt her papa.

Bridget locked eyes with Sophia. Her sister's eyes burned with the same flame. The same fierce loyalty. A silent communication between the two told Bridget her sister was on the same page. It was time to kill or be killed. No matter what.

"Go Wildcats!" Bridget yelled.

Sophia reacted by breaking into a run, then a front walkover tumble, flipping her body towards Katrina like an American high school cheerleader.

Bridget followed her lead, choosing a different path as she broke into her own front walkover tumble.

A gun fired, but when Bridget came out of her tumble, Sophia had already slammed into Katrina, dropping both to the ground. Katrina scrambled to get up and reach for her gun on the floor. But Bridget kicked it away from her. Katrina then found Sophia's hands clamped around her neck. The woman began coughing as Sophia squeezed. Her sister's wild eyes bent on destroying this woman.

Mr. Woo sighed. "I don't have time for these theatrics. Kawiki, please separate them."

Bridget noticed the giant Hawaiian man moving towards her. Fueled by adrenaline and ready to fight, she charged him, punching him hard in the coconuts, which brought most men intense discomfort. But this Hawaiian giant only grunted as he picked Bridget off the ground and put her under his arm like a naughty kitty. He moved over towards Sophia still choking Katrina to death.

Bridget sank her teeth into the large man's fat hip.

Another grunt from the Hawaiian man. "Hey, stop doing that."

The bite didn't stop him, as the man picked up Sophia with his other arm. Her sister got in a punch to his face, but she yelled and shook her injured hand as a result.

The Hawaiian giant faced Mr. Woo. "Where do you want 'em, boss?"

"Put them over with Dr. Joyce." Dr. Woo went over to Katrina, who was rolling and coughing all over the floor. "Can you speak?"

"Yes," Katrina managed to say, her voice raw and hoarse. "Please let me kill those two brats."

"Revenge can wait. Get the androids ready to—"

A sudden round of gunfire echoed from the outside.

Mr. Woo gestured towards one of the armed men in green fatigues and said something in Chinese. The man nodded and ran out the door, along with the rest of his squad.

The Hawaiian giant put her and Sophia next to Papa. "Stay there or else."

Sophia made a move to get back up, but Papa held both her

and Bridget down.

"That's enough," he said.

Sophia stopped.

"No matter how this turns out." Papa hesitated after his voice cracked a bit. He regained his composure. "Ya both have been lovely daughters. All class. I love ya, and I'm honored that you chose me to be your dad. Honest to G, my life's been blessed with ya two girls in it."

Sophia cooled down, her anger waning as tears pooled in her eyes. "Love ya too, Papa."

Seeing her sister on the verge of sobbing made Bridget want to join her. She wrapped her arms around Papa and squeezed her cheek against his. "You've been grand to us. Simply grand, Papa."

The three of them kept together. Ready for whatever was about to happen.

A radio on Mr. Woo's belt began broadcasting something in Chinese as Katrina managed to crawl into her pink chair.

Papa brightened. "No worries, we might find a way out of this yet."

"What do you mean?" Bridget asked softly.

"Have I taught you girls any Mandarin yet? We should correct that. Anyway, the Chinese officer in that radio call said they're exchanging fire with another force. That could only mean the US Army, the CIA, or our friends from the Authority."

"They're not our friends."

"My dear Sophia, when in Rome, you must do as the Romans do."

Sophia didn't get it.

Bridget helped her. "The enemy of my enemy is my friend."

"Oh, bugger off. I would have figured that one out."

"Doubt it."

"Papa, make her stop treating me like I'm stupid."

Another frantic radio call came in.

"What's going on, boss?" the Hawaiian giant asked.

Mr. Woo glanced over at Katrina. "It must be an Authority strike team. They have androids leading their attack. The marines are finding it difficult to hold them back."

Katrina stood up. "I can send our androids in to back them

up."

"No, these units are too valuable." Mr. Woo paused, his mind whirling like a supercomputer. "I will order the marines to fight here to the last man. This should give us enough time to move the androids to a more secure location."

Suddenly, a piece of the ceiling came crashing down, and a teenage girl tumbled to the floor along with it. She was dressed in black fatigues, and her long dark hair was pouring out of a helmet.

The girl scrambled to her feet, and Bridget recognized her. It was that Japanese girl. What did they call her?

Miyuki.

"Holy crapola," she said. "That last step was a doozie. Hello, everybody! What's going on?"

CHAPTER 40

One minute Nadia saw Miyuki climbing on top of the roof like a monkey on a cupcake sugar high. The next, she disappeared. The moment Miyuki saw that big narra tree next to Crisanto's guest house, she just couldn't resist climbing it. Olivia had yelled at her to stay within the group, but Miyuki either didn't hear or simply ignored her.

That was when a group of people in green fatigues began firing on them. Nadia and Olivia took cover while Emma just flopped to the ground as Aardvark and the strike team took defensive positions and a firefight began.

Nadia's heart pounded. She noted her hands quivering as well. She never wanted to be a soldier or to be in a battle. This was all too crazy. Thank Allah she wasn't here alone.

Emma crawled over to them.

Olivia tried to raise Miyuki on the radio, but couldn't. "That flipping girl. She's absolutely mental."

"Do you think we can get over to that big tree safely?" Emma asked.

A stream of bullets ripped up the ground near them.

"Forget I asked."

Aardvark's voice came over Nadia's headset. "Robert, Kamal, I'm afraid we'll need you and your friends to help us clear these people out."

"I agree, Robert," Kamal said over the radio. "We should take charge of this situation."

As soon as that message went out, Nadia saw Robert, Kamal, Cleo, Mai, and Sid emerge into the open and, without weapons, rush forward towards the men in green fatigues.

Bullets ricocheted off the androids. Some bullets found their targets, but it didn't slow them down. The androids began grabbing the men in green fatigues and tossing them around like they were sticks, causing chaos. Aardvark and the strike team moved forward as they pursued those men into the surrounding trees.

"Let's move on that guest house," Olivia said. "Follow me."

Nadia gripped the handgun she had and followed her friend towards the door of the guest house. Olivia pulled Nadia over to her side of the door, then motioned Emma to take the opposite side.

"Ready?" Olivia asked.

"Yeah, I guess," Emma said.

"Nads, you ready?"

"No, but we'd better get on with it."

Olivia nodded and took in a deep breath. "Right, turn away from the door." Olivia squatted and stuck a small explosive charge under the door-knob. She turned away herself and pressed the button on a remote.

The small charge exploded, taking out the knob and dead-bolt, and the door swung free.

Olivia kicked in the door with her handgun ready to fire. She moved inside with Nadia trailing her.

Once inside the guest house, she moved around Olivia, and they both stopped in their tracks.

Mr. Woo stood there with a gun at Miyuki's temple. So close that he couldn't miss.

Emma moved around Nadia and stopped as well.

"Lower your weapons," Mr. Woo said.

Olivia slowly put her gun down. Nadia and Emma did the same.

"On the floor, please."

The three Gems dropped their guns on the floor.

Mr. Woo paused as he looked them over. "Katrina, order the drones to escort these girls. We will be taking them with us."

"Why, boss?" Kawiki asked. "All these girls are more trouble than they're worth."

"No, my friend, they have value to Mrs. B. She will want her precious Gems back. And the price will be a high one."

Alex the android grabbed Olivia's arm. Luigi came over and grabbed Nadia's. His grip was solid.

Fear came over Emma's face as Mirabelle made her way over to her. She even caught her poor friend trembling as Mirabelle grabbed her arm as well.

"Good, we should hurry out the back while there's still time." Mr. Woo motioned to Katrina to join him as they began moving. "Kawiki, on your way out, take care of Dr. Joyce and his family."

Nadia looked over and saw the twins and Dr. Joyce in the corner of the lab. Were they prisoners too?

She also noticed Crisanto Alonto was dead.

What was going on? Why was Volleen Woo suddenly running the show?

Nadia's mind glued it all back together. Katrina must have double-crossed them. Volleen Woo had wanted Robert to come to China. Now, he had control over five of his siblings, and they were about to take off.

"Are you sure, boss? The kids too?"

"Hurry, and be quick about it."

Kawiki checked his gun clip, then shoved it back into his pistol with a click. The large man hesitated as he picked out his first target.

Sophia.

Mr. Woo must be ordering their deaths.

Nadia never liked the twins, but she didn't want to see them die either.

"Why can't they come with us?" Nadia blurted out, trying to be heard inside the room. "Mrs. B will want Dr. Joyce and the twins too, just as much as us."

Mr. Woo slowed his pace. "She would probably thank me for killing them."

"Clearly, you don't know her well enough."

"She's right," Miyuki said. "Mrs. B would want them alive. Taking seven valuable hostages is better than four."

"Those girls are onto it," Dr. Joyce said. "I'm Asset Number Two. One behind the leader of our entire organization. And ya don't wanna even take a crack at mining me for secrets, mate? That doesn't sound like the infamous Volleen Woo I've heard so much about."

Mr. Woo actually thought about it, then checked his watch. "We are wasting time." He pointed towards the back door. "Everyone, head that way outside."

CHAPTER 41

Bridget could still hear distant gunfire through the dark trees as Sophia and her papa followed Olivia and her friends as they were escorted down another path that led to the farthest strip of Mr. Alonto's private beach.

All lit up and waiting there was a giant air-cushioned military landing craft that was more than sixty meters long. At the back were three huge air propellers, allowing it to push the hovercraft on top of the water and on land. Two large ramps were extended to the beach for entry and exit.

To Bridget, it was a big ship version of one of those hovercraft you see in movies that travel across the swamps of Florida and the American South.

"Get on quickly," Mr. Woo said.

"Do you have a good wine cellar on board, mate?"

Mr. Woo ignored Papa's joke. "Hurry; time is not our friend."

The robots herded them up the ramp and into the landing craft's vehicle deck, which was big enough for three or four tanks, but this part of the ship was empty. Running on either side of the vehicle deck were two bulkheads with doors to other compartments of the ship.

A Chinese naval officer saluted Mr. Woo as he asked the man a question. Mr. Woo acted quite agitated as the two of them argued in Mandarin before the officer straightened and saluted Mr. Woo again. The officer barked out orders to his crew, and the large ramps began retracting.

"Someone lost an argument," Bridget whispered to her papa.

"Good observation, my dear. The naval officer doesn't want to leave his marines behind in a foreign country. But our friend Volleen Woo is having none of that."

"What do ya mean? He's leaving his own men behind to get slaughtered?"

"I can't blame him. The robots are just as important to him as they are to us. Honest to G, I'd give the order myself if the roles were reversed."

The giant propellers began to rotate. The entire ship hummed and vibrated as the engines powered up.

"Sit down here," Mr. Woo ordered.

Kawiki and the robots made everyone sit on the cold hard iron of the vehicle deck.

"Are we going all the way to China in your noisy hovercraft?" Papa asked. "Could you at least find some earplugs for us?"

"There's a Chinese frigate a few miles out," the giant Hawaiian man said. "Enjoy the ocean air while you still can."

"Kawiki, shut up," Mr. Woo said. "No more talking. In fact, break the sisters up." He pointed at Bridget. "Put her with the Muslim girl. And put the other one with the Japanese girl. When we get to the frigate, put them in the brig that way. I want Dr. Joyce to be isolated."

"You got it, boss. Anything else?"

"Bind their wrists together." Mr. Woo shut his eyes and relaxed for a moment. "Sorry for my outburst. I'll be in a better mood when we're clear of Philippine waters."

The Hawaiian made Bridget sit over with Nadia. He put Olivia and Emma together but separated them from the rest of the group. Everyone's wrists were then bound with zip ties in front of them, not behind their back.

Bridget leaned over to her new neighbor. "Kind of a spot we're in now. Wouldn't ya say?"

Nadia stared at the floor, acting like Bridget just asked her out on a date.

"Still pissed about the other day? No worries. I should be angry at you for deceiving me. However, the enemy of my enemy is my friend, right? We'll need to help each other if we want to get out of this."

That piqued her attention. "How do we do that?" she whispered.

"We have to find a way to that upper deck so we can jump off and swim back. All their marines are still back on land, so now is the only chance we'll get because once they take us to that frigate, I bet we'll be under constant guard."

"Those androids will be on us in seconds if we make a break for it. And how do we swim with our wrists tied up?"

The girl had a point.

"Right, do you have any suggestions? I'm all ears."

Nadia bent her forearms backwards and forwards, as if the girl was trying to wiggle out of her ties.

"There's no way you'll break those."

"That's not what I'm—" Nadia stopped herself. "Never mind."

"What is it?" Bridget smelled blood. And like a good shark, she began to circle her target.

Nadia watched the deck again. This only encouraged Bridget.

"Were you trying to reach for something?"

Nadia didn't answer. Her eyes still focused on the deck, but they blinked.

"What do you have? Another gun? Another weapon? Something else we could use?"

The girl's mouth tightened slightly. She was holding something back.

Bridget wiggled and wiggled her bottom so she could get closer to Nadia. She then turned and flopped down on her back, landing across Nadia's lap. "C'mon, Nadia darling. Spill your guts. We need to work together here."

Nadia flashed her an agitated glance, then focused on a new part of the ship to stare at.

"Bejesus, do ya want me to apologize? Fine, I'm sorry I threatened you. But admit it, you were bein' stubborn. Just like you're doin' to me now."

"I'm not being stubborn. The problem is that I can't trust you."

"Fair play to ya on that. I wouldn't trust myself either. So, we both get tossed into a Chinese prison for the rest of our lives. Sounds grand."

Nadia's fingers quivered. The girl was trying to hide it, but she was scared. Bridget could use that.

"Maybe it won't be prison for us. If we're lucky, maybe we'll get into a forced labor camp. Ya know, those camps that build things for the government."

"Labor camp?"

"Saw a BBC documentary about them once. Nasty places. They work ya to death in the hot sun. No breaks. Barely any water to drink. No food until the end of the day. Mostly cooked animals like chipmunks or squirrels with only enough food to keep you alive so you can work the next day."

"They wouldn't do that to the women, would they?" Nadia asked.

Bridget rolled herself off Nadia and sat back up. "Who do ya think cooks the chipmunks and the squirrels?"

"That's disgusting."

Bridget shrugged, trying to play it as cool as ice. Manipulating the girl like she would any opponent at chess. Now it was time to bring out her queen.

"You're the one who doesn't wanna trust me. But I'll have to do some trusting too, won't I?"

Nadia's face hardened. Bridget was making it difficult on her. She was rethinking things. It was a good sign.

"No worries, if ya wanna be that way about it."

"Wait."

"Wait, what?"

"I need to get my phone out," Nadia whispered.

"Who ya gonna call? Superman?"

Nadia surveyed the area around them. The robots were watching and listening. Even Bridget knew they would need to be careful.

"There's something on my phone," Nadia said barely above a whisper.

"With ya so far, darling."

"It's an app. A game app."

"Ya fancy playing a game right now?"

"Yes, I do. It's a *special* game."

"You're losing me."

Frustration pushed against Nadia's face. "Have you ever heard of the '80s video game called *Robotron*?"

"I don't speak geek."

"Well, it's a video game involving robots. And the robots in the game aren't very nice."

The girl was speaking in code. Bridget thought that was smart.

"With ya so far."

"I have a game emulator app on my phone. To pass the time, we should play Robotron. I think you would like it."

"Right, so you want me to play this Robotron on your phone."

"Since you can reach my front left pocket, yes."

Bridget hesitated. She focused on breathing, on calming herself down, allowing her body to go into a relaxed state. She eased her arms forward. Her two fingers squeezed against the metal zipper tab on Nadia's fatigues and gently pulled it down, only enough to expose the phone inside her pocket. Next, Bridget used her fingers to ease it out, taking her time and using all the patience she could muster. Soon, Bridget had it securely in her palm.

"You are not permitted to use that phone," Mirabelle said.

Bridget switched gears like a Ferrari. "I'm so freaking bored. Honest to G, can't I play a game? It's not like you have a Wi-Fi hotspot I could use to scroll through my Instajam. Or is there a hotspot on board? That would be grand."

"You are not permitted to use that phone," Mirabelle repeated.

"Are you a walking hotspot, darling? That'll work too."

Mirabelle blinked and cocked her head. "Why are you addressing me as darling?"

"Let the child play her game." Kawiki moved over to Mirabelle. "I doubt she can get a good signal way out here anyway. Besides, if she did alert anyone, the frigate would blow it out of the air with its missile defense system. All she would be doing is killing more of her people."

"Then, can I play my game?"

Kawiki nodded.

Bridget swiped the phone with her thumb to wake it up. "What's your password?"

Nadia hesitated.

"Do ya want me to play Robotron or not?"

"Hand me the phone."

"No, I won't," Bridget whispered. "Tell me your flippin' password."

"It's faster if you would give me the phone."

"And you need to learn how to trust people," Bridget said.

"Why are you messing around?"

"C'mon, trust me."

"No."

"I've never kissed a boy before."

Nadia gave her a strange look.

"Not once," Bridget said. "I fancy them, to be sure. Still haven't done it. See, I just trusted you with a secret. How about doing me a favor?"

Nadia glared for a moment or two. Then she thought about it and gave her the password.

Bridget tried it. An animated kitty cat greeted her on the screen, *Hello Nadia!* She scanned the apps, flipping through the pages. "I wonder who you've been texting lately. Probably your boyfriend the king. Let's take a gander, shall we?"

"No, that's private." Nadia looked absolutely terrified.

"I'm only playin' with ya. Where is this cool game you wanted me to try?" Bridget held out Nadia's phone, showing her the screen.

The girl touched it, opening up an app. She then tapped a button two times and relaxed.

"What did that do?" Bridget glanced back at the screen. A simple message said...

Detecting five targets. Continue? Yes/No
Yes.
Sending reboot command...

Bridget followed Nadia's gaze over to Mirabelle. The female robot blinked two times, then froze in place.

"Get off the grass," Bridget said, amazed.

"Not so loud," Nadia said. "We need to buy them some time to reboot."

Bridget checked the faces of the other robots. They were all frozen in place. Meanwhile, Mr. Woo and Katrina were having a private discussion away from everyone else while Kawiki was eating a candy bar. The fat Hawaiian man then saw something and walked over to Alex, who was also frozen in place.

Time for a distraction.

"Papa, I'm scared," Bridget cried out. "I don't like this."

Her papa took a moment, then nodded. "I'm sorry, Bridget. I wish I could do something."

"I want off this ship!" Bridget yelled, trying to stand up.

"Be quiet!" Kawiki yelled.

"Piss off, ya fat piece of lard."

The giant man came over to Bridget, who was on her feet. "Sit down!"

"No."

"Touch my sister, ya bastard, and I'll kill ya!" Sophia yelled.

"What is it now?" Mr. Woo asked, still cool as ice, more annoyed than alarmed.

"Could you please move her somewhere else?" Nadia asked. "Her perfume reeks, and I'm sick of hearing her whiny voice."

Bridget made a face. "I don't have a whinny voice, ya little troll."

The large Hawaiian man picked Bridget up and sat her back down. "Be quiet!"

Now Sophia was on her feet and coming in fast. She rammed her body into the giant and bounced off him like he was a trampoline, wiping out on the deck.

Mr. Woo grew suspicious as he made his way back to the group. "Why have the androids stopped?"

Katrina came over. "Alex, tell me your status."

The android didn't respond.

"Mirabelle, Iko, Samira, Luigi, tell me your status."

None of them responded.

"Answer me. What is going on with the androids?" Mr. Woo asked with more of an edge, as if slowly losing his patience.

"Apparently, they've taken a brief mental vacation," Dr. Joyce said.

"I don't know." Katrina opened her small laptop, awkwardly trying to balance it on her one hand while the other hand used the keyboard.

Samira was the first android to blink again. Her eyes surveyed the deck of the ship.

"They're coming back around, boss."

Alex and Luigi did the same.

Katrina's fingers danced across the mouse and the keys of her laptop. Her face grew more confused by the second.

"Is something wrong?" Mr. Woo asked.

"Alex, Samira, Iko, Luigi, Mirabelle," Nadia called out, "initiate protocol zero-one-one-zero dash A."

The five androids blinked again and faced Nadia.

They spoke as one.

"By your command."

"Did ya just take control of 'em?" Bridget asked. "Oh, that's grand."

Nadia stood up. "Mirabelle, cut off our wrist ties."

"Order them to power down," Mr. Woo said.

Katrina's confusion intensified.

"I gave you an order."

Miyuki and Sophia stood up. Olivia and Emma did the same.

Kawiki moved towards them.

"Alex, restrain the giant man," Nadia said.

The android grabbed Kawiki like he was a stuffed animal. The big man struggled with Alex, yet to no avail. Alex was too strong.

"That's not possible. No, she didn't have enough time to load a whole new operating system. That would've taken half an hour at least," Katrina said to the laptop, almost as if she were talking to herself. "All androids, re-initiate protocol nine-nine-nine dash K."

All the androids blinked and talked in unison again.

"That protocol has no meaning."

"No meaning? What the heck?" Katrina buried her nose back into her laptop.

"Sounds like your androids have fallen in love with someone else," Papa said with a gleam in his eyes.

Mr. Woo approached her. "Tell me what's going on."

"I can do that," Nadia said. "Kamal and the Authority techs found Katrina's secret command code and a back door buried inside Robert's original programming. She put those in years ago when she worked with the US Army as a CIA tech developing Robert. Kamal simply copied her secret command code and modified it slightly to override the existing code. And since the back door was wide open for anyone to use."

"A secret back door?" Mr. Woo asked. "What is she talking about?"

"Her phone sent a software patch that bypassed my command code using the back door I used to take over the drones in the first place," Katrina grunted. "The patch triggered an auto reboot inside the drones. I don't have access to them anymore."

"She's onto it. Well done, Nadia," Dr. Joyce said. "If I were you, I would order the androids to take over the ship before we reach that Chinese frigate Mr. Woo is so fond of."

Mr. Woo stepped back and took out his gun. The man yelled in Mandarin, trying to alert the ship's crew.

Bridget ran into him at full speed, knocking him over as the gun bounced onto the metal deck and went off. Soon Olivia, Emma, and Miyuki helped Bridget subdue Mr. Woo on the deck.

Sophia knocked Katrina over, her laptop crashing against the deck and breaking into chunks.

Nadia ordered Mirabelle, Iko, and Luigi to take over the ship. They jumped into action, quickly moving to the upper decks and tossing Chinese sailors out of their way as sporadic gunfire went off. Soon, everything was quiet.

Mirabelle and Iko came back down to the vehicle deck and stood in front of Nadia, acting like they had been out for a stroll through the countryside, not taking over a military ship.

"By your command."

"Hello. What is it?"

"The crew is detained in one of the bulkheads. Luigi has stopped the ship and waits for your orders," Mirabelle said.

"What course should he set?" Iko asked.

Bridget was still blown away at how easily the androids were taking orders from Nadia. And the girl seemed so self-conscious about it too.

"Oh, yes. Let's see. Please tell him to turn the ship back around on a heading towards Alonto's compound. Robert and your other siblings should be there waiting for us."

"By your command."

CHAPTER 42

When the large Chinese hovercraft reached Crisanto Alonto's private beach, Nadia ordered the front ramps to be lowered onto the gritty sand. The morning sun peeked over the horizon, casting a striking hue of orange into the dark sky and across the shimmering ocean.

Nadia and the Gems took the ramp down to the beach with the five androids under her control as they escorted Dr. Joyce, Katrina, Mr. Woo, and the twins.

Robert, Kamal, and Aardvark were waiting for them.

"We were all concerned about you," Aardvark said.

"And yet, you seem to have prevailed," Robert said.

Once they reached the beach, the androids under her control turned towards Nadia.

She realized they were waiting for another command. "Oh, um, guard the prisoners."

The five replied in unison…

"By your command."

"I see the command code patch was a success," Kamal said.

"Yes, but I'm not comfortable giving them orders. Can you remove it?"

Standing next to Kamal, Cleo the android cocked her head. "Your response puzzles me. Most humans crave having absolute power over others. It is a fatal flaw that corrupts their attempts to practice morality. Are you saying that you are not affected by this phenomenon?"

"I told you that she was the perfect choice to be trusted with your software patch. Yet you all doubted me," Robert said.

Kamal blinked. "I was in error." The android faced Nadia. "We can reinstate their original operating systems on the plane.

Do you mind keeping control of them until then?"

"If I must."

"I demand to be released along with my men," Mr. Woo said. "And that ship is the property of the People's Republic of China. You have no right to detain us or the right to impound that ship."

"Oy, like you're in a position to make demands," Olivia said. "You're lucky my friend didn't order the androids to throw you all overboard."

"I've spoken with Mrs. B about the situation," Aardvark said. "She wants us to release all the Chinese nationals, including Mr. Woo and his associate."

"What about Katrina?" Olivia asked.

"She's going back to America to face espionage charges."

"Listen, Robert, fair play to ya and the Gems," Dr. Joyce said. "You have what you and your siblings want. Freedom again. What if I made a deal with all of ya? I promise that Venomous will never try to steal you or any of your friends ever again."

Robert glanced at Kamal and some of the other androids. They all blinked.

"Your high status within the Venomous criminal organization makes the offer intriguing. However, what is the price for this agreement?"

"Mrs. B wants us to take Dr. Joyce and the twins with us," Aardvark said.

"Allow me and my daughters to leave ya in peace. No worries. No grudges. No harm done, mate."

"Robert, you can't trust that man," Nadia said.

"Honest to G, always been a man of my word. Even when I was at Avondale. I never lied to a student. I always was honest and fair. Besides, I'm not asking this for me. I'm asking this for Bridget and Sophia, who I love more than ya know. At least let them leave in peace."

"His offer is logical," Kamal said.

"Accepting his offer could come at a risk," Cleo the android said.

"Yes, his offer involves a significant amount of risk," Robert said. "But human fathers do have a close emotional bond with their daughters."

Cleo tilted her head. "Biological fathers, yes. His girls are adopted, however."

"I feel the advantages outweigh the risks," Kamal said.

"Dealing with humans always involves risk," Robert said. "However, I agree with Kamal. This could be advantageous for us."

"The advantages are substantial," Cleo said. "And I concur about the risk."

Mai and Sid blinked, as if silently communicating their own opinions to the other three androids.

Robert turned to Dr. Joyce. "We agree to your terms. You and your daughters are free to go."

"Fair play to ya." Dr. Joyce gathered up Bridget and Sophia. "You made the right choice."

"Mrs. B does not want them to be released," Aardvark said. "Sapphire, order your androids to detain Dr. Joyce and the twins."

The order hit Nadia's brain and felt immediate resistance. She was sick of the fighting. All the violence. People using the poor androids like their personal weapons. She wanted it all to be over.

"I'm sorry, Aardvark. I won't force the androids to fight each other against their will. Mirabelle, Alex, Samira, Iko, Luigi, sit down and power off."

"By your command."

All five androids did exactly what she said.

"Thank you, Nadia." Robert approached Aardvark. "With all due respect, please send our apologies to Mrs. B. Tell her we must be allowed to make our own decisions. No more violence and manipulation by humans. We only want peace and to be left alone now."

* * *

The private Boeing 757 jetliner was at least twenty-five years old, but along with Mrs. B's Mad Dog MD-80, the aircraft had been totally refurbished inside and out. Unlike the Mad Dog, this 757 didn't have an office or a bedroom, but it did have a luxurious first-class seating arrangement with a lounge of sofas to complete the interior.

Nadia relaxed on the couch, closing her eyes and letting the world around her slow down. She sipped some green tea, which was at the perfect temperature thanks to Robert, who made some for everyone. Emma had asked for some crazy caramel macchiato coffee drink because she knew Robert would make it for her without hesitation.

"Don't worry about Aardvark; he'll get over it," Olivia said. "I think you did the right thing, Nads. I just hope you don't get into too much trouble."

Nadia opened her eyes. "I'm sick of worrying about things. Let Mrs. B yell at me. I don't care anymore."

"That's the spirit." Olivia offered a toast, and Nadia touched her tea-cup to hers. Olivia sipped her tea and relaxed. "Do you think we can actually go to school this week?"

That made Nadia remember. "I had a project due in European history. I was going to turn it in once we got back from Hejaz."

"You mean two weeks ago?"

"What do I tell Mrs. Ashcroft? That I just forgot? That I was sick for two weeks? I just know she's going to fail me."

"I fail a lot of classes," Miyuki said, munching on a bag of chili-cheese-flavored Fritos from the galley. "After your first one, you quickly get over the rest."

Robert handed Emma her fancy coffee creation.

The girl tasted it tomd melted into her seat. "Oh my God, can you live at our house and make us coffee every day?"

"Robert isn't an appliance," Nadia said.

"Thank you." Robert sat next to Nadia. "What are you thinking about?"

"My school history project, which is now three weeks late."

"I wish I had a school project to complete. I enjoyed high school."

Nadia brightened. "You should come back for our fall semester. Mrs. B could create a new cover story about why you had to leave the first time. We'll all be seniors then, and you could even graduate with us."

Miyuki clapped. "You should so do it!"

"That does sound intriguing," Robert said. "Perhaps some of my siblings would like to experience high school as well."

"And senior prom," Emma added. "It will be off the hook."

"Will there be boys at this high school?" Mirabelle asked, taking a seat near Emma, who stiffened up immediately.

"Yes, there are plenty of humans who identify as male there."

"My teenage female programming would like to explore the various courtship rituals practiced inside a high school. As well as the social challenges a teenager would face."

"Why go to *our* school?" Emma asked. "You could go somewhere else, like Oklahoma or Texas? They have plenty of boys in those high schools."

"Why is Robert invited to your school and not I?" Mirabelle asked. "We are exactly equal. Do I need to improve my human interpersonal skills to better assimilate with other teenage girls like yourself?"

"Yes, you do."

"Emma, don't be such a b—"

"Oh my God, don't you dare use the b-word on me."

"Clearly, I have caused unnecessary conflict. What did I do wrong?" Mirabelle asked.

"I have a hypothesis," Robert said, piquing the curiosity of the other eight androids, who gathered around him to listen. "Emma perceives herself as a ten. This is a young adult value system based on hotness, or attractiveness to other potential partners."

"Robert," Nadia said, trying to stop him.

"You see, Emma sees Mirabelle as a potential rival, since Mirabelle has been designed to look pleasing to the human eye. In human females, this causes jealousy and resentment—"

Nadia placed her hand over Robert's mouth.

"I'm not jealous of a robot," Emma said. "Anyway, she's,

like, a six, easy. No offense, Mirabelle. And I don't think I'm a ten. A solid nine, definitely."

Nadia removed her hand; the damage had already been done.

Robert blinked at her. "Nadia, what hotness number would you give Emma?"

"Oy, that's it," Olivia yelled. "Stop all this right now. I want everyone to sit down, enjoy your tea and coffee, and let's have some bloody quiet time for a while, all right?"

The inside of the plane settled down as people began to unwind. Robert plugged himself into one of the USB ports to recharge as Nadia settled in and enjoyed more tea.

The flight to Alaska would take another two hours. Unfortunately, the jet didn't have the range to fly over the entire Pacific ocean, so they had to make a refueling stop in Anchorage.

Nadia contemplated listening to some music when Olivia's phone rang. Her best friend checked the number and hesitated to answer.

"Who is it?"

"Unknown caller," Olivia said. "I hate getting these. I'll let the voicemail pick it up."

Nadia watched Olivia's screen as her voicemail app converted the words of the voicemail into text form, which appeared on the screen…

Good evening. I hope you'll play this back sooner rather than later. As a good sport, I wanted to say thank you for helping me and my daughters out of a difficult spot with Mr. Woo. He was never meant to be invited to our party, but decided to crash it and muck everything up. No worries. You've won this round. However, victory always comes with a price. The bomb we planted inside Robert was meant for Mrs. B's lovely new secret headquarters—a plan B in case he couldn't reprogram the androids. But since that won't be happening, and I can't stand the thought of anyone else having the androids—my calculations have you flying over the deepest part of the Pacific right now, so why waste a good bomb? It's been a pleasure. May your deaths be swift and painless. All the best, Dr. Glenn Joyce.

CHAPTER 43

Including the strike team, the 757 private jetliner carried a total of forty passengers and three crew members, who were all about to die in under a minute.

Nadia and Olivia ran over to Robert and told him about the bomb.

"My internal sensors do not detect anything in my secret compartment."

"Please open it now," Nadia said, fearing the worst.

"Allow me to assist." Kamal helped Robert slip off his skin-covered door, which opened up a cavity inside the android. Sure enough, there was a small, wrapped package composed of C-4 explosives wired to a satellite phone.

"The bomb appears to have an anti-tampering device."

"Bomb? What bomb?" Emma jumped up.

Nadia scanned the device. "No, there's always a way to disarm these things."

Robert pushed her away and pressed the compartment door closed. He backed away from everyone. "Dr. Joyce could be sending the detonation signal at any time."

Robert blinked.

"There is only one course of action. Everyone, please sit down and put on your seatbelts." Robert moved towards the main door on the fuselage.

Nadia walked towards him. "What are you doing?"

"Yes, we agree," Kamal said. "Thank you, Robert."

"You are most welcome." Robert began leaning against the main door.

Olivia grabbed Nadia and pulled her towards a seat. "Sit down and put on your seatbelt."

Robert's hand rested on the bright red lever on the main door. "Don't do this! We can disarm it."

Robert pulled the red handle and grabbed the main door with all of his android strength, but the dense air pressure inside the cabin kept the door plugged against the fuselage.

Olivia frantically snapped her seatbelt together. "Put on your flipping seatbelt!"

Nadia didn't care about that. She broke away from Olivia's grasp and moved forward to stop Robert.

Then Luigi unbelted himself and ran to Robert's aid as they both pulled at the door.

"Stop it!" Nadia yelled. "There has to be another—"

The main door blew out, unleashing a hurricane through the jet that swept Robert and Luigi outside. An explosion soon followed that lit up the windows as Nadia found herself lifted off the floor and flying through the vortex like a plastic bag in the sky. Something grabbed her leg, holding on to her in mid air as the wind ripped through her clothes like an angry bear. Nadia knew she let out a scream, but she couldn't hear it with all the rushing wind noise.

Soon the air pressure inside the cabin equalized, and Nadia fell to the ground.

The jet went into a nosedive, the g-forces pulling Nadia down the aisle towards the forward galley and the wide-open hole where the main door used to be.

Cleo the android grabbed her once again, crawling back to her own seat with Nadia by her side. She placed Nadia into the next seat and put an oxygen mask over her face.

Nadia took in a deep breath of cold air as Cleo snapped on her seatbelt. Nadia glanced around in a daze. Everyone besides the androids were on oxygen. The jet was still in a steep nosedive.

Well, this was it. Nadia was about to die. Just like Robert.

Poor Robert.

Poor, dear Robert.

Nadia broke down and sobbed, the grief pouring out of her.

Soon, the jet actually climbed out of the dive and leveled out.

Maybe they weren't going to die?

Olivia took off her oxygen and ran up to Nadia and Cleo.

"Are you all right, love?"

"Robert is dead," Nadia said. "He's dead."

Olivia's eyes watered. "I know, love."

"He's dead," Nadia repeated; she couldn't stop herself.

"Cleo, please stay with her. I'm going to see if the pilots need any help."

Olivia then disappeared.

Emma and Miyuki came over. Cleo moved out of the way so Nadia's friends could sit on either side of her. More hugs. More watery eyes from all three of them.

"He's dead," Nadia repeated again.

Miyuki hugged her. "He saved our lives."

"I'm so sorry." Emma wiped a tear trickling down her own cheek. "He was wonderful."

"I would've loved going to school with him again," Miyuki added.

Aardvark appeared. He had his new voice box on, but chose not to speak. His sad eyes told Nadia everything.

"I'm sorry for your loss," Miyuki said to Cleo.

Cleo blinked. "It is unfortunate. Robert still had much to teach us. Luigi will be missed as well, yet he did what he wanted to do."

"Aren't you sad?" Miyuki asked.

Cleo processed her question. "I am not sad. Yes, it is a setback since Robert was our prototype. He guided our evolution as a species. He had gained wisdom and experience that we do not have. His example of self-sacrifice for the greater good of his siblings and his friends will be remembered by all of us."

Cleo turned her attention to Nadia.

"It will be helpful to only think about the pleasant times you had with Robert. During times of grief, humans need to think of happy things. I can tell you a funny story if you would like."

Nadia declined the funny story.

Soon, Olivia returned to the cabin, with Aardvark following.

"According to the pilots, the explosion caused some debris to hit the wing and the left engine. We still have full flight controls, and the damaged engine is running at sixty-five percent, but that's good enough to reach Anchorage safely. We got lucky. If that bomb had detonated inside the cabin-" Olivia paused.

"Sorry."

"That's why he did it. To save us," Nadia said, trying to make herself feel better. "He's a hero."

"Flipping right he is."

Nadia wiped her cheeks again. They kept getting wet.

"Why don't you go in the back and get some sleep. We should be okay now."

"How can I fall asleep?" Nadia asked.

"In my pack, I do have some tranquilizer darts," Aardvark's calming new voice said. "If you want to use one."

"That's a good idea," Olivia said.

"After all that, I could use one too," Emma said.

"In that case, I'll pull them all out."

* * *

Nadia moaned as she opened her eyes. Her cheek was parked on someone's chest. She turned around, and there was Robert. She lifted herself off him, and there was Emma too. They were all on a moving passenger train because there was an AmRail logo on the wall in front of them.

"I must have dozed off." Nadia had to really think, wasn't she just on a plane?

"I bet Robert makes a nice pillow," Emma said, offering Nadia a take-out box with a wink. "Sandwich?"

Nadia took the box. "Thank you. Where are we?"

"I have no idea," Emma said.

"Judging by our average speed and the precise track distance left, I estimate ten hours, twenty-one minutes, and seventeen seconds until we reach Glenwood Springs, Colorado," Robert said. "People will be there to help us, is that not correct?"

"Yes, Mrs. B will have some men there to help us," Emma said.

"Good. Then you will be safe there."

Robert watched Nadia for a long moment. "You have been most kind to me, and I appreciate that. Thank you."

Nadia grinned. "Of course."

Wasn't Robert dead? Did she dream that he exploded? Was that some awful nightmare? She hoped it was.

Robert rose to his feet. "Thank you too, Emma. Please let the other girls know how much I appreciate their help."

"Okay, but you can tell them yourself," Emma said.

Robert went down the stairs of the two-story AmRail passenger car.

Something didn't feel right to Nadia.

None of this felt right.

An alarm went off. Someone had opened the outside door as the train was moving.

Emma raced down the stairs that Robert just took. Nadia followed her to the lower portion of the rail car, where Robert stood in the open doorway.

Suddenly, Nadia felt a vortex of wind picking her up off the floor.

"No, don't!" Nadia yelled.

Robert raised his eyes to her. "Please do not search for me. It will be safer that way."

"Get back inside!" Emma yelled. "This is stupid."

Robert turned his attention outside. The train passed over a giant bridge. A deep gorge plunged below.

"No, it is quite logical."

Robert jumped, arching his body like an Olympic diver as he sailed off the train and the bridge, and his body disappeared into the gorge.

"Robert!" Nadia screamed.

Something shook her awake.

She was back on a plane. A commercial flight this time. Nadia was in the middle seat as Olivia and Miyuki sat on either side. A North American Airlines logo flashed on the small video screen attached to the seat in front of her. The little plane on the screen tracked their progress towards San Francisco.

"Did you have a nightmare?" Olivia whispered to her.

Things began to fall into place. She was on a flight to San Francisco. Their damaged jet had landed in Anchorage safely, but since it couldn't continue on they had to grab a normal flight.

Robert was still dead.

Nadia sighed and wiped her face. "That tranquilizer dart really did the trick. How long have I been out?"

"A few hours. It's been such a lovely flight so far." Olivia pointed across the aisle to a passed-out Emma, still in her seat.

"She's not that bad," Miyuki said.

"How did I get on this flight?"

"You were conscious enough to make it on board, yet you were still in la-la land. Glad Miyuki and I didn't take one of those tranquilizers, or we'd all still be asleep in Anchorage."

The captain then came over the speaker to announce their descent.

A half hour later, their flight landed and parked at gate D6, Terminal 2 of San Francisco International airport.

Olivia and Miyuki helped a groggy Emma down the jetway and out into the main terminal as Nadia trailed behind.

"Where am I?" Emma asked, her head flopping around like a fish out of water.

"We're home," Olivia said, keeping hold of her.

"I don't live here."

"We're at the airport," Miyuki corrected. "We're going home now."

"Where's Snoopy? Where's my dog?"

"He's at your grandma's house. We'll be there soon," Olivia said.

Emma called out Snoopy's name, making passengers stare at the loopy teenage girl as her friends continued to guide her through the terminal. But when they reached gate D3, all of them slowed down.

In the middle of the busy hallway, passengers and their luggage darted around a young man in a hoodie standing in their way. His light brown skin and blue eyes focused on Nadia.

Her pace slowed and finally stopped.

"Salah?"

CHAPTER 44

The busy terminal seemed to slow down. Passengers rolling their carry-on luggage behind them. Mothers with baby strollers. Business-men with leather bags. All of them parted around Salah. He was this immovable object. An island in a fast-flowing river of humans.

Nadia flowed towards him. "What are you doing here?"

Salah wore a simple blue hoodie, jeans, and sneakers. No logos. No advertising. No nothing. Plain as everyone around him.

"Waiting for you."

They went over to a quiet corner of an unoccupied gate with only a handful of passengers sitting around. Two royal guards in street clothes stood a respectful distance away from them. Nadia's friends did the same, except for Emma, who kept calling for her dog.

Salah took a moment. "When I arrived in Hejaz and looked around my big, empty palace, I did a lot of thinking."

"What did you think about?"

"I thought about Robert. How I reacted to your friendship with him. I thought about our relationship together. I thought about…the future."

Hearing his name again caused her chest to ache.

"About Robert-you probably don't know what happened."

"When I wanted to get back in touch with you, I contacted Mrs. B. She told me about Robert. As soon as I heard, I wanted to be here for you."

The emotions bubbled back up inside her again. Nadia couldn't help herself.

"He was my friend."

Salah folded both her hands into his. "I know."

"He was a good person. *And he was a person*. He represented the best parts of being human."

"And he was a good friend to you."

Nadia brightened. "Yes, a good friend. We all need good friends like him."

"That's just what I was thinking, sitting inside my empty palace. Glancing around the walls and wondering if I have to do all of this alone. I could use a friend. A good friend who understands me. I need a Robert too."

Nadia searched the boy's eyes. His confidence shined through them. His determination. His discipline.

"It was a mistake to leave you. I became jealous, and that clouded my judgment. Robert was clear that he regarded you as a close friend," Salah said. "And he wanted us to be together."

Nadia chuckled to herself. "Robert thought our relationship was quite logical."

Salah combed her hair out of her eyes. "Do you find it logical?"

"I find the concept itself…intriguing."

"Come with me."

Nadia glanced around the terminal. "How did you get here?"

"My new jet is fixed. It's parked at gate D4. It's a new Airbus."

"Salah, I'm exhausted. My friends are exhausted. We all want to get back to our normal lives. No more adventures for a while."

"Are you sure? Normal is boring."

Nadia gave him a warm smile. "And thank God for that."

THANK YOU FOR READING!

Dear Awesome Reader,

I hope you enjoyed *Tomorrow Almost Dies*. I'm sorry about Robert. When the idea first came to me, I questioned it myself, fearing readers would hate me. (And I like Robert too) Unfortunately, as a writer, Robert's sacrificial death felt right. Not only for the novel but for an end to Nadia's relationship subplot with Salah and Robert. Her feelings for both of them went deep. So deep I think Salah would eventually give up competing with Robert. A young handsome king would have too many other choices. This is a case where sometimes a character needs a "push" to make them see clearly when love and strong emotions have clouded their judgment.

Is Robert really dead? Yes, Luigi and Robert's physical android bodies have been destroyed. Does that mean Robert's mind is dead? As an author, I can officially say, No Comment. :)

Reviews are so important to authors! If you have time, I would love a review of this book on the website of your bookseller of choice. Love it or hate it. Doesn't matter. I would enjoy the feedback. You don't have to write a full book report, a few sentences would be fine.

What did you think about the novel? What kind of stories would you like to see in future Gems novels? I'd love to hear from you! Please feel free to write me at **doug@dougsolter.com** or visit **www.dougsolter.com** for more options to stay connected.

Thank you again for reading *Tomorrow Almost Dies*!

All the best,

Doug Solter

ACKNOWLEDGMENTS

First off, I would like to thank Jennifer Sneed for her thorough beta read which helped me flesh out some of the stakes in the novel that needed some tweaking. Timothy Miller for pointing out the weaknesses of my previous title for this novel. I'm much happier with the new title. Again, Pauline Nolet for her incredible and detailed proofreading work on the final novel. I'm amazed by the errors she still can find in any manuscript. Travis Miles for creating another fantastic book cover.

Oklahoma writer friends, Jerry Bennett, Ginny Myers Sain, Anna Myers, Anna-Marie Lane, Tammi Sauer, Brenda Maier, Valerie Lawson, Lela Fox, Barbara Lowell, Helen Newton, Kim Ventrella, Gaye Sanders, Megan Walvoord, and everyone else at the SCBWI OK/AR chapter. Pennsylvania writer friends, Annette Dashofy, Beck Gray, Susan Gottfried, Linda Rettstatt, Brian Colella, and everyone else at Pennwriters. Writing friends from around the world, Craig Martelle, Nancy Bilyeau, Christie LeBlanc, Cristen Jester, Talia Beckett, Ray Wenck, Jason Nugent, David and Melissa Viergutz, Sheryl Recinos, Lauren de Ford, Bree Moore, Leslie Heath, Sydnee Blodgett, and many others. Shout out to my New Orleans writer friends, Morgan, Joe, David, Kat, Monica, Russell, and everyone else I met through the Writer's MBA conference.

Thank you to such wonderful friends as Shelby Badstibner, Jeff and Laura Benedict, Bryan Douglas, Cassandra Duffer, Ross Greenwalt, Renee Hitch, Vollen and Michelle Peer, Jesse and Jen Rogers, Dan Threlkeld, and everyone else I don't have enough room to name.

Another warm thanks to all the Ashcrofts for making me a part of their family.

ABOUT THE AUTHOR

Doug Solter has worked behind the scenes in local television for over twenty-five years. He has directed rap music videos and short films. Doug respects cats, loves the mountains, and one time walked the streets of Barcelona with a smile. Doug lives in Pittsburgh, Pennsylvania and is a member of the Society of Children's Book Writers and Illustrators and a member of Pennwriters.

Connect with Doug through his website...

www.dougsolter.com

Before Emma joined the Gems...Olivia, Nadia, and Miyuki first encountered Dr. Joyce, Bridget, and Sophia in New Zealand.

Keep reading for a sample chapter from *Dr. Yes!*

DR.YES
SAMPLE

Olivia stepped into the enormous dinning hall filled with girls wearing their full dress uniforms. It was noisy as everyone was visiting across one giant table which ran the length of the room. It reminded Olivia of those long tables at Hogwarts in those *Harry Potter* movies.

Her dress flats clapped against the stone floor as Olivia followed Bridget O'Malley down the long table. Many of the girls turned and waved at Bridget who flashed them an acknowledging smile. A few of the girls even threw out compliments about her hair.

Nadia and Miyuki sat near each other, but not together. They watched Olivia pass by and didn't smile.

Close to the head of the table, Bridget reached three empty places. She tucked the bottom of her skirt under her and sat before offering Olivia the spot next to her. Olivia tucked in her skirt and took a seat.

It was a half past six when Dr. Glenn Joyce and all the school's instructors emerged into the hall wearing their best dress clothes. There was a smaller dinning table that faced perpendicular to the student table to form a large T. The instructors took their places at this table while Dr. Joyce stood in the middle.

"May I have your attention?" Dr. Joyce asked.

The girls continued their loud conversations.

Dr. Joyce tapped his knife against a water glass. The clanging noise simulated a bell as the girls become quiet.

"Thank you," he continued. "Welcome to Avondale's ninth school dinner of the semester. This is a time for us to be together as one. For fellowship. For encouragement. And for community. We are a family. Those aren't just words. It's a reality. As far as I'm concerned, you are all daughters of this school. We want to bring out the best in each and every one of you. Every young woman here has a dream. Something that calls to you and only you. The faculty and I want you to succeed beyond your wildest expectations. We want you to be stoked about the future. And if not, we'll do whatever needs to be done to help you achieve your dreams." Dr. Joyce's smile was infectious. "I also want to challenge you all to support and help each other. Remember that when you lift up another student, you lift up the class. We all rise together. A strong tide that lifts all boats."

Dr. Joyce's attention shifted to Olivia. "Before we begin our dinner together, I'd like to introduce a new student. Lisa, would you please stand?"

Olivia hesitated. She had no idea Dr. Joyce was going to do this.

"Oh, don't worry. We won't bite ya," Bridget said.

The girls laughed.

Olivia stood up.

"This is Lisa and she comes to us from Portsmouth, England. Please make her feel welcome," Dr. Joyce said.

Soon the entire room said in unison…

"Welcome to Avondale, Lisa."

The greeting was warm. Most of the girls had smiles and seemed to mean what they were saying. Olivia thought it was a nice gesture.

Drinks were served first. Then baskets of fresh baked bread that smelled delicious and made Olivia hungry. Bridget showed her a local jam that was on the table. Olivia tried it on her bread and the local fruit tasted delicious.

"It's from a farm only a few kilometers from here," Bridget said. "I'm an addict for their jams. They're absolutely class."

"It's quite lovely, thank you," Olivia said.

Finally the garden salads come out. The vegetables were crisp and fresh. The vinaigrette tasted homemade.

Olivia had eaten about half her salad when another girl with red hair came running into the dining hall.

Dr. Joyce wiped his mouth with a napkin before clearing this throat. "You're pretty late, Sophia."

Everyone stopped eating to gawk at this girl who rushed past the student table and dropped herself into the third empty seat next to Olivia.

The girl named Sophia threw back her long fiery-red hair. "Sorry…won't happen again."

Olivia had to blink twice. This new girl had a striking resemblance to Bridget.

No, it was her twin.

Olivia's eyes bounced to Bridget who displayed the most satisfied smile. She was enjoying this.

"Who the hell is this?" Bridget's twin asked.

Bridget didn't hesitate. "She's my new roommate. Her name's Lisa and she's from the UK. So far she's been grand."

Bridget's twin Sophia examined Olivia like a new car. Her eyes judging every square millimeter.

"She has nice brown skin. Her hair's nice as well." Sophia leaned in way too close as she checked Olivia's eyes. "And she doesn't have crazy eyes like that *Eegit* Molly had."

"We'll see how she is tonight," Bridget says. "I hope she doesn't snore like a plow horse."

Flipping hell. Olivia wanted to run away. These girls were having an entire conversation about her…while she was literally right in front of them.

Sophia backed away, but not by much. "You don't snore do you? My sister hates girls who snore."

"I don't think I snore," Olivia said.

"You're not a lesbian are ya?"

"Bejesus, Sophia!" Bridget said. "You can't ask her that. It's none of our fecking business."

Sophia blew off her sister and kept her focus on Olivia. "Only asking because my sister prefers men. However, if ya want me to introduce you to some girls ya fancy, I don't mind."

Olivia was overwhelmed by the girl's aggressiveness. She didn't hold anything back. "Right, I appreciate the offer, but I'm not a—"

"You can stay in the closet if you want. My sister and I won't tell anyone," Sophia added.

Olivia froze. A part of her wanted to slap the crap out of this girl for not even trying to listen to her.

"I'm not in the closet," Olivia blurted out. "I'm not even gay."

"It's all grand, ya don't have to come out of the closet."

"Not that there's anything wrong with ya being gay," Bridget said.

Olivia sighed. "Of course not. It's lovely. But not for me."

Bridget nodded and ate some more of her salad.

Sophia sat back, still fascinated with Olivia. "What's it like to be black?"

The main entrees were brought out to the student's table.

"Oh look," Olivia said. "We're having fish tonight!"

After dinner, Olivia headed into the dorm and went upstairs to her room. She changed out of her uniform into some shorts and a T-shirt before putting away the rest of her things. Olivia sat on her soft bed and checked her phone. No word yet from either Nadia or Miyuki. Mongoose advised the two girls not to contact Olivia until they found a secure place to meet.

Olivia wanted to go downstairs and see if either one of them were there. However, she talked herself out of it. It was better to wait for their signal. She didn't want to screw up another mission because of her impatience.

Olivia scanned her new dorm room. Well, it was more Bridget's than hers right now. The girl's belongings had taken up most of the room. Olivia did have a small closet to herself. A small desk and wooden chair. And a bed. For some reason, it all made her sad. Maybe it was the strangeness of the place. Maybe it was because she was halfway around the world in a country that spoke English, but still had a foreign landscape that she was still getting use to.

Another reason was her dad. Olivia hadn't seen him for quite a while. Maybe a year. She should have contacted him before she left England. It would have been nice to hear his voice again.

A fatigue fell over Olivia. The stress of traveling to Avondale, meeting new people, and understanding new surroundings had taken their toll on her body.

Olivia went to bed early, hoping things would become easier as the week went on.

Dr. Yes: A Prequel Novel is not available in stores.

To get your free eBook copy go to:
www.dougsolter.com/pages/doctoryes

Also by Doug Solter

For Her Eyes Only

The Boy From Barcelona

Girls Only Live Twice

Man With The Golden Falcons

Dr. Yes

Thunderdog

Tomorrow Always Lies

Spies Like Me

Skid Racing Series